ALSO BY
CECIL CASTELLUCCI

CECIL CASTELLUCCI

Stone in the Sky

ROARING BROOK PRESS

New York

Text copyright © 2015 by Cecil Castellucci
Published by Roaring Brook Press
Roaring Brook Press is a division of Holtzbrinck Publishing
Holdings Limited Partnership
175 Fifth Avenue, New York, New York 10010
macteenbooks.com

Library of Congress Cataloging-in-Publication Data
Castellucci, Cecil, 1969–
  Stone in the sky / Cecil Castellucci.—First edition.
    pages cm
  Sequel to: Tin star.
  Summary: "In this follow-up to TIN STAR, the desolate planet below the
Yertina Feray space station is discovered to have overwhelming amounts of
an invaluable resource, which suddenly makes the station a major player in
intergalactic politics"—Provided by publisher.
  ISBN 978-1-59643-776-0 (hardback)—ISBN 978-1-250-07368-6
(trade paperback)—ISBN 978-1-62672-151-7 (e-book) [1. Human-alien
encounters—Fiction. 2. Space stations—Fiction. 3. Science fiction.] I. Title.
  PZ7.C26865Sto 2015
  [Fic]—dc23

                                                        2014040877

Roaring Brook Press books may be purchased for business or promotional
use. For information on bulk purchases please contact Macmillan Corporate
and Premium Sales Department at (800) 221-7945 x5442 or by email
at specialmarkets@macmillan.com.

First edition 2015
Book design by Andrew Arnold
Printed in the United States of America

1 3 5 7 9 10 8 6 4 2

To the suns that warm. Human or star.

1

• •

No one is safe when the warning sirens on a space station blare.

It could be anything. Imperium battleships. Meteor storm. Asteroid. Pirates. Or maybe my mortal enemy, Brother Blue, the man who killed my family and left me for dead.

I stood in the arboretum staring at Quint, the planet that the station orbited. It was a terrestrial planet, a bit smaller than Earth and mostly made of rock and metals with a gray looking ocean. There was a rust-colored fertile line, the Dren Line, which cut the planet as though it were wearing a belt. It was there that the planet had the tiniest hint of color. It was my favorite part to look at.

I was light years away from the girl I'd been on Earth. I could hardly remember who she was. At first, I had not wanted to go to space. My mother had dragged my sister, Bitty, and me away from Earth, which was reeling from climate change and pandemics. My mother had been charmed by Brother Blue's promises of a fresh start by expanding to new planets and of Humanity living in the stars through his organization, the Children of Earth, and eventually so had I.

I had believed in him.

After our colony ship, the *Prairie Rose*, left without me, it blew up en route to Beta Granade, the planet we were supposed to colonize. My mother and sister were dead not even knowing that I had been abandoned here on this space station. They died thinking that I was being taken under Brother Blue's wing, being groomed to have a high place with the Children of Earth, aiding in the formation of past and future Earth colonies that didn't even exist.

Before he left me stranded on the Yertina Feray, I had been keen on helping him with his mission. Once I'd left Earth, I'd always imagined that I would be a settler. I'd grown to love the idea of it.

What a joke that dream was now. He'd fooled us, and in a way, I was dead, too.

The strobe lights continued to pulse in time to the sound of alarms, which indicated that all inhabitants should get themselves down to a shelter immediately.

"We should not tarry, Tula," said Thado, the arboretum caretaker, as he pressed a button with his long tentacle-like arm to close the lead panel over the window. The curtain would help to minimize the station's radiation levels and protect the precious plants he cared for. My view of Quint disappeared.

I felt blinded, just as I was by so many things that had happened so far in my short life.

I heard the door slide open and the familiar steps of Tournour's boots. He'd come to make sure that I was accounted for and to let us, his friends, know what the actual danger was before he went about his duties.

"Solar flare," Tournour said. Thado blew air from his blowhole in relief. There were so many things in space that were worse than a solar flare, not that that was something to be shrugged off. But to me and my friends, the Imperium attacking us would be worse.

Tournour approached me and squeezed my hand.

"Tula, you have to get to a shelter." I looked at up at him. His antennae were very still, showing his full attention. Since he had made his feelings known to me, there was something about his face that reassured me that everything was going to be all right.

"Is there anything I can do to help you?" I asked.

He shook his head. I fixed my eyes on the triangle patch of skin between his antennas, which flushed a little darker when he was near me.

"Standard protocol. Annoying but necessary," he said, squaring his broad shoulders. "I'll catch up with you when the all clear sounds."

As we walked quickly to the exit, he calmly clicked his communiquer and started issuing commands to his people. Tournour was the chief constable, and the Yertina Feray Space Station was in his care. He took that job very seriously. When he was on duty, he had a grace about him that commanded authority. He walked with a straight back that made his long limbs look longer, and I followed his orders immediately when he was like this.

Thado was right on our heels. He was a Dolmav and to me he always looked like a sea creature, swimming through the air as he caught up with us. Despite the fact that I was Human, these two aliens were my only real friends on the space station, and they would not let harm come to me if they could help it.

I knew after what they'd seen me through that I would always do the same for them.

As we exited the arboretum, Thado pressed a basket of trests, my favorite fruit, into my hands. They were green and

3

thick skinned with purple seeds on the inside. They were annoying to eat and their juice stained everything, but they were sweet and high in the vitamins many species needed and did not get enough of in space. They were also easy to grow, and that was why most space stations and ships grew them. Best of all, they staved hunger away for most aliens. They had become a staple in most alien diets. He knew they would be welcome in the underguts shelter where I would take refuge from the storm.

"Thank you," I said. It was these small kindnesses that had kept me alive these past three or four years and had helped me to carve out my life bartering favors and goods.

"Good that it's a storm and not the Imperium passing by," Thado said.

Even though he and Tournour worked for the Imperium, they had no love for it. Here on the Yertina Feray we were far enough away from the center of things that they could afford to resist in their own tiny ways. But it would be good for no one if we were inspected.

"Or invading," I said.

The Imperium was a military governing force that they had to obey. The Imperium had taken control in a coup a few years back from the League of Worlds, and it seemed to roll over planets, stations, and species.

There were five Major Species, or those who had more than twelve colonies scattered throughout the galaxy. The balance of power shifted among these five—Brahar, Loor, Dolmav, Per, and Kao. Those with more than five colonies but fewer than twelve were considered Minor Species. Below that, species were barely considered spacefaring. But under the League of Worlds, those could petition for planets to colonize and in that way they could grow in time to be Minor Species and eventually have some voice in the way the galaxy was governed.

The Imperium wanted to cease colonial expansion. The Brahar were the instigators of the coup, preying upon those officials in the Major Species who fed on greed. They changed the way things were done in the galaxy. First, it was the razing of planets, which was unheard of in the past. They started with the planets that housed simple organisms; they went in and took every resource, rather then earmark them for expansion by Minor Species. Then they took worlds where there was potential for intelligent life to bloom; where the League of Worlds would leave those planets alone, the Imperium did not. And there were rumors of culling the planets of the species that they determined to be less desirable.

Under the Imperium, every species was out for itself. Brother Blue had managed to get Earth to avoid the Imperium razing by exploiting the five-planet loophole, making it seem as though Earth was fully Minor. Only there didn't seem to be any Human colonies at all. That's what I'd inadvertently discovered when he stranded me here, and what made him ask me to kill my friends Reza and Caleb.

I hadn't done that, of course. I'd put them into cryocrates and shipped them off to the Outer Rim.

Everyone, including me, was afraid of the Imperium. No one could travel freely anymore without a special pass. No species could speak up without being silenced. It was seemingly unstoppable. Tournour and Thado worked undercover, collaborating with the Imperium to keep us safe on this far outpost.

"Tournour works quite hard at making sure the Yertina Feray isn't even a blip on the Imperium radar," I said.

5

"I'm thankful every day for that," Thado said. "He makes my unfortunate collaboration with them bearable."

I nodded.

"Be safe, Thado," I said.

Living in space was not safe. One could only hope that the metal that housed us would stay together and protect us from the dangers we faced daily.

"As you," he said. I knew he was giving me a blessing in his language, but the nanites that swam in my bloodstream and in my brain to help me translate sometimes failed when it came to sayings, idioms, or songs. Universal Galactic was not a poetic language, so when an alien wanted to give you a truism, they spoke their mother tongue. The nanites helped to fill in those gaps.

The nanites still amazed me. To think that I had small intelligent nanobots swimming through me regulating the gases in my lungs and attaching to my brain stem to help me translate and speak to other species was nothing short of a miracle. Every species had their language, and sub-languages, but the standard for all aliens to use was Universal Galactic. Universal Galactic was not easy to learn, but for almost all species it was doable.

The nanites helped with the precise understanding that was necessary when negotiating or governing. They were expensive to get, though, and not everyone had them. I only had them because my old Hort mentor Heckleck had stabbed me with his barbed tongue to inject me with them. I was lucky to have them. It gave me an advantage despite being a Human, a species that most aliens disliked dealing with.

Thado and I parted ways. He went up, and I went down to the underguts.

I could have chosen to be assigned, like him, to the shelter where the more affluent waited out these kinds of cosmic events in luxury. Instead I chose to remain assigned to the station's underguts shelter where there were too many aliens crowded into too small a space.

The underguts was where all of the rabble like I once was ended up. It was housed in the very bones of the station. It was a shantytown of metal bins and desperate aliens who had no means to live in the residence rings and no currency or way to leave the Yertina Feray. Most of them would beg for jobs from the few ships that docked here. They may have been looked down on, but I knew that they were the backbone for the whole underground economy here. I had lived there for my first two years on the station, scraping together an existence first by being an errand girl for Heckleck, and then striking out on my own dealing in barter and favors.

I felt a pang for a minute thinking about Heckleck. Were he alive, he would not go to an underguts shelter if he could help it. *A good time to get a good price for things is when people are facing their mortality. Rich people have the most to barter when they think they are in peril.*

Heckleck was always looking for a good deal.

The underguts shelter was no place of luxury. It was the dregs of the station, near the shantytown. Even though I had gotten myself out of the underguts, when a lockdown happened, I always threw my lot in with them.

I had a soft spot for the forgotten and overlooked. Because once upon a time that had been me.

In a way it still was.

When I got to the shelter, a thick-metal-walled room deep in the center of the station, I could smell the fear on everyone.

Aliens were sitting everywhere they could. There were no beds in this shelter, so aliens would string up hammocks and put makeshift bedding on the floor. It was crowded and uncomfortable. I didn't have to check to know that there was not one Human in the bunch. When I first arrived on the Yertina Feray, it was nearly two years before three Human Youth Imperium cadets became stranded on the station. That was when everything changed for me. When I discovered the depth of Brother Blue's betrayal.

But those Humans had been gone for over a year, ever since I sent Reza and Caleb, who had become my close friends, to the Outer Rim, frozen in deep sleep in cryocrates. I had no choice—I had to save their lives, although my fear was that those crates had become their coffins. The third one, Els, had met her death here on the station. Brother Blue had killed her for what she knew and because he thought she was me.

I squared my shoulders. This was not the time for regrets. This was the time to make sure that I made it through another day.

I signed in with the Brahar guard and tried not to shudder when her reptilian-like scales brushed my hand. They reminded me of a purse or a belt. The Brahar were cold blooded and cold hearted. It was their world that had set the Imperium into motion, and so they seemed to always be in charge whenever there was an emergency.

"We've run out of salt paks," she said.

I knew that this shelter had probably never had them. She waved me away as the next aliens checked in and the long last siren wail signaled that shelter doors would now close. There was no leaving now until the all clear sounded.

I walked around the shelter and began handing out the

trests to the aliens holed up in there with me. We would be huddled together for at least thirty hours, and the aliens in the underguts were always lacking in the essentials that I now had.

I didn't want to forget where I had come from, so I freely handed out what I could during these lockdowns. Real fruit was always a welcome treat on a space station, but during the long uncertain hours of waiting in a shelter, it was a piece of comfort.

It made me feel good—*Human*—to be able to help others in some small way. I had made it clear long ago that these were not favors owed to me, but I was no fool. I knew that my good will went a long way in keeping me in every alien's good graces. I liked to think of it as insurance. It was hard enough being Human. And if Heckleck had taught me one thing, it was to always have favors in the bank that you could call in.

When the last trest was handed out, I settled in, finding a space where I could. Then there was nothing to do but sit with my thoughts.

2

This space station, the Yertina Feray, was likely the only home I would ever know.

At times, that depressed me.

I had always hoped beyond hope that the colonies Brother Blue had promised the Children of Earth really did exist. I said the names of the colonies to myself in a pattern to pass the time. *Killick. Kuhn. Marxuach. Andra. Beta Granade.*

But I knew that if any people were living on those planets, it was probably only a handful of Brother Blue's stooges, who manned radio stations to give the illusion that anyone was there. I knew the truth, but I had no one to tell. If I did, Earth would be in danger of being destroyed. And as much as I wanted to take Brother Blue down and expose him for the lying conniver that he was, I would not doom Earth.

Brother Blue and his organization, the Children of Earth, had been scamming people like my mother into giving him everything for a chance to settle the stars for decades. And when the Imperium rose to power, he had taken advantage of his scam to trick the Imperium into thinking that Humans had five colonies and were an up-and-coming Minor Species. He did it as much to get power and riches as he did to save his own skin. But I had to admit that he had saved Earth in the process.

I wondered what had happened to those other colonists who'd bought into Brother Blue's tall tale. Had their ships blown up like the *Prairie Rose*? Or had he let them loose into the universe to wander like the other Humans who couldn't go back home?

There were only Humans on Earth and Humans who wandered. I was neither. Or maybe I was both.

Solar flare.

Solar flares were nothing to sniff at. They could be dangerous to the station depending on where we were on our rotation around Quint. If we took it full force, electrics could be fried, ships could lose navigation, and radiation levels could swell. For some species that was not a big deal; for others, even a minor shift in radiation levels was catastrophic.

I soothed myself with this thought: it was a known problem with set solutions. There was time to take shelter once the sun erupted since it would be hours before its radiation reached us.

It was the unknown events that were terrifying—asteroid or meteor showers, or something that compromised the station. We were only a bulkhead thickness away from space and nothing, except perhaps for some hearty bacteria, could survive outer space. And then there were the alien threats, like the Imperium and its plans or the increasing rumors of attacks by Pirates on small ships on trade routes. One unknown event thousands of light years away was sometimes way more dangerous than a solar flare.

It made me angry that Earth had fallen to the Imperium after having been isolationist for so long. When the Imperium came, half the planet wanted to fight, but the other half was afraid, so when Brother Blue swept in with his five colonies and a way for Humans to be folded into the galaxy, they took it. They were now under its thumb. The Imperium protected Earth from being razed like other worlds. Then again, every planet that could colloborate did. The planets and species that had fought had dwindled—or disappeared.

Brother Blue.

His name, even the color, filled me with a furious fire of pure hatred.

One day I'd out him, maybe even kill him, for the things he'd done. One day the time would be right, and I'd expose him. Earth would know that there were no Human colonies on the planets he'd claimed to colonize: *Killick, Kuhn, Marxuach, Andra, Beta Granade.*

The map is always changing.

The thought of that always made my self-preservation kick in. It galvanized me even though I knew killing him would likely bring about my own death. Meanwhile, time marched on, and that day always seemed to slip further and further away as years passed and Brother Blue's position in the Imperium and with Earth Gov became more and more solidified.

Brother Blue was out there, free, and I was stuck here, broken. I would have to ruin him if I ever wanted peace.

I closed my eyes to calm myself, repeating one of the lessons that Heckleck had taught me when I was first on the station.

"Think of the big picture, Tula Bane. One week. One month. One year. Five years. Ten. One hundred."

By the time I got to one thousand years away from this moment, I had regained my calm. The all clear blasted, and we emerged from our safe shelter cocoon.

I took the lift and walked to the living quarters to get Trevor, the mining robot that I looked after for Caleb, and to wash the thirty-plus hours of alien sweat off of me. Life on the space station returned to normal. We all pretended that there was no more danger.

But nothing was ever normal on a space station, and by the time I reached my quarters, the whole station was buzzing.

During our lockdown, an unknown non-Imperium ship had crashed on the planet Quint.

3

．．．．．．．．．．．．．．．．．．．．．．．．．．．．．

The difference in my life from last year or from when
I was first abandoned on the Yertina Feray was that I had el-
evated myself from living in the underguts of the space station
and bartering to stay alive to being an almost respectable citizen here.

For so long my only goal had been to leave and, if I could,
kill Brother Blue. But I had softened. Circumstances and experience had changed me. Or perhaps I had just grown up.

I had managed to talk my way into my own living quarters
on one of the residence rings as well as secure space for a water,
salts, and sweets shop on the entertainments deck.

If there was one thing that I had learned was true in the
universe it was that no matter how bad things got, people always wanted their home-world water and their home-world
sweets. And every species needed salts. All were welcome in
my place, and in a pinch, one could always trade me a favor
for some low-grade water to drink.

I called it the Tin Star Café, although I hadn't tasted anything that resembled coffee since I was on Earth.

"What's coffee?" aliens would ask me. I would try to explain
it to them, although truth be told, I could barely remember it
exactly except for the smell. Coffee was something that my
mother and father would drink in the morning, and I would

get a taste of it on special occasions as a child. But I could still remember the smell of it, and that was something. The aliens would shake their heads and say a different word for a different thing that did the same thing from where they were from. When a ship came in with that item, they would bring it to me to taste. None of them were coffee, but all of them were interesting.

The Tin Star Café would be the best place to get information on the castaway below, and I was as curious as everyone else. It was an event. When you lived on a nearly empty space station along a trade route that no one really used anymore, any event was significant. The Yertina Feray used to be less desolate when there had been mining on Quint, but those days were long gone. No one ever went down to the planet anymore; it was so depleted.

When I'd left the underguts, I hadn't taken advantage of all of the empty quarters. My living space was not large—just a small room—but it was mine, and it was better than the metal bin I'd lived in for two years in the underguts. Having real quarters made me a bit sad, though. It seemed to cement the fact that I was here to stay on this station.

"On, Trevor," I issued a command to Caleb's robot, which was in rest mode in the corner of my room, and then stepped into the sonic shower to clean myself. It felt good after having been squashed in with aliens for so many hours.

Trevor had other uses besides music, news, and companionship. He was, in a way, my protector. One word, one secret word uttered from my lips, and Trevor could do great damage to whoever menaced me. He had arms that could mine through bedrock. He had data that went back 500 years. He had no voice, but I swore that he had personality.

I had found him in a warehouse when the Yertina Feray had been in transition between governments. I had painted a face on him, but until Caleb had fixed him, he had done nothing but turn on and off. Now, Trevor did so much more, but with his painted on face, he looked almost comic and docile.

Until you noticed that he had knives tucked in his hands.

Trevor began a steady outpouring of news from the galaxy. I had programmed key words for him to scan, so the news was read out in a jumble as he skipped around doling out tidbits of information. My heart always sank at any news report about another planet that had fallen to the Imperium. Every victory for the Imperium felt like a wound.

While I washed and dressed, I listened to the stream of shipping news trying to learn what items of use would be coming into the station and what would move off. Knowing what was around to barter, even though it wasn't my trade anymore, was a habit I could not shake.

I had also programmed Trevor to find any hint of what had happened to Caleb and Reza on the Outer Rim. Where were they? Were they even alive? Every time I thought of how I had poisoned them to sleep and shipped them out in cryocrates to the far rim of the galaxy, I was wracked with guilt.

It had been hard to be the only Human on the Yertina Feray, and when Reza, Caleb, and Els had arrived, I had not wanted to know them. But they had been more than friends to me; Caleb, with his soft ways and his heart on his sleeve, a friend that I could talk to in a real way. And Reza. I had tried to push the idea of love or romance away. What did I need of that when all that fueled me was hate? But Reza had changed all that. With his warm, brown eyes. With his strong arms. With his deep kisses.

And then there was Els, who had betrayed us all. She was the real reason I had sent Reza and Caleb away to the Outer Rim.

But now she was dead, and they were gone.

I had tried to save them when Brother Blue demanded that Els and I kill them to prove our loyalty. I had used Els to get close to Brother Blue, but things didn't go as planned. She had been killed because of what she knew and because Brother Blue thought that she was me.

What had I done?

Earth had been in civil war, half of it wanting to remain isolationist—Earth Gov—and half of it kowtowing to the Imperium so it wouldn't be stripped. We had been caught in the middle of it. These were things and machinations too large to understand.

Caleb and Reza were lost and probably dead, but I couldn't stop hoping that I'd hear news about them. That they would get word to me and tell me that they were all right.

I had meant to send Reza to Earth and Caleb, along with his robot Trevor, to the Outer Rim to search for allies for Earth, thinking that would give the rebellion its best chance. Instead I had sent Caleb and Reza both to the Outer Rim and Trevor had been left on the docking bay.

What had I hoped when I sent Caleb and Reza away? That somehow Reza would spark a revolution to form a united Earth? Unfortunately, until recently Earth was still mired in infighting, with the power tipping back and forth. Now, the rebellion—made up of those who had wanted to remain isolationist—had been quelled and the Outer Rim remained eerily quiet. Except for the news of Pirates.

If Caleb were still alive, would he have found a group of

aliens willing to press in from the Outer Rim and help Earth overthrow the Imperium and its tyranny over species and worlds?

I had done it all wrong. I had stumbled in my mission to kill Brother Blue. I had been cowardly, and I played dead once again. I had used my precious travel passes on what was likely little more than frozen corpses by now.

I was not as clever as I'd thought.

I shook off the dark thoughts and familiar feelings of failure and hopelessness. There was work to be done. There was a life to be lived. I was young, and if my old mentor had taught me anything, it was that time had a way of making the right moments for action travel toward you. In the long game, long was short and short was long. Patience was the key.

There was nothing I could do about the past. I shut off any part of me that missed Reza or Caleb and focused on the beats of my moment-to-moment survival. There was still a war going on, and I was still the way most aliens got their necessities. That was worth something. That was what I could do instead of dwell on the regret of what had not been done.

"Reports on station docks," I commanded.

Trevor switched to listing the ships that were docked at the station and the ships that were leaving or scheduled to arrive. Only two. Every ship carried water. All life needed water. At least those two ships would have water that I could trade for. I listened to any hint of the identity of the crashed ship, but there was no mention of it, as though it was not large enough to merit a mention. That was interesting unto itself.

Heckleck had always reminded me, *"There are volumes of information in silence."*

"Music," I commanded Trevor.

He began to play a soft Hort music, full of bells.

I patted Trevor on the head. His painted-on face did not express anything, but it made me feel connected to the robot. This was something that we all did, not just Humans, I'd noticed. We endowed inanimate objects with personalities. It was a universal thing. Aliens had pets, dolls, and nicknames for computers. I loved that we all had something in common. It was what I looked for. If an alien was too alien, I could always start there, with the things we anthropomorphized.

When I was ready to leave, Trevor shut down the music and rolled along behind me. Trevor was not my servant. He was more like a pet.

If I were still on Earth, he might have been a dog.

4

• •

Even though the station kept a twenty-six-hour day
and there was no day or night per se, there was a natural
rhythm to the hours we all kept. The Tin Star Café was either
open or closed, but mostly, with the help of a young Nurlok
named Kelmao, it was open.

Most aliens made do with the various protein paks for basic
sustenance, but when it came to indulgences, a sweet, salt, or
water was the only true piece of home. At the Tin Star Café, the
aliens came in and drank their water, ate their sweets, got
their salts, and, of course, they talked. It was a few tables, a
bar where my intergalactic sweets, salts, and bottled water
were on display. On occasion, I'd serve real food, which was
hard to come by on a space station.

Stretched high along the entire back of the room was a window. Through it I could see a glimpse of Quint, and, of course,
I could also see the stars.

On the sill I had placed my alin plants. From their pots, long
tendrils of the infrequent yellow bloom and green leaves cas-
caded down behind a protected plate of glass. I didn't want
anyone touching my plants. Alin, even from poor-producing
plants such as mine, was hard to grow in the galaxy. It had vast
medicinal properties that made it worth stealing. The plants
bloomed when they could, which was almost never. I had three

plants now, two were cuttings from my first plant, which had kept me alive when I first arrived on this space station.

Trevor rolled to the corner and began playing some contemporary Loor music.

Too many low tones, I thought. Without antennae I couldn't appreciate the full beauty of the piece, but others could appreciate it. Soon enough the style of music would change.

There was only one kind of music I didn't care for anymore.

Human music.

It reminded me too much of what I had lost.

In my place, I was proud that those species who traditionally did not get along—gutter rats, ambassadors, pirates, and the rare travelers—sat next to each other and played simple parlor games: sticks and stones, zero ones, and poppop bon. If they poisoned or betrayed each other, it didn't occur at the Tin Star Café. Instead, it happened at my competitor, Kitsch Rutsok's. I think Kitsch was proud that his place had such a rough reputation.

Let him keep it, I thought. As long as I stuck to treats and specialties and not the things that he dealt in—imbibing, gambling, and other perverted comforts—he mostly left me alone.

The castaway on Quint was the only thing that anybody could talk about. Quint had once been a planet full of ores used for various technologies. The ores were mined by aliens with robots like Trevor to cut the rocks and earth. No one had been on the planet for two hundred years. There was no reason to go. There was nothing there.

"Any news?" I asked a Per whom I knew was from the Ministry of Travel. It had a drink in each of its four hands.

"Not on any of the manifests. It's a small ship."

That made me feel better as it eliminated an Imperium ship

from the possibilities. The stranger was someone wanting to fly under the radar, which was not uncommon to visitors on the Yertina Feray. We were far enough away from the central core systems and unimportant enough these days to be a place to come to and disappear from the rest of the universe.

As the crowd ebbed and flowed, rumors abounded as to who it was.

Rebel. Slavers. Traders. But no one knew.

The poor soul had obviously gotten caught in the solar flare and had its ship's electrics fried. With the station on safety protocol, an SOS would have gone unheeded. Not being able to dock, there was only one place to go.

Quint.

Throughout the day my eyes kept unconsciously drifting up to the window so I could see outside. It offered no great view like the arboretum, but it was my window, and so its view pleased me.

Who was down there? I wondered. *Were they still alive?*

"You won't be able to see them," Tournour said, interrupting my daydreaming.

I loved the sound of his voice. There was a tone that Loors had that Humans could barely hear, but I imagined that was what made his voice sound so warm to my ears.

I hadn't seen him since we'd all been on lockdown. His antennae moved slowly from side to side, indicating that he was concerned about something, but not too worried. In the past year, I had come to know and depend on him in a way that I had never done with anyone before. He was the only thing I had left. Somehow, we fit together, the two of us, cast out from our homes and secretly trying to fight the Imperium.

Even if it felt like most days I had nothing, I still had something.

One thing.

"I was looking for the color blue," I said.

"It's out there," he said. "But you should leave that color be."

He was trying to steer my heart away from whom it hated most.

Tournour ordered a bottle of Loor water and sat down, signaling to the other aliens there that all illegal transactions should be put on hold. Aliens either left my place and went to Kitsch Rutsok's, or settled down to more casual social interactions. Tournour was of the law.

He placed his currency chit on the counter, which I pushed back to him. It was a game we played. Whatever he ordered, it was always on the house.

"He ruined everything in my life. He abandoned me on this space station and tried to kill me," I said.

"Twice," he reminded me and took a long swallow of water. He put the bottle down and smiled. Loors, despite their antennae, triangle patch of colored skin, and lack of eyebrows, were more similar to Humans than most aliens in their expressions. With a Loor, a smile meant a smile.

I smiled back.

"You don't sound glad that Brother Blue kept his word and made sure that we're forgotten," he said.

"When you say it like that, you make it sound like I should be thankful for something that man did. I will never be thankful for anything that he does."

"He kept his word," he said. "That's more than most."

I started to get agitated. Most days it was something that

I pushed to the bottom of my thoughts. It was either that or let the powerlessness I felt about Brother Blue drive me mad. Tournour shifted, and I could see him holding himself back from trying to calm me down. It was a strange thing about Loor biology that when they were mated to someone, they would release a scent when their partner was in danger or upset. It was a way of bonding. Sometimes it made me feel uncomfortable to have the responsibility of his heart, as much as I needed his care.

"I just expected . . ." I continued.

"What?" Tournour took my hand. He knew the things I was frustrated with. Being here. Being the lone Human. Feeling powerless. Thought of as dead. Being worldless. He was a careful observer of everything but also, of all things, me. He also knew that I was from a species that needed to state and restate the obvious all of the time. He'd learned, through my careful instruction, that sometimes I just needed to vent. That it didn't mean I was angry or in danger. It was a necessary Human emotional release. I let my breath out in a big sigh and changed the subject.

"What's the news on the castaway?" I asked.

"Hard to say," Tournour said. "We don't know if the alien is alive or dead. There is a distress beacon on Quint, so we know where it is, but it's automatic. We've had no word from an actual alien, and we don't have the resources to send someone down there."

"So if they are alive, they will just live there on Quint? Alone and abandoned?"

"Assuming it has the nanites to help its lungs with the atmosphere. And assuming its kind can."

Not every species benefitted from nanites. They only

regulated the gases of most species so that complicated masks or suits were not required on some stations, ships, and certain planets. Of course, it all depended on your physiology. Many aliens had nanites and still had to wear masks. Nanites were still useful for language if not breathing for those species.

Tournour knew that I didn't like to think of things being left behind and forgotten.

"Eventually someone will go down there to get them, alive or dead," Tournour said softly. "It's just not a priority. I don't want to make a request to the Imperium because it would put us on their radar."

The rules of rescue meant that a ship that could assist in an SOS could salvage any and all parts and ware from the wreck in exchange for safely returning the survivors, if any, over to the closest habitable planet or space station to be questioned, treated, and then sent on their way.

"Seems like a hard lot," I said. It was bad enough having been abandoned on the Yertina Feray as the only Human these past three years, but to be the only being on an entire planet. That could break even the strongest soul.

"They'll be found soon," Tournour said. "No one will leave scrap anywhere for long. It's too valuable. Every time a ship comes to dock at the Yertina Feray they are asked if they have the capability to retrieve and rescue the crashed ship."

The music changed again. A Nurlok lullaby. Some Nurloks at a corner table began to sing along, and I could not help but feel soothed.

I lifted my wrist and shook the gold bracelet with the charm of Earth that I had taken off of Els's dead body a year ago. Tournour put his hand on it and played with the charm as I kept talking about my hate for Brother Blue. He cocked his head, and it made me think he loved the sound of my voice as much as I loved his.

I looked at his dark eyes, no whites in them. Sometimes looking into his alien eyes made me long for Reza's Human eyes—deep and brown. They were eyes that I could understand. Eyes that I missed.

But I could not deny that these alien eyes of Tournour's filled me in a way that was uncharted. Feeling guilty, I let go of his hand.

"I wish I could cut this hate from you. I can't understand why you hang on to it," he said, thinking that my sudden shift in mood was because of Brother Blue, as it was so often. I didn't correct him. I didn't want to tell him how much I missed Reza sometimes. It felt like a betrayal.

"Don't Loors hate?"

"Yes," he said. "But it doesn't consume us the way it does you Humans."

We were so very different. It was when he couldn't understand me that I remembered he wasn't Human after all. He was alien.

"Caleb and Reza, if they are alive, are now long awake."

"I'm sorry that we don't know what happened to them," Tournour said. "Communication is not simple with the Imperium in control."

That was true, but it was also true that Tournour was the one who made sure that the communications array was in disrepair and not upgraded quickly enough. He liked to keep the station quiet. That was one of the ways that he kept the citizens of the Yertina Feray safe. If no one could hear you, it's almost as though you don't exist. Ever since the Imperium had put Tournour in charge of the Yertina Feray, he kept us as quiet as possible. It was not unlikely for aliens who docked here to comment on how surprised they were that the station was still in operation.

"You did what was the best option at the moment," Tournour continued. "Instead of everyone being dead, you all lived. Isn't that good enough?"

"No," I said. "Never."

I almost hated myself for sending Reza and Caleb both to the Outer Rim. I traded in favors and promises, and I didn't like to break them. I was disappointed in myself.

I looked out the window. Quint was back in view.

I longed to be on a planet again one day. Any planet. But for now, with the Imperium in power and travel restricted and my being banished from Earth, there was only the wild and unlivable planet below to stare at from this station, never to set foot on.

"I love to watch your face when you stare at Quint," he said.

I laughed. Tournour was learning to change the subject. He was clumsy at it. Awful, even. But it touched me that he tried so hard to make room for my differences. I hoped that he felt that I tried, too.

Reza had always been open and wide in his physicality. He was dark all around in a way, and there was a loudness about him that brightened a room. Tournour was long limbed and graceful. There was a chiseled aspect of him, the triangle patch between his antennae, the angles that his body formed, and his sunken cheekbones. He smoldered most in his quiet moments. They both appealed to me despite their great differences.

It was hard to let Reza go. He'd meant so much to me when he crashed into my life. And it was hard to forget the way that he held me. But I was giving in to Tournour.

5

A few weeks later there were rumors that a ship had gone down to Quint, but there was no word if anyone had been found alive.

It was late for most and early for some when an ominous figure stood in the arch of the doorway the next day. I imagined that this was the captain of the salvage ship. I'd heard that they were Pirates, which made sense. They were always looking for easy loot. I remembered hearing that they had found something, maybe someone down there. I tried to remember if I had heard that they had come back already.

The creature was wrapped up in yards and yards of fabric that covered its arms, head, and face. It wore protective dark goggles, and even though I could not see its eyes, I felt unsettled by the way the creature stared at me with a fixed gaze. I wondered how large its eyes were.

The being, a biped, staggered to a chair and sank into it like it could barely walk. Perhaps the gravity on the station was too heavy for its species. Nanites could regulate breath and help with language, but not much could be done about gravity.

"If you want to come in you have to be uncovered," I said. It was a rule that Kitsch Rutsok had and I followed. Not that this creature was exactly in pirate wear, but it was covered from head to toe. Pirates covered themselves in flamboyant fabrics and bright colors so that their individual species could not easily be identified, but in a bar on a small space station, that could cause problems. Uncovered discouraged trickery. If you were seen, then you were accountable for your actions.

The creature nodded and slowly started to unravel the bandages that covered its face.

Trevor sat in the corner playing music. The tune had just changed to an Earth song. The stranger stiffened at the same time I did. Some species' ears were sensitive to the tones in another species' music.

I could no longer listen to Human music without thinking of Reza and Caleb.

"Change," I commanded. The popular music of the Brahar came on. I started to hum along, singing the strange Brahar words whose meaning was loosely translated by the nanites in my head.

> ". . . The sun setting. My love is a pig. Wonder.
> Wonder . . ."

"Water," the stranger croaked in perfect Universal Galactic. "Sweet. Expensive."

I knew that voice. This was no stranger. It was Reza. He was alive.

I watched as the being in front of me slowly removed its coverings. First I saw his dark brown eyes boring right into me. Then came his face, his skin was even darker than when he'd left, probably from being sun soaked on a planet. Then he shrugged the fabric off of his shoulders. He was skinnier than he'd been before, but his muscles were harder, his jaw sharper. Everything that had been open about him looked closed.

My eyes had a hard time adjusting to what I was seeing. My heart jumped and froze at the same time. But even more than that was the fact that it was still shocking for me to see another Human. It was like seeing something that nourished your whole being. Something so familiar that your whole heart leaps and thinks that everything is suddenly right again.

"Reza?" I asked. Reza had been the castaway. He'd been trying to get back to me. I reached my hand out to touch him to see if he was real.

"Water," he said, darting away from my touch.

Not *hello*. Not *I'm here*. Not *what did you do to me*? Not *I missed you*. Not *let me hold you*.

I understood. He was angry. He hadn't woken up on Earth. He probably thought I'd lied to him.

"I can explain," I said.

Surely he could forgive me. After what we'd had together, he would forgive me. Love had to count for something. All this time I had been holding on to my feelings for him because they were good feelings. I had tried so hard to fill myself up with something that was other than hate. I had spent this whole year hoping and now here he was.

"Where's Caleb?" I asked.

He glared at me. Then he coughed. It was an ugly cough.

I both wanted to reach out and recoil. He was someone I knew and a stranger at the same time. I found that I was at a loss. If he had been warm to me then I could've followed suit. But an impregnable wall had come up between us. I understood that he could be furious with me. What had happened while he was in cryosleep could not easily be explained.

He leaned closer to me, and I could smell him. As much as

Tournour had his own particular smell, it was nothing like this. I could drink in Reza forever.

He threw a rock onto the table. I didn't pick it up. A rock was not very valuable.

"This isn't worth anything," I said, reaching for the rock as he pulled his hand away. I never knew an action of not touching could hurt so much. An intense sadness filled me.

"For the plants." He pointed his covered hand to my windowsill.

I reexamined the rock and discovered that it was actually a clump of dirt. That *was* worth something. Real soil would have mineral elements in it that were hard to find on a space station. My alin plants were hard to keep alive. I could use this, but my pride kicked in. I wasn't going to give him expensive water for it. I took my cheapest bottle of water and put it on the table.

We stared at each other for a moment. One of us would break. One of us would have to break. A move from either of us and in a heartbeat we could go from stranger to friend.

My mind was screaming at me to ask him questions. To throw my arms around him in relief. To push my pride out of the way and make the first move. This was Reza, whose heart beat at the same speed as mine. I had a million questions. Why was he alone? Why was he sick? But instead, the training that Heckleck had taught me kicked in.

Never assume that someone you care for is still on your side until you see how they behave.

So far, Reza was behaving like an enemy.

Everything about the way that he sat looked different from what I remembered. As though he had aged. Or been injured. He had a hunch in his shoulder. This was not my Reza.

He pushed the cheap water away from him and then he

took a small bag out of a fold in his makeshift robes and plopped it onto the counter. I didn't touch it. I knew it wasn't currency.

We were waging a battle of wills, and I saw the few people in the bar lean forward, wondering exactly what this Human was up to. Everyone knew that I was a tough person to barter with. They wanted to see if I would go easy on one of my own.

I wouldn't. Especially not him. Especially not after a greeting like this.

"I only accept currency chits," I lied.

His brow rose as though he were surprised. The me he used to know would have bartered. I understood then. He was measuring me up, to see what kind of person I had become. I bit my lip. I could already tell that I'd done everything wrong in our exchange. As someone who was so good at bartering with aliens, I was proving myself terrible at it when it came to Humans. I wanted to laugh at myself. But that would probably be misunderstood and only serve to make things worse.

When you realize you are losing, lose all the way.

There was still a heat between us despite the chilly interaction. I could tell that he thought I would bend, and I wouldn't give him the satisfaction. It pleased me when he looked surprised. Like I had reached him in some way.

"You'll accept this," he said.

He opened the bag up and poured a few of the pollen pearls onto the counter. In all my time growing my three alin plants, I'd only collected a few random pollen balls of low quality and little use on their own. Though they'd traded well with the Per doctor in the med bay who used it as a tea.

Now it was my turn to look surprised.

"Where did you get that?" an alien at the end of the bar shouted, knocking over her bottle of water in excitement.

"Quint," he said to her, turning away from me.

As the room exploded with excitement, I felt weak and sank my weight into the counter, which was the only thing holding me upright. Everyone left in the bar pressed in around us, wanting to see if the alin pollen was real. The tiny bag was worth an unimaginable amount of currency.

There are very few things in the universe that are rare and wanted by everyone and alin was one of them. Alin was not indigenous to Quint. It came from a planet that had long been forgotten and destroyed. It did not grow well, and it was difficult to pollinate. When it did bloom rarely, it produced the pollen that was so coveted by species across the board. The pearls of pollen were highly healing. They could be made into oils that soothed some species. They could be used as teas that helped other species. Pollen pearls could be made into a paste. Or a suspension. Or a broth. They could be smoked or eaten. Pollen pearls were a flexible, universal drug that interacted differently with many species, but for each, did something specific and wonderful. Since alin was so difficult to grow and even impossible to simulate, it was coveted by all. It had been brought to Quint by some miner, and it had done well on the planet, but never really bloomed.

The aliens were crowding around Reza, asking him a million questions. Cursing themselves that they had not thought to go down to Quint. Although, why would they? There had been nothing down there to go to since the mining stopped. And most people who came to this system were just on their way somewhere else.

"Something happened. It's grown wild. It's grown hearty.

It must have adapted to the quiet of Quint," Reza talked with authority.

"Who knows how a planet infected with other nonnative species will react?" a Nurlock chimed in.

"The churning of the land those centuries ago must have brought whatever the alin needed to thrive to the surface," a Per mused.

Whatever had happened, the alin had begun to produce. To have a few plants produce was not unusual. To have fields of it meant there would be a boom on Quint. It was strange what one little blooming yellow plant could yield.

All around me, the first plans were being made. It was like watching a storm come in. It was a wall of unknown forces at work. It was exhilarating and terrifying. Those with ships ran out of the bar, and others began negotiating terms for ships to get to Quint. Others hit their communiquers and frantically shot orders to their shipmates.

The shift in the atmosphere of the Tin Star Café made Trevor alert, knives whirring. People were yelling with excitement and making plans. Only Reza was calm.

"Off, Trevor," I commanded. It powered down.

"Caleb really modified that thing, didn't he?" Reza said.

Reza and I looked at each other, and it felt like the first moment that we were really seeing each other. His brown eyes were deep and hurt. The skin around his eyes had lines like an old man's. I saw that he looked harder than I'd remembered him. As though all of the beautiful openness that I loved about him had snapped shut. I wondered what had happened to make him so tough.

Whatever it was that had happened to him, I was afraid it was my fault.

"What are you wearing?" he asked as though he were finally really taking me in.

I looked down at myself. I had long ago ditched the simple clothes with the many pockets that I used to wear when I lived in the underguts for a more fashionable style.

I blushed. I suddenly felt self-conscious standing behind the bar in my finer colorful threads that flounced.

"You know, I couldn't believe it when the Brahar who rescued me talked about a Human female running a water bar on the Yertina Feray," Reza said. "An old gutter girl who'd risen high. I couldn't believe it was you. I had to see for myself. And here you are, all cleaned up and full of power."

"Where's Caleb?" A lump formed in my throat. Had Caleb died on the planet below? I couldn't bear the thought of Caleb being dead.

Reza took a deep breath.

"He's out there," Reza said, waving his arms in front of him indicating the whole of the galaxy.

"He's alive?"

I gripped the counter. The guilt I had been feeling for almost a year overwhelmed me.

"I assume he is. We parted ways on the Outer Rim."

Relief flooded me. I had not killed them. They were both alive. I leaned forward needing to know more.

"Why did you part ways?" I asked. I would never want to be alone out there.

"We had a disagreement about what our plan should be once we figured out our situation."

The situation I had put them in. I knew that they had been at odds before I had put them in the cryocrates. They had both wanted to save Earth from different directions.

"I thought you weren't staying here on the Yertina Feray," he said. "Now it looks like you've settled in and done well for yourself. I'm actually surprised that you're not in Bessen with Els. I had half a mind to go straight there first."

It startled me that he didn't know that Els was dead. But of course he wouldn't know that. He'd been in cryosleep when Brother Blue had killed her in the cargo bay and I had cowered in a corner.

"Els is dead," I said. "Brother Blue killed her. I barely made it out of that situation alive."

I could see Reza register this information. It opened him up, but only for a second.

"Well, I suppose Els had it coming," he said. "She was a slippery one."

I touched the gold bracelet with the charm of Earth that hung on my wrist. I had taken it off of Els's dead body. Part of the reason for keeping it was that it kept me real. It reminded me to never be like her. We felt the same way about Els. Her manipulations. Her lies. She was willing to kill Caleb and Reza, and I was willing to save them. If he didn't know that, he knew it now.

That he had been looking for me didn't escape my notice. I wondered if despite his anger, he thought we were still connected. Perhaps that was a way to reach him. It was like negotiating with an alien. I needed to find out what it was that he wanted. Once he had it, he would soften. But first, he had to know the truth.

The truth was, I was the most powerless Human in the galaxy, and if he couldn't see that, then being on the Outer Rim and all alone on Quint had addled his brain.

Ever since Caleb and Reza had come into my life, I had

tried to shed my coldness and embrace my warmth. But now, with him standing in front of me acting so strange, I could not remember how to be Human. This reunion was not going anything the way that I had imagined. I felt myself shutting down and relying on the behaviors learned from Per, Nurloks, Loor, Brahar, and other aliens in complicated situations. Having longed for a Human in my life again, I was failing miserably even though the one that I cared most about stood in front of me.

I had still not touched the pearls of pollen on the counter, and the aliens in the bar were now howling at me. They were shouting and laughing and pointing at me as though I were delirious for standing my ground. They all knew that I bartered for water, salts, and sweets, but here I would not budge. Not until I could sort out what I was feeling.

I hadn't lost my mind. I was as clear headed as ever and I was following Heckleck's instruction for negotiation: *When there is something that everyone will go crazy for, stick to the thing that you know is valuable. Keep a level head in an insane time. Always be fair, for few will be fair. Steadiness is the real worth and the truest measure.*

Currency would keep its value. I would stick to that.

It did not take too many leaps of imagination to know that if Reza had that much alin pollen he was willing to part with, he must have more, and he must have gotten it from Quint. Everyone in this bar would be going down to Quint to get some. Soon after that, others would come. Everything I did now in this moment would dictate what the rules were when the alin pollen started arriving at my place. If I had learned anything in my years of bartering on the Yertina Feray, it's that I knew I had to stand my ground now.

"Where's my water?" he asked.

"I told you I only take currency chits."

"Give him what he wants!" the aliens around us yelled.

If people wanted the hard stuff, to get intoxicated, or to find comfort in the arms of someone for the night, they went to Kitsch Rutsok's. At my place, everyone had a clear head or they were thrown out. It would be the same with currency. There was going to be a rush on Quint, and if they wanted to spend pollen madly, let it be there, not here.

"I know I don't have a currency chit, but I had hoped you would exchange that pollen for a bottle of sweet water," he grinned in a way that made every part of me flutter. "For old times sake."

"Can somebody buy this Human a drink?" I pulled my gaze from his face and turned to the aliens crowded around the bar. "This Human doesn't have a currency chit."

It was strange to not say his name. *Reza. Reza. Reza.*

I couldn't say his name. As though to name him were to acknowledge that I was hurt. If he were a stranger I could cope.

It took a moment for someone to speak up. They had to calculate the cost of the expensive water that Reza wanted and what it might be worth down the line. A small Per came up and put its chit down with one of its four arms and nodded to me. I put the most expensive, sweetest water I had onto the counter, and Reza snatched it up and slapped the Per on the back.

"Your pollen," I said as Reza was leaving, pushing it toward him.

"Your tip," he said, scooping up his bag of pollen but leaving the clump of dirt behind for me. He left to join the Per at their table without so much as a glance back at me.

In that moment, my heart broke.

I watched as the bar became full and crazed with action, but it was as though it were in slow motion or underwater. Sounds seemed far away, and my face felt hot.

Finally, Tournour entered, and I felt myself breathe again. Instead of coming to me, he went directly to Reza with an angry look on his face. I had never seen this mood from Tournour, and it frightened me a bit.

"There you are," he said grabbing Reza roughly by his arm. "You have to go to the med bay first. You have to clear quarantine."

Then an unmistakable look passed between Tournour and I that made it clear that there was a bond between us.

Reza stood up, knocking his chair over and coughing that awful cough.

"I just wanted to see her first," he said.

"Now you have," Tournour said.

Reza was no longer looking at me. He was already heading out the door.

The music changed back to Earth music. This time, instead of turning it off, I let it play.

6

I was in my favorite spot in the arboretum. Head leaning on the window. Bare feet in the dirt.

Thado glided along the rows of vegetation, leaving me to stare into outer space in silence.

I sometimes believed he considered me to be one of his plants or trees; something to be watered and nurtured, a thing that he could help to thrive in this harsh, artificial environment. In his arboretum, there was life. There was something about leafy greens, the way that the air in here was a little bit different. The way there were small sections with slightly different atmospheres that made this place almost holy to me. It was my sanctuary. I think the green in here thrived because Thado's kindness ran so deep. He'd helped me more than once by providing me refuge. By trading fruits and vegetables with me so that I could keep living. And best of all, he never complained when I took my shoes off and stood in the dirt to look out the window.

I heard voices in an intense conversation somewhere behind me. I only began to listen as the voices became louder. Thado was giving soil advice, and that interested me. Every alien heading down to Quint came to pry gardening secrets from him, and he always refused. I wondered who had managed to get him to talk.

When I turned, I saw it was Reza punching Thado's information into his datapad.

I shook the dirt off of my feet and joined them. This was my chance to fix things.

"Reza," I said. "This is silly."

I did not have to elaborate. We were the only Humans here, and I knew that he must feel as I did, comfort in a face that could be understood. A face in a sea of alien faces looked more real than real because it was familiar.

He turned to me. There were an unbearable few moments of silence that seemed to stretch into years. I reminded myself that this was like any other negotiation I had done in my life. If I waited, if I stood my ground, if I insisted, then we could possibly move forward. It didn't always work, but when it did, the deal was all the sweeter.

But there was nothing easy about confronting him. I had been brave and I had been a coward about many things in my young life, but this moment felt like I was standing on the edge of a cliff where I could lose my footing in an instant. Either things between Reza and me would ease up or they would worsen. There was no way to find out without pressing the issue, which felt like the most frightening thing I could do.

I took another step toward him.

"Reza," I said, quietly this time. Like I was saying his name just for him.

Thado had moved away, but over Reza's shoulder I could see Thado looking at us, slowly pruning a plant that was pruned enough and checking to see that we were all right.

I could tell by the way Thado was watching us that he liked something about both of us, as different as we were. It never occurred to me that he could be Reza's friend, too. But of course he could be.

The seconds ticked by, and I took another step forward. I got into Reza's personal space—the zone that threatens some species and declares intent in others. I was an arm's length away from him now.

Reza took a deep labored breath and pulled at his long hair. For a moment he looked like the boy that I had known a year ago, but then he looked uncomfortable, and I could see him shutting himself off from me. His whole body tensed up. I was losing him.

I took another step forward. I could pull him in for a hug. I could stand on my tippy toes and kiss him. The air around us felt alive.

At last Reza spoke.

"I have to go," he said. "I just came here for some advice on a fungus that's grown on some of my acreage."

"Stay," I said. I reached out and touched his arm. He pulled away but I didn't let it confuse me. "I can explain everything if you just listen."

I could tell from his face, which was so easy to read, that he was caught between caring and wanting to know, and not caring and drawing his own conclusions.

I realized that was a Human thing, to keep up a falsehood to justify your feelings and actions. Wasn't that what I did with Brother Blue? Purposefully made him into a devil? He was a devil, but I kept him there. To so many others, Brother Blue was a savior.

I tried to figure out how I could explain everything, every action I had done that had taken us from there to here, but I couldn't find the words.

"You have Trevor working as a glorified jukebox in your water bar," Reza said. "Caleb would be angry."

"I can't imagine Caleb getting angry at anything," I said.

"You wouldn't recognize him if you met him now," Reza said. "He's angry all the time."

"Like you?"

"I'm not angry all the time," he said. "I'm just angry at you."

That stung, but it was fair. At least we were talking.

"Trevor's more than a jukebox," I said. "He has a kill function."

"Of course he does," Reza said, laughing and shaking his head.

"I'm sorry," I said.

Reza made a noise. A Human noise that I remembered meant disappointment, anger, and disbelief. It was a terrible noise made with tongue and teeth. A cluck or a tsk whose wordlessness made it sound worse.

I had missed Reza and Caleb's presence when they were gone. I had imagined what it would be like if and when I ever saw them again, and the reality was so different from what I could have possibly thought. I imagined Reza returning with Earth united, and Earth Gov in charge again instead of the Earth that collaborated with the Imperium. I saw him blazing a trail toward making Earth a force in the galaxy; as a planet and a species with real colonies, as a planet that welcomed its own back home. I had imagined Caleb heading a ragtag team of minor species to Bessen to eliminate the species caste system, taking down those in power.

I imagined that they would become the leaders that I knew them to be. And that they would do so much good, not just for Humans, but for all life forms.

"You don't know what happened out there," he said.

"Tell me," I said. "Tell me so that I can understand."

"When I joined the Imperium Youth, I had aliens as squad leaders. I mingled with them. When I came here, it was hard that the aliens didn't like me because I was Human, but I thought it wasn't so bad. But that was because of you. Out there, on the Outer Rim? There are aliens out there. And they are very strange. And most of them have never met a Human, and if they have, it's been the Wanderers, whom they despise."

"But you all had the same cause," I say. "Surely that got you somewhere."

"Most of them didn't speak Universal Galactic. I couldn't communicate with anyone."

Reza closed his eyes as though he were trying not to remember.

"We were alone, and it was horrifying," he said. "Everything out there was unfamiliar, disturbing, and full of horror."

I knew that the Outer Rim was at the very edge of explored space in the galaxy. It consisted of many suns and planets and species that had barely any contact with Bessen and the known spacefaring races. Of course, as the known galaxy grew, the Outer Rim pushed farther out. It's how places like Earth were discovered.

It struck me then about how hard it was for those explorers who made first contact with each other. How a person's whole universal view could be altered from it. Reza was in crisis out there. There hadn't been any salvation out there. I had sent them to hell.

"Caleb wanted to be there," he said. "I wanted to be home. Caleb figured out how to make it work for him. I couldn't do it his way."

"You both never saw eye to eye," I said.

"You don't understand," Reza said. "The Outer Rim changed him."

There was a look in Reza's eyes that was slightly wild. I recognized that look. It was the way I saw my eyes in the mirror right after I was left here. Back then when I couldn't understand what was happening and couldn't see how I could survive.

I was wrong about everything, and I didn't know how to make amends.

"I have to go," he said. "A ship is waiting."

"You're going back to Quint now?" I asked.

He nodded.

"You're always welcome at my place," I said. "Your next sweets or salts are on me." I tried to smile. I tried to make it light, but I could hear myself and I sounded desperate. I was ashamed.

These were the kinds of moments that I wished I still had a mother to turn to for advice, or a sister to sit and talk with. Instead, I fumbled along this path of trying to grow up and I didn't know how to come of age.

He looked down at his feet and mumbled something. I couldn't tell if it was an acceptance of my invitation or a goodbye. He shrugged and turned away from me.

I watched his retreating figure, heartbroken.

Being Human was messy, but now I could own up to my confused feelings. And though I was not good at being Human, I was good at being messy.

I hadn't envisioned failure and silence, but now Reza was as close as Quint. That was something.

Thado floated over to me. I could feel the hot air from his blowholes.

"He's very intelligent for a Human, as you are," he said.

I nodded.

"He cares for you," Thado said.

"How can you tell?" I asked. I needed to have confirmation that Reza would somehow be in my life no matter how much I'd messed it up.

"He angles himself toward you," Thado said. "Creatures in conflict angle away. Like trees that hate shadow."

I put my hand on Thado's smooth, rubbery skin.

"Thank you," I said. "I owe you one."

"Always glad to have a favor owed from you, Tula Bane," Thado said.

7

Word about the alin blooming on Quint spread through the station like wildfire. The news brought with it an excitement I had never experienced on the Yertina Feray before.

The whole station was coming alive in a way that it had only known in the past. I recognized it for what it was.

Life.

Eyes were wild. Fortunes yet to be made were being plotted. Alliances that would eventually strain and break were forming. It was there in every tip of the glass at the Tin Star Café. In every currency chit swiped. In every forced smile and heated conversation. Hope was in the air. Possibility abounded. It infected even me.

Soon the ships came. Hundreds of them arrived at the Yertina Feray, and it was a sight to see them coming. Every day new ships docked full of eager fortune seekers. There were familiar species but also types of aliens that I had never seen before were arriving.

"It's madness," I said to Tournour.

"I am not going to be able to keep us off the Imperium's radar," he said anxiously.

I could see how it was bothering Tournour, but there was

nothing either of us could do. How can you stop a rush? You can't. It's relentless in its flow until it stops.

The rabble had come first, but when the truth of it had spread out to other systems, more sophisticated types came to the Yertina Feray with dreams of making a fortune down on Quint. And with them, came the people who saw a fortune to be made in the supporting of those heartier types. Gigolos and whores. Seedy merchants. Con artists. False prophets. Robot vendors.

Suddenly everyone wanted a Trevor unit to bring down to the planet with them to get whatever it was that they could find. Claims were only good as long as you could work the area and even though a robot could not do the delicate work, it helped to keep a claim open. Some people went for alin specifically. Others thought that there were additional things to be found there.

In order to keep a slight peace, only authorized ships were allowed to go down to the planet below. If anyone else tried to land, they were shot with a pulse that burnt out their electronics, and their ship was quickly hauled back to the station. The rush to get planet-side immediately meant that most of the ships that docked were then abandoned. If they were not claimed within a week, they were uncoupled from the Yertina Feray and set adrift. It was chaos out there. Ships floating away, empty.

Wherever there was a window, you could see them drifting.

After decades of being a ghost town, the Yertina Feray was bulging beyond its capacity. Old wings long abandoned were reopened.

I walked through the old parts of the station with wonder.

The design in those wings, the styles were so different from what I was used to. I had explored some of these halls with Heckleck a few years ago, but to see them alive and bursting with population was a whole different thing. My world felt expanded. It was easy to imagine what the Yertina Feray had been like in its heyday. There were families who had come. There were adventurers.

Reza led the prospecting. I learned that as soon as he was well, he moved out of the med bay and then went straight back to Quint once he'd gathered enough equipment. I couldn't help but wonder about Reza and how he was doing down on the planet. No longer alone, but invaded by the desperate, greedy, and hopeful who crowded the planet, sifting for alin.

He only left his claim to come back to the Yertina Feray for more supplies, to trade his collected pollen, to take on workers to help him expand, and to meet with Thado in the arboretum for agricultural advice.

All of these new aliens arriving meant that it was harder to run into Reza, even though his name was on everyone's lips. I felt frustrated and caged; it seemed that everyone was coming and going except me.

He was always careful to avoid me. He lived in the under-guts when he was on the station even though he could have stayed in the most luxurious quarters. He never came to see me, and it hurt.

"Since he came back to the station, you haven't been yourself," Tournour said. "It makes me sad to see you sad."

I looked at Tournour. It was too strange to talk of my hurt heart with someone who I had feelings for, too.

"He was my friend and now he's angry with me," I said. "It's unsettling."

"He was your mate," Tournour said matter of factly.

"*Mate* is the wrong word," I said.

"What is the right one, then?" Tournour asked. *"Partner?"*

Partner was wrong. Tournour was more my partner than Reza ever was, but Reza's was the face I wanted to kiss. Was that just because he was Human and Tournour was not? I looked at Tournour again. To me, his face was handsome. To me, he was the being that I orbited. Then what was Reza? Boyfriend seemed wrong. Lover seemed wrong, too.

"There is no word for what we were. Just more than friends."

"He's not even on the station. So I don't understand why you should care so much anymore."

Tournour was looking at me with such intensity, as though he were trying to unlock the secrets of Human emotion. I could explain it to him one million times, and he would still be confused. I could not be angry with him for not understanding how intricate and complicated it all was.

"Yes," I said. "It hurts that he's cut me off."

"Human relations are so confusing. With the Loor it's all chemical. You are chemically bonded to a person or you're not. It's very simple. There is no gray area. With you it seems like you can feel a million opposing ways about one thing. It must be exhausting."

If he had been another Human, he might have felt jealous or threatened by Reza's arrival on the station. But Tournour didn't seem jealous at all. He was truly interested in Human dynamics, always seeking to understand how I moved through the world.

We were made in such opposite ways.

"But you feel," I say. "You feel love and hate and sadness and jealousy."

"Yes, but it's tied into our bodies."

"How is it that you feel for me when I'm not a Loor?"

"I cannot explain it," he said. "It just is. All beings have a chemistry, and we react well or poorly to it. I do not like the Per, but I have met Per whom I feel for because they are not offensive to me. There is something about Humans. Your species smells like family.

"I can see with my eyes that he is a handsome Human male," Tournour said. "And I could call myself a bit attracted to him. He smells as nice as you do."

Tournour wasn't making my conflicted feelings about Reza any easier. I could understand jealousy. I couldn't understand sympathy.

"But how do you know that you like me?" I asked.

It is a question that I asked him all the time. He put his hand on my face, his antennae folded toward me, and he bowed his head.

"I feel for you in my heart as much as in my biology."

I cupped his hand and took the moment in. It was new for me to feel love and I was still suspicious of it, but Tournour's care filled the hole that Reza was currently ripping.

His arms encircled me, and I leaned my head on his shoulder. This was as close as we got, and it felt good. But I couldn't deny that it was different than being physically with Reza. That was what my body longed for now that Reza was so close. I wanted to talk to him with my body.

"Are you feeling better now? Are you comforted in a way that is helpful to you?" Tournour asked.

I smiled. Having a relationship with an alien was tricky. Tournour put his hand on my back. He was so busy with all of the rush craziness and yet he still made time for me. It was a hard thing to reconcile that intimacy could mean so many things.

"Yes, Tournour."

I kissed his cheek. He blushed. Kissing was not something that Loors did lightly.

"I must excuse myself to go on my rounds. The station never stops," he said, and quickly left.

I headed to the Tin Star Café, which was the only place where I could get a good idea of everything that was going on.

8

• •

Since it was where Reza, who was now a legendary
figure, had started the rush, the Tin Star Café was the center
of it all. Aliens felt that meant there was magic here. So it
was where all of the claims swapping took place. Kitsch Rutsok's and the new establishments that had sprung up were
jealous of how well I was doing.

Along one wall of the Tin Star there was an electronic map
of the planet. I flipped it on, and the colored lights swirled. On
the map, claims were electronically updated as they swapped
hands.

Quint was not that large. It was half the size of Earth,
but that was still a lot of space. Every last inch of the planet was
being bartered over, and in a rush, every inch counted. It
was something to watch, that map. The claims changed hands
so fast that the board looked like a moving piece of living
art. There was only one claim that stayed steady: Reza's. It
was large and lay in the largest part of the Dren Line, which
was the most fertile part of Quint. It was comforting to look
at it. Looking at that line was like looking at him.

I was in a prime place to see how all of the allegiances rose
and fell. And I took note of who was taking the most advantage of Reza's position as a rich speculator—by the way they
used his name or tried to undermine him—and I gave them

the worst waters. Or the water that was slightly off. Or the sweets that had just soured. It was my tiny revenge. I made it clear that any kindness to Reza down on Quint would be rewarded in small ways. It was the only way I could think of to help him. I hoped that one day he would come into the Tin Star Café to pick up some salts and forgive me.

But I had my life to live, and this new economy on the Yertina Feray caused its own problems. Part of me had to reutilize my bartering skills in order to make sure that everything ran smoothly. Every day had some bit of craziness to it now. I had just solved one problem when another arrived.

Kitsch Rutsok suddenly burst into my place with his goons behind him. His scaly skin looked shinier than usual, and I knew that meant he was in a rage. His tongue spat out toward me and vibrated as he spoke.

"You've stolen all of my customers," he hissed.

"I've stolen no one," I said. "Aliens do what they will, and your place is always full."

"Not as full as it used to be," he said.

"There are more places to go now," I said. "You're not the only game on the station."

"But I'm the first, and I'm the best," Kistch Rutsok said. He said it out loud to everyone, as though he were advertising himself.

"That you will always be," I said. "Everyone knows of your reputation."

"I wish you'd keep your Human friend in your place," Kitsch Rutsok said. "He comes into mine with his dust and bad energy and smolders in a corner. I'd offer him one of my comfort girls, but no one really knows what to do with a Human."

That stung. I wished that Reza would come to my place. To

me. I knew that being the start of something could be a burden, and I knew that talking with a friend was the relief. I could be that friend—that comfort—if he'd only let me.

"He's got free will," I said. "He can go where he pleases."

"But he's Human," Kitsch Rutsok said. "You could reason with him. Influence him."

I laughed.

"Perhaps I would feel better if you paid me a tax since I was here first," Kitsch said. "After all, you likely learned how to run a place from me."

I laughed again. "Go back to your place, Kitsch," I said. "Don't bother me anymore, or I'll use what I know about you as payback."

That made him quiet down. I knew too much about the illegal things he did. While he might be able to strong arm a tithe from the new aliens who were setting up shop, he could not force me to give him currency credits.

"Besides, we sell different things," I said. "We have no competition."

"Yes, you sell hopes, and I sell dreams," he said, changing his tune. "You just have a better class of clientele."

"Are you jealous?" I said.

It took a minute for the nanites to translate the precise meaning to him.

"Me? Of a Human?" Then he laughed, his scales rippling up and down his body, while his sly reptilian-looking eyes squinted and teared up. The Brahar only cried when they were laughing.

"Then we both have what we want," I said. "Now leave me alone."

Just then, Tournour entered the bar and took a good look around. Everyone hushed when he came in, as though somehow

Tournour would ruin the excitement of the times. He nodded to me and then sat down. Once everyone was certain that he would not interfere with their dreams, the excitement flared up again.

"It's a bit calmer here than in your place. There, people are already spending money that they don't have," Tournour said to Kitsch Rutsok.

"Then I'd best get back to it," Kitsch said. "I wouldn't want to miss a single drop of currency."

Kitsch left with his goons, but I knew that a line had been drawn. Territory had been staked up here on the Yertina Feray just as much as it had been down on Quint. I could have the business of Quint on my back wall, and sell my treats and sweets, but the gambling and the whoring would belong to him.

I opened up a bottle of premium water for myself. I imagined my old friend Heckleck and what he would do at the news of the rush. He would know exactly how to place it, how to trade it, and how to make the best of it all. I wondered how I could turn it into getting me back onto the path of destroying Brother Blue.

"I'm just back from Quint," Tournour said. He was overwhelmed ever since the Yertina Feray administration was suddenly charged with handing out claim stakes to the once uninteresting planet below, and I had seen very little of him.

I was jealous that Tournour had gone down to the planet, but with the rush in full swing, infrastructure had to be put into place.

"What's it like?" I asked. Although I could have easily staked a claim and jumped down to Quint to harvest alin pollen, I only daydreamed about doing it once or twice. But in the end, that kind of madness wasn't for me. I still had a larger mission in my life, and it didn't involve becoming a speculator. I repeated the names of the colonies to myself so that I would remember what my path was. *Killick. Kuhn. Marxuach. Andra. Beta Granade.*

"It's an explosion," he said. "It's beautiful. I suppose with everything else stripped away, the alin had a chance to bloom."

"I'm going down as soon as I can to lay a claim," said the old alien at the bar next to Tournour.

"You do that," Tournour said. He drained his water and tipped his antennae toward me and did what passed for a Loor wink.

"What's down there?" I asked. I had imagined my own booming town, but I supposed that really the image that I still had so firmly in my head was the vision for the town I had hoped to grow on Beta Granade with my mother and sister and the other Children of Earth colonists. That was a hard dream to shake.

"There is a shantytown down there. Mostly tents. But Reza has built himself a little cabin. It's quite sweet," Tournour said.

"You saw him?"

"Of course," he said.

I searched Tournour's face to see if he'd noticed how I'd sounded desperate when I'd asked about Reza. A Human would have picked up on this and been annoyed with me. But Tournour wasn't ruffled at all.

"He seems to be doing well. A little thin, I think. I was worried for him, so I insisted on taking him out for a meal. We had a good time. He's quite amusing. We did a lot of laughing together."

They were supposed to be rivals, but here Tournour was

showing him kindness. It stung me that they got along when I felt torn in my feelings for them.

"Does he have enough sweaters?" I asked.

"I don't know," Tournour said. Then he jotted something down on his data pad. "I'll make sure to tell him you want to check on that when I next see him."

"No!" I said. "Don't tell him I asked about him."

Tournour looked completely confused.

"I don't understand. You did ask about him."

"Yes, but in general. I was really asking about the planet. The town. Not him specifically."

Tournour processed what I was saying, and I could see him chalk it up to one of my strange Human emotional quirks that were beyond his comprehension.

For the past three years when I looked at the empty Quint from the arboretum window, it filled my imagination with possibilities. I knew that while it was cold and barely fertile, it was livable for a Human. Livable in the way that the arctic or the deep desert was habitable before the Earth warmed up. Now Reza was down there alive, walking around, eating, sleeping, and looking up at the stars from that planet. He was looking up at me.

Truth be told, I was jealous. It bothered me that he was down there. When I looked at Quint, instead of seeing the oceans, the clouds, the rust belt, or the landmasses, I imagined his shadowy figure lumbering across what I had begun to feel was my special place. My lonely world. My stone in the sky.

Now with all of those people down there, it was as though my own heart was being invaded.

And I preferred for my heart to be untouched.

9

The one thing about the rush is that there was no time for anything else. No time to think about Reza. No time to spend with Tournour. No time to wonder about Caleb. No time to mourn my mother and sister. No time to hate Brother Blue. Everyone wanted something from me: a rack of water, a trade for an introduction, a currency advance for gears and parts.

The quality of items that arrived to be bartered on the station rose as the empty wings filled up and the wealth from the alin began to flow.

Everyone wanted more than what their goods were worth. Everyone tasted riches just within their grasp, and they were impatient to start accumulating their wealth and spending it. Prices were inflated, and I noticed that those with the worst attitudes felt that their claim would be worth the most. Most of them I saw days, weeks, months later, defeated and broke. Then they would sit and be glad to trade someone their useless depleted claim for a glass of mediocre water.

I argued with everyone. I did not budge. I held the line. I charged high prices to keep up with the rest of the madness on the station and with Kitsch Rutsok's outlandish prices, but I never refused a person their water, salts, or sweets. All of my years of trading favors to survive made me bend in strange ways. They could pay what they wanted, and mostly I found that they paid me fairly. It wasn't that I was a soft touch. They knew they owed me, and they knew that while I preferred to deduct from currency chits, I could still always be paid in favors or information, just not in pollen.

In the middle of arguing with a particularly obnoxious Hort by the bar, a silence came over the room as someone entered. It struck me because it had not been quiet in the Tin Star Café since the beginning of the rush.

"What's going on?" I asked, straining my neck over the throngs of aliens to see what had everyone's attention.

I started to move away. The Hort put her appendage on my arm to stop me from moving.

"An alien who wants to stay alive never leaves a Hort in the middle of a negotiation."

I shook her off.

"You'll take your stub off me or you'll never come in here again," I said.

She knew that my threats were not empty and that a ban from the Tin Star would be worse for her down the line than an interrupted negotiation. She removed her appendage and let me pass. She would never dare kill me.

The door opened again, and Kitsch Rutsok came in with his goons. They had knives prominently displayed. Guns were not allowed on the station or on spaceships, since a stray laser or bullet could tear through the hull and cause damage and death for more than just the intended.

"No knives in my place," I said, following Kitsch, who was making a beeline for the claims board. His face told me that something was going terribly wrong. I put my hand on him to slow him down but he shook me off as he headed straight for an alien. It was only then that I noticed that near the claims wall there were two bipeds in bright Imperium uniforms of high rank with their backs to me. I had heard through Tournour that the Imperium would be sending some people to check into the situation on Quint, but he had said that wouldn't be for a few more weeks. I hadn't seen them come in because these days it was so crowded it was difficult to see everyone that came into the place. But I was surprised that these Imperium delegates looked like Humans. Tournour had inferred that it would be low ranking clerical workers. He'd made certain that it would be nothing more than a formality.

"You can't do this," Kitsch Rutsok said. "I've paid my taxes. I've paid my hush money, and I've paid my Imperium operating dues. I've *paid*."

"You should be glad that with all of the illegal activities you engage in you are not paying more to stay open."

I knew that voice. When he turned around to face us, I couldn't speak.

It was Brother Blue.

Kitsch signaled to his goons who flanked him.

"Hey," I said, finding my voice. "Take it outside!"

"Whatever this Imperium stooge is doing here, he's going to make your life a living hell, too. You should let me cut him," Kitsch said. "Maybe then they'll send another whose hands are not as sticky as this Human's."

"Get out of my place, Kitsch," I said, hoping beyond hope that Brother Blue would follow him outside. Kitsch didn't leave, but some of the tension in the air dissipated.

I hadn't recognized Brother Blue at first because his hair was short and his face was cleanshaven. He looked like a younger man. His eyes met mine, and I could see that he looked just as surprised to see me as I was to see him. He managed to compose himself faster than I could.

"Tula Bane? You look rather well for someone who is dead," he said.

When he actually said my name out loud my heart leaped to my throat. I stumbled backward and placed my hand on a chair to steady myself.

I turned to look at the young woman with him, almost thinking that it would be Els. That somehow Els had made it out alive after he had shot her, but it was not. It was a Human girl, a little older than I was. She was Asian with bobbed dark hair and perfect bangs. She had eyes so dark that they seemed to have no irises. She had not one curve on her. I did not recognize her. There was no reason I would. She smiled at me, and not knowing what to do, I nodded my head stiffly in return.

Brother Blue went directly up to the claims board and pulled out a data plug and plugged it in. Immediately the map changed, and a new map was overlaid onto every claim that had been made.

"Attention, people of the Yertina Feray. My assistant and I are here on behalf of the Imperium. It has come to our attention that Quint is once again a viable planet and worth our interest. Upon looking at the claims list of two hundred years ago, the map of Quint is being divided. I have been placed in charge of this endeavor."

The bar exploded.

All the aliens looked to me. This was my place.

"We have a system," I said. My voice sounded thin and

pinched. Once again he was besting me and there was nothing that I could do. "You can't come in here and make claims on staked claims."

They had sent the Imperium here to mess with virtual claims. We were firmly on their radar now. It didn't take any more than looking at how the Yertina Feray had blossomed in a few short months to see that there was real money to be made here. Of course Brother Blue was the one who came. He was the type of person who knew how to exploit something that was booming. I wondered if they were down on the planet doing anything to the prospectors on Quint. My thoughts flew to Reza, and I grew as worried for him as I was for us.

"Calm down. We are not here to mine the whole planet, but we are happy to lease you our spots. We are basing our claim on the old maps from when the planet yielded different substances."

Brother Blue pointed to the map. The places where we all knew alin didn't grow but where the lodes had been best for mining were all claimed by Major Species. Large tracts of the planet were claimed by the Per, the Brahar, the Loor, the Moldav, the Kao. The Dren Line was where the ores had poor yields and so those claims sported the names of many Minor Species, some names that were familiar to me, Hort and Nurlok, for instance, but many I'd never heard of: Freng, Volla, Gej, Ypsem. I wondered if they had never managed to grow their stellar colonies, gone extinct, or if the Imperium had made them go silent.

"No one has heard from the Gej for a long time," I said. It was feared that they, with their peace-loving ways, had been the first to fall. We'd all heard that the Imperium had been

64

razing planets with less than five colonies for resources. I had once tried to sign up for that kind of work. I shuddered at the thought now.

Brother Blue looked at me.

"So you are correct," he said. Then he lifted up his datapad and the claim on the coveted Dren Line that once said Gej now said Earth.

He smiled at me.

"You see. I'm still helping Earth's expansion," he said to me.

I wanted to vomit.

"What about those other claims by Minor Species?" an alien with a gourd-like head asked.

"What does this mean for us?" a Nurlok behind me yelled.

"Those of you who have claims may all keep your claims as long as you pay a healthy fee for the privilege," Brother Blue said. "And if you can't, then your claim will be turned over to the Imperium. We'll transport in some of our workers. And of course, anyone here is welcome to sign up for work with the Imperium."

He went on to say that workers on a claim could only be of the same species, or non-Human, meaning that more than half the speculators would have to scramble to find or trade workers or their own kind to keep their claims.

I held my mouth shut. Because it dawned on me that Brother Blue claiming the Gej claim for Earth had actually protected Reza. He'd made a mistake. It lifted my spirits to see that Brother Blue could fumble in his mad grab for power. He would realize it later, but there was nothing he could do about it. He'd set the rules.

I scrambled back as the others surged forward, pressing in on Brother Blue. I hoped perhaps they would tear him to pieces. Before anything could happen, Tournour came in with his officers, who placed themselves strategically around the bar to keep the peace. The crowd was infuriated, and I was torn between wanting to lead the mob to tear Brother Blue apart and to find safety immediately. He still frightened me. I had soothed myself into thinking that I had let him go because I was waiting for the right moment to kill him. But the way I trembled made me think that I was still just as much of a coward now as I had been when I'd seen him over a year ago.

He still had a hold over me that I couldn't shake.

I had to think. I couldn't think with all of this action going on around me. But what could I do? What were my choices?

Tournour pushed his way over to the claims wall.

"Brother Blue," he said.

"Ah, the constable is here. Let's have calm," Brother Blue said. "Constable Tournour, I'm here on behalf of the Imperium."

"I'm sorry I wasn't there to meet your ship," Tournour said. "I was told the Imperium delegation was arriving next week. I didn't know that it would be you that they were sending."

It was not often that I saw Tournour ruffled, but Brother Blue being here clearly was as much a surprise to him as it was to me.

"I thought it best not to give you time to clean up before I got here," he said. "I like to see the mess. Much more informative."

"We agreed that the Yertina Feray would be left alone," Tournour said.

"I agreed, and I kept my end of the bargain. But things change," Brother Blue said, "especially when wealth is involved."

"We have it under control. I've been sending reports. We can handle our own affairs."

"I know you say you have the Imperium's best interests at heart. But, no," Brother Blue said. "You don't have it under control. The Yertina Feray has become too bustling a place now for a young Loor like you to handle. You need my help. Imperium help."

He punched his datapad again. Imperium guards made up of all the Major Species entered the Tin Star Café and lined up along the walls. It reminded me of the quiet way we had been invaded when the Imperium had first taken over. Heckleck had gone into hiding when they arrived. But it was clear by the sheer numbers of guards that this was wholly different.

Tournour looked cuffed, collared, and leashed. He could not protect the station from the Imperium. His officers were outnumbered in the Tin Star. We'd been seen, and things once noticed don't easily disappear again.

Brother Blue and Tournour looked at me. I tried to make myself as small as possible.

"It's really a simple matter," Brother Blue said. "These claimants are free to do what they want once they pay the appropriate fees to the Imperium. We'll be setting up a proper claims office, and I'll be here with my assistant to oversee it. Those who don't have claims or lose their claims are welcome to work on Imperium-seized land. Loor with Loor. Per with Per, etc. We're in control now."

Then he showed a datapad that had the official Imperium order on it. It was clear that we would be scrutinized for compliance and that we would get away with no deviation from the law. Everything that Tournour had done to keep us on the edge of this regime vanished in an instant. Tournour, as a member of the Imperium, could not refuse. He nodded and entered his digital signature to mark that he'd received the order.

"Besides," Brother Blue said, "we had a deal based on the fact that I thought you said the girl was dead. It seems that you lied. That will have to go into my report about you."

"She was dead," Tournour said. "You examined her yourself."

Brother Blue sneered. What Tournour said was true. It was Brother Blue that had made the mistake.

My heart went out to Tournour. It was easy to forget that he was considered to be just a little older than I was. I wished that in this moment I had something that I could do to calm him down. This was the reason that he needed to be partnered with his own kind. What could I do? Nothing. My very existence was causing him even more trouble.

My blood boiled. How was it that Brother Blue was winning again? How could the galaxy be that unfair?

"I suppose she's tougher than I thought," Brother Blue said. "We'll have to fix that immediately. Mark down a request for a trial order against this Human girl."

"For what crime?" his assistant asked.

"For inciting a riot," Brother Blue snapped at her.

His assistant looked at Brother Blue and hesitated for a moment before marking his wishes into a datapad. Then Brother Blue made a signal with his hand and all hell broke loose as the Imperium guards took their batons and hit those constables closest to them in the guts. Once Tournour's officers were disabled, they moved forward in a line, methodically bashing people with their sticks. They seemed invincible.

Kitsch Rutsok and his goons pulled out their knives and

then the hidden knives that others wore on them started coming out.

Trevor came awake and was menacing those around him. Cutting both Imperium members and my clients.

"Trevor, off!" I commanded. I had to say it twice before Trevor heard me. Chairs and tables were swung and knocked over as fights broke out in all corners of the Tin Star. Fists and other alien appendages were flying. The Imperium kept moving forward, dodging thrown bottles and uprooted stools.

Tournour pulled me by the elbow and led me away from the chaos to the safety behind my bar. The divide of the counter and the aliens made me snap back to my senses. I appreciated the restraint that Tournour had shown by not spraying me with his calming scent. I wanted to have my wits about me, and he knew that it bothered me when he did it without my consent.

"Are you all right?" He asked in a low tone as we crouched behind the bar.

"No," I said. "I'm not."

"Let me calm you down," he said. "It will clear your head."

"No," I said. I wanted and needed my own Human adrenaline.

He reluctantly nodded. I wondered if it hurt him to withhold the scent.

"I have to go out there and stop this," he said. "I have to go do my job, or I'll be on trial next."

I nodded and watched as he activated his riot field and threw himself into the fray.

It was over so quickly. The Imperium neutralized the situation. Kitsch Rutsok and his goons were being cuffed and led away. Customers looked dazed as they tried to pick their way through the broken furniture and the shattered glass to avoid arrest. I could see three of my customers dead on the café floor, one of them, the Hort I had been arguing with.

When I saw a chance, I bounded out of the door and ran to my quarters.

I was clearheaded enough to know that my time was limited. This was the moment to act. He was here, but I wasn't ready like I thought I'd be. That's the trouble with moments. They never come when you are ready.

There is never a right one.

There is only *this* one.

10

Later that night, Tournour came alone.

Tournour did not make a habit of entering my room uninvited. He shook me awake. It was unusual, but not something that I hadn't expected to happen one day. Trevor perceived no threat as he knew Tournour as a friend. We both remained calm.

"We have to come up with a plan," I said.

"I know," he said. "Do you trust me?"

"I do," I said.

"Then tell Trevor to power down and follow me outside."

Everything would be all right. I turned to Trevor and issued the command.

I put on my shoes, pulled on a sweater, and followed Tournour outside. I could tell he was nervous by the way he carried himself.

Once outside, I was greeted by a flock of Tournour's men, all with knives drawn and pointed at me. I was surrounded. I knew why he didn't want Trevor with me. If Trevor had come, blood would have been spilt.

"What is this?" I asked.

"Three died at the riot you instigated at the Tin Star Café. You're under arrest for murder."

"No," I screamed. I turned to his officers. "You were all there. You saw what happened."

Each one of them stayed silent. Each one of them averted their various-looking alien eyes.

"I didn't kill those men," I said to Tournour.

"Don't make this harder on yourself," Tournour said. "I have to do my job so that the job can get done."

His eyes were looking straight into mine. They were saying *trust me*.

It is very difficult to have faith when your arms are being cuffed behind your back. Tournour worked for the Imperium. He was following orders. *Brother Blue's orders.* Tournour read me my rights according to the Imperium, which were no rights at all.

My confidence began to waver as I was marched through the station's halls. It was a commotion like I'd never seen before. Everywhere, everyone had stepped out of their abodes to watch as I passed, but instead of making the usual noise, there was silence. There was no jeering. There was no shouting. There was no gesticulating. Everyone was quiet. They looked at me, catching my eye and I knew two things: Tournour must have arranged the commotion. They all knew that I was being arrested this evening, and they all knew that this was wrong. They might have been quiet, but they were on my side.

My heart went out to Tournour. He was forced to be a puppet in this charade. I both admired his dignity but hated that he didn't fight back. More than that, I knew that he was scared for me.

"I'm scared, too," I whispered.

He pushed me forward forcefully, and as he did, he released the scent. I breathed in the musty odor and immediately felt

72

calm and clear in a way that had me hyper focused. I only wished that there were something I could do to calm Tournour down.

I was brought into the interrogation room to discover Brother Blue's aide was there.

She stuck her hand out to me in a Human gesture to introduce herself. A handshake. As though she were my friend and not my enemy. I refused to touch her, and after a moment, she let her hand fall to her side. She may have been one of my species, but to me, she was an alien.

"I'm Myfanwy Yu," she said. "I'll be both your Human representative and also Imperium observer."

"Isn't that a conflict of interest?" I asked.

"You are to have a counsel of your own species in order to ensure no speciesism."

"I can choose any Human to observe?"

I would feel better if Reza were here. At least it wouldn't be someone in Brother Blue's pocket.

"There isn't much of a pool of Humans to choose from," she said.

"There is a Human on the planet," I said.

"Yes. I heard that, but it's too hard to get anyone back up here in a timely manner. Since Brother Blue has called against you, the task falls to me."

Myfanwy Yu. I knew that name. How did I know it? Then it hit me. She was the girl that Caleb pined for. She had been an Imperium Youth like him and Reza, only while their ship was being sent to the false colonies and sabotaged before they got there, she had been sent to Bessen, to serve at the Human Embassy there. It made perfect sense that she was here. Perhaps this was to my advantage.

Hekcleck always said *the only real wild card in any trade is love. You can never factor in for it.*

Myfanwy adjusted herself in her seat to make herself comfortable. I leaned forward.

"We have a mutual friend," I said. "Caleb Kamil."

"Yes, I do know him," she said. "But that won't distract me from my task at hand."

She didn't even light up when I said his name. She did not twitch or show any hint of emotion. Could she really be the love of Caleb's life?

Love was confusing. But it was not indifferent. As still as I could keep my face, if someone asked me about Tournour or Reza some part of me would light up. I was trained to look for these kinds of little betrayals in aliens. I could only think that I had not enough practice with reading Human faces. Still I would try to pull on this thread and find her sympathy.

"He's spoken of you to me," I said.

"We were at the academy together," she said, pushing at something on the datapad. "I barely knew him."

That surprised me. Caleb spoke of her as though she were the love of his life. But there were all kinds of powerful ways to love someone, even unrequited. Even unnoticed. I waited for her to speak again. As I did when I was bargaining for the upper hand in barter. She waited a good long time before she spoke.

"For the record please state your full name," she asked.

"Tula Bane," I said.

"My information says that you came to outer space with the Children of Earth initiative. What planet were you headed for?"

74

"Beta Granade," I said. "On the *Prairie Rose.*"

"That ship burned with all hands on deck."

"Not with me," I said.

"You survived the crash?" she asked, surprised.

"No," I said. "I wasn't on the ship."

"Why not?"

"I'd been left here."

"Why?"

I couldn't tell her the truth. It wouldn't help me right now to accuse Brother Blue.

"I don't know."

She made a note in her datapad.

"Why did you stay here? Why not try to join one of the other colonies?"

That startled me. I examined her face. She was being serious. Could she really not know that they were scams that Brother Blue had pulled? I was beginning to think that I was in a lot more danger than I thought.

"I couldn't . . ." I was at a loss. ". . . reach them. I had no credits. The Imperium came, and I found it difficult to get off the station."

"I understand that returning to Earth was not an option, but you didn't try to join the Wanderers?"

I didn't answer because it had never struck me as a real idea to join them. It was more like they were an abstract idea of how I could get to Brother Blue one day when I left here.

"I didn't know how to find them," I admitted.

Tell the truth as much as you can, Heckleck always said.

"You've been here for a few years, yes?"

I nodded.

"How did you survive?" she asked.

"Barter," I said.

"The Imperium frowns on black market activities," she said. "That will have to be another charge to your crimes."

She made another note in her datapad.

"Why did you start the riot?" she asked. "Do you resent the aliens that you live with?"

"No! And I didn't start the riot," I said.

"That's not what the eyewitnesses said."

"You were an eyewitness," I said. "What did you see?"

"I'm here as a neutral party," she said haltingly. "I can't be called upon as a witness."

"Who is called then?"

She flashed her datapad to me, and I could see some of the names.

They were aliens that I knew who were down on their luck. Who hadn't had much of a break in the rush. Or lived in the underguts. I couldn't blame them for saying they saw something. They were trying to survive. They had likely weighed the worth of staying loyal to me. And if there was one thing I knew was that a favor owed to the dead was not worth anything at all.

I needed to change this conversation quickly before I drowned.

"How's Earth?"

I saw her wince at the mention of home. She looked up from her datapad.

"Earth and her colonies are thriving under the Imperium," she said. "Earth is stable. All rebels destroyed."

"What colonies have you visited?" I asked. "What do they look like? I've always wondered since I never made it to mine."

Killick. Kuhn. Marxuach. Andra. Beta Granade.

Her eyes snapped to me.

"I'm the one asking the questions," she said.

"Which one have you seen?" I asked.

"I have not yet had the pleasure," she said. "I was to accompany Brother Blue to Kuhn last season, but I came down with a stomach virus the night before and could not leave. But they are thriving."

I was about to open my mouth and tell her what I knew. I was going to tell her to check my data plug for the information. At least if I was going to die, I wanted someone of my kind to know that I knew about Brother Blue. If it was the last thing I did, I would plant a seed of doubt in her mind. It would be a slow poison from within. If the Imperium found out, then she would be in jeopardy. Her ruin was a small comfort. But at least it would be something.

Really I was just taking swings in the dark.

Before I could speak, the door slid open and Tournour stepped into the room with barely a glance at me.

I wished we could be alone. I wished he would tell me that he'd killed Brother Blue and that he was now going to kill this Human girl. But to kill them with all the Imperium Guards around only meant death. And while I had not cared about that, Tournour had tried to show me that patience, which I did not have, and strategy, which I was slow on, was the only way to get what you wanted, and to live.

He took a seat in one of the large chairs and looked bored, as though he didn't care for me. Not even his antennae were paying attention to me.

As close to Tournour as I was, in this moment I knew that I had to pretend he was no friend of mine now. I had to face him as an enemy.

I steeled myself.

One thing that I knew about Tournour is that he would fight to keep the Yertina Feray safe, and right now I was in the way of that. That was one difference between the Loor and the Human. The Loor always had the greater task in mind. If it meant taking me down, he would do it. I was just one Human, even if I was his.

But Humans would fight for each other.

I laughed. Neither way was better or worse.

I was being interrogated about every aspect of my business. I was glad that I had always insisted on being paid in currency chits. It made it easier for me to still seem legitimate and harder for the Imperium to find too much fault with me. They cited me for how I acquired the waters I sold; for not having proper ways to store and serve the different kinds of fresh foods; for the friendly gambling that my customers did when they played their simple games; for undeclared income from the bartering I did. The list went on.

Myfanwy was relentless at digging in every dark corner that I had. As she entered notes into her datapad, Tournour sat stone-faced. I was exhausted and wanted to make it stop. I wanted to be in the arboretum with Tournour, with our feet in the dirt. I wanted to be questioned about simple things, things that would make us both smile. Or bring us closer together.

To make things worse, Tournour would occasionally interrupt Myfanwy and make a point that dug my hole even deeper.

"We are satisfied," said Myfanwy.

"When is my trial?" I asked.

"The trial for execution will be set for tomorrow."

Now I understood why I couldn't catch a break with Myfanwy. In her eyes I was already dead. Tournour wouldn't try to help me because the best thing I could do for him now was to have all of my errant ways be revealed so that they would not have any reason to turn on him, too. I was securing his position as essential to the station.

But what about me? I thought. *I want to live, too.*

Tournour threw me into the brig himself. He had done this to me before to keep me safe. But it didn't feel that way this time. My absolute fear was rising fast.

He was the last one to leave the room and he turned to face me as the cell door slid shut. And only I saw his lips move.

"Trust me," he mouthed.

I lay down on the hard bench with my face to the wall. I didn't want to be seen as I wept.

11

It was hours later when I thought that all hope was lost that Reza burst into the room where I was being held.

At first I didn't recognize him. It seemed out of place to see him back on the station, in the brig, holding a knife in one hand. He punched the guard at the console and then wrapped the guard's arms, legs, and mouth in some of the rags that he wore.

"What are you doing here?" I asked. I sounded angry, but inside I was feeling light. Hopeful.

"Getting you out."

"I thought you were on Quint." I said.

"I'm back."

Reza looked at me and smiled, then put his finger up to tell me to wait a minute.

He hovered over the console, pecking at the terminal buttons, taking an awfully long time at whatever he was doing. I wanted to get out of my cell before someone came in.

"Hurry!" I said. I worried that we'd both get killed.

He shook his hand at me to keep quiet.

"This is suicide," I said.

"I'm trying to remember the code," he said. "I'm good at strategy and force, but I forget codes," he said. "I need to concentrate here."

It was frustrating to not be able to see what he was doing. I imagined that if I could see, I could help. But that wasn't necessarily true. I had social skills, but I had never learned computer programming. Heckleck had taught me a few basic override commands. How to overide a simple door was one of them. *It's always good to know a few ways in and out of a place.*

But this was a brig. I couldn't lock pick myself out of this one.

"Look you need to know something. This whole station is completely under the Imperium's thumb. They're coming for the alin. Tournour is with them right now," I said. "Just leave me here. He won't be able to help you if you get caught."

Reza stepped back from the console and sang himself a little tune. Some mnemonic device and after a moment, he punched the numbers in slowly. The door that jailed me slid open.

He stuck his hand out for me to take. That electric spark was still there. It was nice to touch a Human.

"Who do you think called me back up here, came up with the plan, and gave me the code?" he asked glancing up at me with that look that I loved most about him.

Tournour. Of course. This was his plan. He told me to trust him. He was always going to get me out of here.

I laughed.

"The guard didn't struggle, as though he knew he was going to be attacked."

"It was all theatrics," Reza said. "This station isn't completely under the Imperium's thumb. You've got friends. But Brother Blue has all his papers to order an execution after your trial. We have to go. *Now.*"

We exited the brig, and standing guard at the door was Trevor.

"You brought Trevor," I said. "How did you get it to work?"

"Tournour activated it," he said. "He thought you'd need it."

I was so happy to see the robot that I threw my arms around its metal body and hugged it even though it could not care less that I was feeling anything.

"We don't have time for that," Reza said, pulling at me. I instructed Trevor to follow us.

It was the quiet cycle, the time when most aliens were asleep. But even so, there was always something going on. Aliens should be present and walking around. The station functioned around the clock. But the station was especially eerie this time.

"Where is everyone?"

"There's been a power grid glitch. Everyone is to stay inside," Reza said.

"Really?" I said.

"No," Reza said. "Tournour."

"What's the plan?" I asked. "Where am I to go?"

"I don't know," Reza said. "We didn't have time to think that far ahead."

It was strange to think of Tournour and Reza plotting my fate together. Although if my fate were in anyone's hands, I was glad that it was both of theirs. They approached problems differently, but together they would likely think of almost every angle.

Despite the clear path, we weaved through sections that while it seemed to be the long way around, I knew were the safest, sneakiest way to get to the docking bay.

When Reza diverted from the way I would have gone, I knew that likely it was because he had information that I did not. I had to trust him even though I knew the station better than he did.

"Tournour and his guards could chase us and never catch up," I said. Confirming why I thought we were going the long way.

"That's the idea," Reza said.

But even I could tell that it was taking too long. We were only halfway there when the all-clear sounded.

"Well, it couldn't have lasted forever," Reza said.

I turned cold as panic flooded me.

The halls were filling up, making Reza agitated, and Trevor more alert, but everyone who passed us averted their eyes, telling me that they would not say they had seen me. I knew that I had bought this precious extra time with those favors I had accrued over the years.

How much would I owe when I got back?

Then it hit me. Would I come back?

I could see a patrol coming down the main hallway.

"Twelve o'clock," I said.

We weren't too far from Kistch Rutsok's, and I could see him standing outside of his place waving people inside, trying to get big business. Kitsch Rutsok's voice was so loud. We were going to get caught.

"Tell Trevor to head to the docking bay," Reza said.

I gave the command and watched as Trevor rolled away from us.

Kitsch's eyes caught mine. I stared at him, thinking that he would be glad to witness my arrest.

Reza pulled me into a public data nook and pushed me up against the console wall.

This little nook would not cover us from the officers' view no matter if they were on Tournour's side or not. They would not be able to ignore us. Capture was inevitable.

But I'd seen something change in Kitsch Rutsok's eyes. Although he hated the fact that I was his direct competition, he did something for me in that moment that I would never forget. Instead of waving everyone inside for business, he started telling everyone inside his place to come outside. His big booming voice changed pitch, and I watched in amazement as his arms pulled at aliens to crowd the hallway.

"The data nook is over there," he said. "Make sure to fill your currency chits!"

The aliens who I didn't know, or whose faces were unfamiliar, kept going into the bar; but the aliens who had lived on the Yertina Feray for years poured out of the bar and started coming toward the nook that Reza and I were crouched in.

I saw a little Nurlok that I knew well. Kelmao, who had helped me in the past with the Hocht I had against Caleb, and occasionally helped out at the Tin Star Café, noticed me. Then she turned to the Nurlok nearest her and spit through her whiskers. The other Nurlok spit back, and they started to fight and the crowd formed a ring around them, hiding us as the patrol went by.

The data console jabbed into my back as Reza pushed closer to me. I twisted my body toward it, a plan forming in my head. If I was going to get off of this space station there was only one place to go, to Togni Station and take the space elevator down to Bessen. From there, I would have the best chance of taking a swipe at Brother Blue's reputation. He would be here. I could hurt him.

My determination to avenge all that he took and kept taking away from me was reignited.

The patrol came up to the crowd. They knew I was missing, but they didn't seem in a particular hurry to find me, even though I could hear them questioning the crowd. Kitsch Rutsok led the crowd in ignoring the officers and goading at the two Nurloks. It was like an impromptu Hocht. They threw punches and then started to run down the hall.

"Officers! You waste time looking for a measly Human when you've got two Nurloks causing trouble right here! I should issue a complaint and have you fined for not doing your jobs!"

The other aliens joined in yelling at the officers who finally took off after the Nurloks.

We were alone in the hall now, except for the few who had lingered behind to still cover us. Everyone that had been on the station since before the boom seemed to be in on ensuring my escape, some had even given me pieces of their clothing to help disguise me.

I entered in my secret code and retrieved my data about Brother Blue.

"We don't have time for this," Reza hissed.

I put my finger up to tell him to wait.

"I can't count on Trevor being at the docking bay, and I need my proof if I'm going to have a bargaining chip down the line," I said.

I punched in the numbers to remotely access my data and ordered a data plug of the file that I kept on Brother Blue. It was encrypted, and only I knew the code, but when I decrypted it I could show the discrepensies that I knew for certain about him. Some of it was what I had accumulated. Some of the data was what Els had tried to bribe Brother Blue with. Silently I thanked her, even though she had caused me so much trouble and had died for it. In a few minutes, the console 3-D printed a data plug for me.

Now I was armed.

"Go, go!"

It was Kistch Rutsok pulling at us to leave the nook.

I shook the dreadful thoughts out of my head and put one foot in front of the other.

"Thank you," I said as we passed Kitsch Rutsok.

"Live," he said. Not looking at me.

I tried to calculate how many favors I would owe for this. My mind spun at the thought of the unpayable debt for life by so many people on the station.

"What's at the docking bay?" I asked Reza as we ran down the halls. There was no time to go any other way than the direct way.

"There is a Per ship willing to take you off the station," he said. "After that you're on your own."

"I know how to do that," I said.

12

• •

Finally, we were at the docking bay.

Trevor was there waiting for us. I was so happy that it'd made it.

Reza and I rushed to the hangar where the Per were waving us in frantically with all of their arms.

"The alarm has been sounded," the Per captain said. "We need to leave now if we are going to leave at all."

I was really leaving. After three long years on the Yertina Feray, after all of that wishing, the day was finally here and I didn't want to go. I sent Trevor onto the ship ahead of me and then turned back to Reza.

"Come with me," I said.

"No," he said. "I have to stay here. I can make money. A lot of it. If I can get it to the resistance and overthrow Earth Gov and stop this collaboration with the Imperium, then somehow, maybe I can help Earth."

I loved that he was still fighting for Earth. Even after it betrayed him, even after it had fallen to the Imperium, he still believed in it. It was as if he knew that though things were seemingly good on the surface, the dependence on the Imperium was a deal with the devil. Reza believed he could be the one to open Earth's eyes to that.

How much further along would he be with his dreams right

now if I had not mistakenly sent him to the Outer Rim, but back there as I had planned a year ago? Would he have done anything as noble back on Earth? Or had my mistake, assigning travel passes to Caleb and Reza during their cryosleep, somehow saved him so he'd be ready for this moment? Maybe my mistake had really given him his best shot. Maybe he knew it too from the way he was looking at me. Like he still had some fight in him.

He clenched his fists and brought them to his eyes. "Besides, if I go with you, Brother Blue will know who is on your side. We've got to keep him guessing. This is everyone's best chance."

I knew he was right, but I didn't like it. I caught my breath. I was leaving. And I might never see him or Tournour again.

"Tournour will have to be your enemy," I said.

I didn't like to think of the two I really cared about being on opposites sides.

"It'll be all right," he said.

He took my hand in his and squeezed it. All I could think of was that his skin felt so familiar, and I might never feel it again. His thumb ran itself along mine. Time slowed. These few seconds were forever. They were all we had.

"I shouldn't have been an ass when I arrived," he said.

"I was a jerk, too," I said.

I looked into his deep dark eyes, and I got up on my tippy toes, and I kissed him. At first it was hesitant, but then he slid his arms around me, and I knew that we had both said what we couldn't say. *I'm sorry.*

"You have to go," he murmured as he pulled away from me.

"Tell me where Caleb is," I said.

"I don't know."

"You must know something. A clue. A trail. Don't let me be alone out there in space."

"I honestly don't know," he said. "Besides, you don't want to meet him again. He's different."

"We're all different," I said.

He looked down at his feet and then after a moment back up at me.

"Please," I said.

I could see that he was trying to keep something from me.

"We have to go," the Per captain said worriedly.

"The *Noble Star*. Look for the ship *Noble Star*. He might still be with them."

I nodded. We hugged. I held him longer than I should have. Unless I found Caleb, he would be the last friendly face I would ever see.

"Come on, come on, come on!" The Per captain pushed me up the ramp as it was closing.

The door sealed shut, and we were separated by the metal and glass, and a Per crew member put one of her hands on me, pulling me away from the door.

"Please, Tula Bane, you must strap in for takeoff," she said to me. The ship started rumbling as the engines engaged.

I tore myself away from the door; from Reza standing on the dock staring at the closing airlock, from Tournour some-where in the station dealing with the fallout of my escape, from my home.

I was frightened. I felt the ship uncouple and float. I sat down and strapped in just as the engines engaged.

I looked around at the ship. It was a standard cargo ship with a skeleton crew. Probably running passengers to the

Yertina Feray for the rush, but now empty on the way back. I could see the cargo of alin hastily strapped down next to where Trevor had been secured. This was how my trip was being paid for. It was probably Reza's first crop. Another thing I owed him.

The ship accumulated high speed and pushed toward the inevitable light skip we'd have to complete to pull free from this solar system.

We were off.

I was in space again.

13

. . . .

There is a certain kind of calm to a voyage in space.
I wondered if it was the same in the old times for those who sailed on the oceans of any planet. Of course, oceans are choppier than windless space, but space had its own storms and challenges. What it did hold in common with an ocean voyage was the endless view of the same thing outside of a window for days, weeks, and months, even years on end. It allowed the mind to roam.

I was restless, and no amount of blackness could calm me.

These Per knew I wanted to get to Bessen. I'd told them my first night on board.

"When do you think we'll get there?" I asked.

"We'll get there when we get there," the captain said.

But they didn't want to go to the heart of the Imperium with their cargo only to have it confiscated. I had to get off of this ship.

Being a solo traveler on a spaceship was never totally safe. That was why so many aliens traveled in packs. It was why the Humans wandered. I was grateful every moment for Trevor. Trevor rolled with me wherever I went and for the most part, I was left alone by the skeleton crew of the Per ship.

I appreciated their quietness and how they tried to make me comfortable, even though their ship was not made for the

Human form. The whole ship was made for more arms than I had, and sometimes it was hard for me to reach or open different things.

Since I wasn't part of the crew, I meandered through the ship and looked out the windows at the stars when they were visible. Part of me knew that they left me alone because of Trevor. They had seen his knives whir once or twice. And part of me knew that they wanted to ensure they could still dock at the Yertina Feray. Tournour owed them a favor now, and even though they'd been paid with an early harvest of alin, with the rush on Quint, it was becoming a desirable thing to have an in on the station.

My safety ensured their future when dealing with alin.

These Per were looking to make trades right away while the prices would still be high. Alin was still rare because it was the growing season, and the first shipments would get the prettiest price.

They knew they were lucky and would tolerate me until their cargo ran out.

Think, Tula. Think. I said to myself as I wandered the empty ship.

Going back to the Yertina Feray was a death sentence unless I had help. I knew that.

Although I had spent the last three years surrounded by aliens, I was reminded that the citizens of the Yertina Feray had become familiar to me. On the Per ship, I felt a new kind of loneliness.

I tried to remember that despite that feeling, I was not friendless. Tournour was my friend. Thado was my friend. Reza was my friend. Caleb was out there somewhere, and if he could forgive me, then maybe he could be my friend.

He was the only one who I could go to for help now.

The *Noble Star*.

It surprised me that he was on a ship and not a planet. From the way Caleb had talked when we were on the Yertina Feray, he'd seemed to lay his bet on finding a race on the Outer Rim that would want to ally with Earth and come to the center with an army. But Reza had said that things had changed out there. I couldn't count on what I thought, only on what I knew.

I had a place to start. The ship's name was *Noble Star*. Now I just had to find it.

I haunted the communication room, sitting for hours searching for news of the ship. I scoured all systems and found nothing. It was as though the *Noble Star* did not exist. If only I had a planet that it was from, or a species to attach the name to. It was like looking for a needle but not knowing what or where the haystack was.

I knew that Reza would not give me a false name, and that there were plenty of ships that came from the Outer Rim that were not on any official registry. Not every planet from the Outer Rim with spacefaring life on it was part of the Imperium. That was what was also so appealing about the Outer Rim. But that was what was frustrating my efforts to find Caleb now.

Of course there could be another reason. The *Noble Star* could be a pirate ship. I didn't want to think of that. Pirates were nasty things, and I never liked to deal with them when I was trading for Heckleck or serving in the Tin Star. They were heartless. They attacked ships and stripped them. They spent their loot on perversions that I could not even think of. The only thing that was true about pirates was they were hard, rough, and had no empathy. They were so cold that the usual tricks I depended on for my trading didn't work. They wore outrageously colored costumes with shapes to distract from their form so that their species was hidden. There was no differentiation of species in their ranks. It was as though they'd all been wiped of any physical identity.

That could never be Caleb. Sweet Caleb could never turn to that kind of life. He was too generous. Unselfish.

Unless something terrible had happened to him.

But Reza had said as much, hadn't he? He'd hinted at the horrors they'd faced on the Outer Rim. Reza had made his way back to me because he hadn't wanted to break. I knew that now. It was the only thing that made sense.

But what if you were broken? I had to believe that even if Caleb had turned into someone like that, he'd still have heart enough to lend a hand to an old friend.

I had no time for doubts.

I sent messages hoping to catch the ship's attention, but it was like sending a message in a bottle. And if the Per knew that I was trying to contact a pirate ship, they likely would kill me on the spot regardless of their agreement with Tournour.

Meanwhile, I had nothing to do and nowhere to go but hope that sometime soon we would cross paths with either the *Noble Star* or a ship that was headed to Bessen.

I had nothing to do as they went about their business, and I tried to make myself as invisible as possible. As generous as they were, I could tell that I was wearing out my welcome from the slurs that the Per crew would mumble when I passed them in the halls or the mess. I had to find another ship that was willing to go to Bessen. And I had to find one soon.

I looked at their manifests daily until finally I saw on the roster of places that a Brahar ship the Per were trading with was going to Bessen.

Bessen.

After weeks of dreariness, my heart lifted. Humans did live in the consulate on Bessen. At least I knew that I would be safe as long as Brother Blue was not there. Perhaps I could buy myself some time. Earth's embassy was there. Perhaps there was a way for me to blend in with them. Pass myself off as coming from Earth. I started to listen to all the Earth transmissions I could whenever the communications array was pointed toward our sun. I studied what news I could get and tried coming up with a story that might slip me in with any Humans as a new recruit. I didn't know how many were stationed on the moon but felt that since I did not have the tattoos of a Wanderer, whatever story I told would be more believable.

Revenge was a powerful motivator.

14

. . . .

The Brahar ship light skipped into the system that housed Bessen soon after I boarded. We were to arrive at the moon in the middle of the sleep cycle, but I woke up early in order to see the outer planets as we jumped by them. Finally, we were circling the Loor home world, Tallara, where the moon Bessen orbited.

Staring at Tallara, the planet that Tournour was from, made me feel as though I were with him somehow. I had hoped that I would receive a message from him, but I knew that it wasn't safe, and though I had thought about sending him word when I was looking for the *Noble Star*, I resisted. Silence was the best way to let him know I was all right. Besides, I was sure that he knew that the Per ship had gotten away with me on it. I didn't want my heart's need for contact and comfort to put him into danger. But seeing his planet suddenly made it feel like he was with me across the light years, and I felt stronger.

The clouds and the blue water were familiar. My eyes teared up at the sight of it. As much as I had loved looking at Quint, it was drier and colder; Tallara looked so warm and welcoming, it made me long for what had once been mine.

For the first time in years, I missed Earth.

Tallara looked like Earth, but with more land masses and

smaller oceans. I knew that the Brahar home world, also in this system, was an even drier place. From here, that planet was only a red star in the sky.

We were to orbit while the Brahar captain did some business on the surface. The city was the large domed city that sat on the face of the moon, and from the sky, it looked much like the Yertina Feray but laid out flat on the smooth surface. Here it housed the embassies of every kind of species, both Major and Minor. There were also all of the offices that did the various incarnations of government work. To take over the galaxy, one had to rule Bessen. The whole of the known galaxy was represented here.

There were many ships in orbit around the moon, ships that were too big to dock with Togni Station, which had the space elevator. I could see a steady stream of small shuttles going to and from the station in a coordinated dance to dock with the space elevator that would take people down.

I'd never seen a space elevator before. It stuck up out of the moon like a pin and ended in the shuttle port that orbited in sync with the moon.

"I'm ready to go down," I said to the captain, my bag packed, ready to try to infiltrate the Human consulate.

The Brahar crew members laughed at me.

"You need the proper papers," one of them said. "And you don't have any papers at all. You're not even supposed to be on this ship."

My heart sank.

It was true. I was lucky that they had taken me. It was only because they were headed back to their own system that they had agreed to. As instigators of the fall of the League of

Worlds, they were a more protected species when it came to navigating Imperium bureaucracy.

Of course I couldn't just waltz down to Bessen from Togni Station. And if I did, I couldn't go and speak to the highest ranked Earth Gov representatives. Even if I claimed to be a Wanderer, they wouldn't care.

I cursed not having found the *Noble Star* before I got here. I needed help and I didn't have it. Bessen had been a good idea, but I'd failed to stitch all of the pieces together to succeed in my plan. I knew the rules and how to bend them to my way on the Yertina Feray. But this was space's center, and I knew nothing about it.

"Where will I go if I don't find a pass?" I asked.

He pointed out the window to Togni Station and the space elevator.

"You can probably catch someone there willing to give you their papers for a price," he said. "You have a few days before we drop you there."

Defeated, I went to the mess hall to eat and think, but I could feel all the Brahar with their eyes on me, whispering about their bad luck to have been stuck with me on their trip.

Think, Tula. Think.

I did what Heckleck always told me to do when defeated. *Take stock of what you have, even if it's nothing.*

I had some currency on my chit. I had Trevor. I had information about the Yertina Feray and Quint. I had no home. I had desperation.

That was more than nothing.

I started asking my ifs.

If I had to go to the Togni Station without a plan for a way down in the elevator in place, I would need a pass.

If I got a pass to get down the elevator to Bessen, I would need a place to disappear to when in the city.

If I made it to Bessen and managed to move about, I would need a contact that could light a spark to make a fire in the Human Embassy.

It would be hard as a Human on Bessen to go knocking on doors. I needed to use these few days I had left to open one for me if I managed to get down there. If I could reach someone at some ministry, they might get me a pass to go on the space elevator and that was the first step.

When you can't see the long game just think of one step.

There were many ministries on Bessen. Surely someone would give me a pass if I used my skills in bartering.

Times were such that no one would report a strange call from a Human. They would log it as miscellaneous and would make it disappear.

It would be impossible for me to get anyone with high authority to talk to me, but I knew my best chance would be to go lower. Receptionists, clerks, janitors; those were the people that Heckleck always reminded me were the ones who would be most willing to barter. They had the most to gain from under-the-table dealings. And to my advantage, they likely wouldn't know for sure if I was with the Human contingent on Bessen or not.

I took a deep breath and started making vidcalls. I would call everyone except Humans so as not to get caught. And I would start all of my calls dark so they could not see me until I was certain that they were not Human. The first place I signaled was the Office of Extraplanetary Excavations.

I punched the screen and a female Loor filled the screen. She was not looking at her console; she was packing her bag, obviously getting ready to leave.

"Yes?" She said. "It's almost closing time. You'll have to call back when my secretary is in."

This Loor seemed bored and disinterested. I pressed my camera button so the Loor could see me.

"Hello, my name is Tula Bane."

The Loor looked up at me.

"You're Human."

I nodded my head affirmative.

"Have we met?" she asked. "On Earth?"

She'd been to Earth. This was not a low-level worker. Maybe this would work out better for me.

I shook my head no.

"Not a Wanderer," she said, examining me and likely noting that I lacked the tattoos that Human Wanderers had to mark their voyages.

"Not Imperium." She motioned to my outfit, which was not the uniform that the Humans who worked at the Embassy wore.

I shook my head again.

When something unexpected happens, the truth is often the right way.

"I'm solo," I said.

"No one is solo in space," the Loor woman said. I'd lost her, and her hands began the movements to cut our communication off.

"I belong to the Yertina Feray," I said. It was what Tournour had always said about me. Even though I had been sent away, it felt truer than belonging to anywhere else. Unless I belonged to myself.

"Where did you say you were from again?"

"The Yertina Feray," I said.

That got her attention. Like everyone else, she would be aware of the rush on Quint.

"It's on the outermost . . ."

She waved her arm at me, indicating that she knew where it was. I was familiar enough with the Loor to know that her antennae told me that something about her attention had shifted in my favor.

"I'm representing the claim holders on the planet Quint," I said. It was a lie, but I needed something to keep the wedge I had with this Loor open. I could see that she was interested in me.

"What do you want?" she asked.

"I'm looking for a pass to come down and talk to someone about the tracts of land for sale."

I checked my list. Office of Extraplanetary Excavations.

"There's land and work to be had. I thought I would offer it to your department first," I said.

"Claims on Quint aren't an issue," she said. She looked old and tired. "We Loor have had a claim on Quint since back in the days of ore mining."

"The Loor do, but how about you? People like to speculate."

I bit my lip. This could be a big mistake. Even though many government officials were corrupt and not averse to making a little on the side, I could also be wrong.

"The Imperium has a representative on the ground, dealing with the situation," she said.

"Your office?" I asked.

"Another office," she said.

I could tell by the way she was acting that she would not begrudge me my attempt to lure a pass from her with a claim.

"Your representative is Human," I said, taking another chance. "How does that best serve the Imperium?"

Her antennae waved softly as she took her time to answer the question.

"We are satisfied."

She was being careful. I gave another little pull.

"The Yertina Feray has a complaint that the representative is Human."

"Do you have a problem with a Human being there?"

"Yes," I said.

Her antennae folded toward me and leaned to the left. I'd intrigued her.

"That's not my department," she said. "You'll have to take that up with the Office of Interspecies Harmony."

I laughed. Everyone knew that speciesism was *de rigeur* in the Imperium. You just had to be the right species to ignore that it existed.

"Speciesism will not be tolerated," she said.

"Tell that to the Hort, the Vizzini, and the Calwei," I said. "And the Humans."

The Loor looked up at me and studied my face through the vidscreen. Her antennae were now definitely on alert.

"The Imperium has been a good thing for Humans," the Loor said. "Earth is in the fold. There are five human colonies, and you're on track to becoming an important part of the Imperium. Your people should be grateful we don't interfere with your affairs."

"I don't have anything to do with those Humans who collaborate," I said. Here it was, I had to take a chance. "I told you, I'm solo. And I'm against them."

The screen went dark.

Somehow the conversation galvanized me. I called the Office of Interspecies Harmony. They were useless. I tried a new ministry: The Office of Biodiversity Information. Then another: the Imperium Opportunities Office. Then on and on. It was a thankless task, but it felt good to be active. Like I was fighting for my life.

With each place I left the same statement: I was against the Humans from Earth.

Something had dislodged, and my instincts told me that even though I did not know what I was doing, I was on the right track. Eventually something would happen. I could feel it in my bones. When you are in the dark, you never know from which side the light will come.

I wore my voice out trying to find someone at each agency that would talk to me. They kept shifting me around to another office worker until finally I had no one else to talk to there and had to begin again somewhere else.

While I might have been agitating aggression against the Earth Gov Humans and hopefully undermining Brother Blue in some way, my time was running out. I had still not managed to get a pass down to Bessen from Togni Station.

Time after time when I mentioned a pass I was shut down, told to call someone else, or hung up on. I felt defeated. I wanted to turn off the vid and head for sleep. It was late, and I was too tired to begin another round of pleas to lower agencies.

Just one more, Tula, I told myself. *Just one more call.*

Eventually, I was so exhausted that I fell asleep at the console.

A few hours later, a Brahar crew member shook me awake. "It's time to go," she said.

I still didn't have a pass. I was going to be stuck on Togni

Station space elevator. I may be leaving the ship, but I would be stuck in limbo once again. The Yertina Feray had been bad. This would be worse.

"Can't you take me to Brahar with you?" I said. "I'll give you all of the currency on my chit."

The Brahar shook her head.

"A message was received for you from below. You're to meet your contact on Tallara. I have the coordinates."

"My contact?"

"A Loor, I suppose." The Brahar picked at one of its scales, not at all interested in my troubles.

I had spoken to many a Loor that day, all from different ministries or agencies.

"I don't understand," I said. "I'm not going to Togni Station?"

"A shuttle is docking as we speak to take you down," she said.

Although I was no stranger to plans being changed, and I knew that I had overstayed my welcome with the Brahar, suddenly being in the belly of a spaceship with those who didn't like me felt safer than going down to a planet to meet with an unknown someone alone. Meeting on the planet meant that whatever happened was unofficial. Unofficial was in my interests but now that it was here, I was scared.

That was bad. Unless things were changing.

There was nothing to do but to go meet whatever fate had in store for me.

"I'm ready," I said aloud to give myself confidence.

I boarded the shuttle and five hours later I was landing at a remote spaceport on Tallara.

When I stepped outside and my feet touched the ground, I fell down.

15

• •

It was strange to be on a planet again. The sky confused me. The clouds cut the sky like sharp, violent objects. The sun was very bright, and the shadows were everywhere. Bessen, unlike the moon I knew and remembered from Earth, was clear and brown in the daytime sky.

I held on to Trevor for support. The air was humid and heavy. And I could barely walk.

Before me stretched a long, red dirt road lined with trees— long, spindly things with fungus-covered trunks and sharp pointed leaves. I could see purple fruit hanging from the branches, but I could not identify them so I did not know if they were ripe. What struck me, as I tried not to throw up, was how much brighter the colors were here than on a ship or on the station. In the arboretum, I thought I knew what the color green was. Seeing the vegetation on this planet made me realize what green really looked like, and it made me miss Thado and his ramblings about planetary flora and fauna.

I quickly noted that the spaceport was a private one. It consisted of a single landing pad with an old empty-looking building covered with vines that crept up the side of the walls. An old Loor was sitting on the porch in a mechanic's jumpsuit eating the purple fruit I couldn't recognize and spitting out the seeds. He didn't look up at me when I approached him to ask if he was the person I was to meet. He just stuck his hand out and pointed to the exit.

Way down the fenced lane, I could see a hexagonal house. There was no one else waiting for me, so I headed toward it to meet whoever had called me here.

I dragged myself to the gate holding on to Trevor. It was a slow process.

Wherever I was it looked rural, as though I were far away from any urban center. I couldn't hear any of the busyness that a city or a close-by dense population made. There were only the sounds of insects, birds, wind, and the cries of animals on what I assumed was an unseen farm.

I took a deep breath. The air was real. Overwhelming. Sweet. Sticky. There were new smells everywhere. Chemicals from the landing pad. Dirt. Leaves. Rocks. Animal manure.

The sun was warm on my face. It felt so much like my sun. How had I managed with only Sunspa lamps? They were nothing compared to the real thing.

My legs shook as I stumbled forward. I was not sure that I could make my way down the lane by myself, and Trevor was too awkward to hang on to for long amounts of time. He rolled too fast for my slow steps. I let him go as I moved to the side of the road and was sick into the scrub-like grass. Then I pulled myself up to hang on to the fence posts and started dragging myself toward the house. It was a near impossible task. But I had no choice. The shuttle had taken off immediately after I left, as though it didn't want to be here any more than I did. It was already long gone.

Planet sickness.

That's what I was suffering from. I'd heard about it before, first in Kitsch Rutsok's and then in the Tin Star Café. Travelers

106

were always laughing and telling stories about new space voyagers, who hadn't heeded the warnings of landing on new planets after long journeys.

It wasn't the gravity of the planet that was making it difficult for me to walk. Although it was slightly heavier than the Yertina Feray, I knew that was a little lighter than Earth. It was the sky I could not get used to. It was the birds. It was the wind. It was the trees. It was the sound that a planet makes. Even in the quiet of the country, it was deafening.

I was so used to the dome of the station that the sky troubled me. The largeness of it and the color, an unreal-looking indigo, confused me. It was as though the sky wanted to scoop me up and fold itself around me one million times.

As I got closer, I could see a Loor standing in the doorway of a house, observing me as I approached.

I stumbled again. My inner ear ached, and the ground in front of me spun. My balance was off. I felt a wave of vertigo wash over me. I gripped on to another fence post on the path to the house to steady myself. Trevor had stopped so that I could catch up. I pulled myself a little farther along the post, dizziness overwhelming me. When the fence ran out, I commanded Trevor to glide beside me, so I could find my balance. Eventually I stared at the ground, so I did not have to face the sky.

"How long have you been in space?"

I looked up. The Loor was female. She'd come down the road to meet me and was now offering me her hand. She was covered in scarves so I could not see her face or her antennae or the form of her body, but I could tell by her voice that she was female. Not that I cared. I gave her my hand, and she put her arm around my waist to help me walk toward the house.

I was grateful that I had someone to lean on. Someone who knew how to go slow. Someone who walked, not rolled.

"Years?" she asked.

I nodded, unable to speak for fear of vomiting again. As we walked, it was as though I could feel the planet spinning on its axis. I could feel us orbiting the sun, which the Loor called Blan. Everything was moving.

"You'll be fine in a day or two. You've got planet sickness."

I nodded.

"You'll get used to it."

I nodded again, wanting to believe her. But I felt so sick that I had my doubts that this feeling would ever go away.

We reached the door at last, and she let me go in first as she opened it and ushered me inside.

"Please sit down. Food and drink will settle you."

She disappeared as I sunk into the couch. I looked up, curious for a clue about where I was. Before my vertigo overtook me again, I noticed that the room was tastefully decorated with sleek angled furniture in all shades of blue. There were flowers on every available table space. In the corner there was a wooden sculpture of two Loors heads leaned into each other, antennae entwined. Red, yellow, and blue circular windows lined one wall. The sun streaming through them made beautiful hues on the floor.

She reappeared with a tray. Her scarves were a bit looser now, so I could see her face. She looked familiar.

Usually when I dealt with an alien, I knew within minutes what they wanted. On the Yertina Feray it was easy. But I could not begin to guess what this Loor wanted me here for. With the scarves on her head covering up her antennae and the loose shift she was wearing it was hard to read her body language. She could read everything about me. I tried to still my body movements and my facial tics so as to not give anything else away.

I realized I was in the presence of a master negotiator.

There was only one reason that she could possibly want me here. I must have said something that either spooked her or intrigued her when we spoke on the vidcall.

I had spoken to so many people the past two day cycles that I couldn't remember what I'd said to whom. So I couldn't imagine what I'd spun to get her interested in me.

When you are lost, be direct. Heckleck's teachings reminded me. I broke my rule and spoke first.

"You're from the Office of Extraplanetary Excavations."

"Yes," she said, serving me a plate of snack-like items and a bowl with a steaming clear orange liquid. "My name is Hendala."

"You severed the connection," I said. Most of those I'd called had gotten me off quickly, but she had gone dark. There was a difference between hanging up and severing a connection.

"We're here talking now, aren't we?"

I nodded and took a sip of the warm liquid in front of me. It was a smoky broth that I knew Tournour was fond of.

"Why are we meeting here?"

She looked at me suspiciously.

"You are a Human unaffiliated with your own representative who was trying to make backroom deals about something that my office is not in charge of but would like to have a piece of. It would be inappropriate for me to meet with you in any kind of official capacity."

"I didn't want to talk officially," I said.

"What did you want?" she asked as she folded her long arms

in front of her chest and leaned back in her chair as she took me in.

"I wanted a pass to get down to Bessen from Togni Station."

"Where you would have raised many red flags and likely have been killed," she said. Her antennae had not moved, and I knew that meant she was apprehensive about me.

"You don't know that," I said. "I have a way of blending in."

She laughed, and I could see her antennae had softened under her scarf, signaling that she was slightly more at ease with me.

"Do you even have papers?" she asked.

I shook my head in the way that Loor used to say no.

"You're not very smart. You're like a shosho in a glass shop. Causing havoc in its wake."

It took a moment for the nanites to translate the word *shosho*, but I knew she meant some kind of large, lumbering dumb animal.

"A Human doesn't blend in on Bessen. There are far too few of you that are seen in public spaces. To have one rogue Human wandering around the city without an Imperium uniform the way some of you wander around space would be obvious."

"I fit in on the Yertina Feray," I said.

But I knew she was right. No matter how un-Human I felt sometimes, I could not deny my biology. I was a Human. I would stick out as I always had.

"You've been pressing and prodding every ministry on Bessen for a pass down from Togni Station," she said. "Did you mean to draw that much attention to Earth? I've had twenty inquires about excavation possibilities there today."

I sucked in my breath. It was one thing to ruin Brother Blue. It was another thing to condemn Earth. Before Earth Gov joined the Imperium, it had been isolationist and there was a policy to not accept anyone back who had left the planet. That was why the Wanderers, descendants of the first intergenerational ships, wandered and why I no longer had any great love for my planet since it had ignored me. Even now, return to Earth was only possible for those Humans who had left under Imperium rule, but the thought of it being harmed in any way was still unbearable to me. I should have been more careful.

"I just wanted a pass," I said, opening my arms in front of me to show vulnerability.

She cocked her head to the side.

"Being loud in a time of quiet can have a disastrous effect."

It sounded like something Heckleck would say. Something I would hate to admit was right.

"What would you have done with the pass once you were on Bessen?" she asked, her hands smoothing her skirt down.

"I meant to draw attention to the alin on Quint. To speak for the Yertina Feray Space Station. For the claimants."

The claims were the only card I had.

Despite it making the room spin again, I leaned forward in my chair.

"What authority do you have to speak for a space station or for the people speculating on Quint? You don't even work there."

I could see her antennae moving beneath the fabric of her shawl swaying from side to side in agitation.

"I am a citizen. I'm from the underguts," I said, touching my heart.

"You're not even on their roster of citizens," she said. "How did you come to be there?"

Her hand stabbed the air as she pointed at me.

"My colony ship left me there."

"On its way to its colony?" she asked, leaning forward.

"Yes, but the ship exploded soon after, and I was declared dead."

"So you're a dead Human with inside information," Hendala said. "Still a shosho."

She paused. I had to defend myself. I was not a shosho, whatever that was.

"Everyone on the Yertina Feray has dealt with me in some way before. I own and run a sweets, water, and salts shop."

Her broad shoulders relaxed.

"Smart. Everyone longs for those homeworld things in deep space," Hendala said. "Go on."

"Before that, I lived in the underguts of the station. I ran errands and barters for a Hort named Heckleck. They couldn't trust him, but they could trust me. I strike a fair deal."

Her antennae peeked from under her shawl and folded toward me in a way I remembered Tournour doing; it meant curiosity.

"So you're trusted by the low and the high?"

I nodded. Talking was still a little difficult. I took another sip of the broth.

"I know the way deals are made on the Yertina Feray," I said. "I know how we survived before the money came. The speculators don't want to pay all the fees. I wanted to bring attention to that."

She nodded.

"Before the rush, the Yertina Feray was a ghost town, and Quint was abandoned," I said. "Now every wing has reopened. Ships arrive in droves every day."

I had her interested. I could tell from the way that her body

112

settled itself and her head turned that she was beginning to trust that I knew what I was talking about.

"Is the rush really that big?" she asked. "Certainly alin pollen and its medical use derivatives have become more available since this boom, but I haven't noticed anything along the lines of what you are saying."

That surprised me. I had assumed from the cargo I'd seen on the Per ship that more would have followed.

"It's the new economy on the station," I said.

She leaned back, taking it all in. I could see from the slight tics in her face and shift in color of the triangle between her antennae that she realized I was the one telling the truth about Quint and the alin.

"If it's truly that big a trove, then I understand why you would use the alin to tempt someone to get a pass down to Bessen."

"Yes," I said. "There is money to be made. And I do have connections. I am friendly with Reza Wilson, the being who discovered that the alin had bloomed big."

"I don't doubt it," she said. "I've heard he's Human and has made a fortune. "

Now I was the one who blushed. I'd omitted his species so that there would be no prejudice, but of course if everyone had heard about the alin, then they'd heard that it was a stranded Human who had discovered it.

"If it's as big a bloom as you say, then I'm surprised that there are not others who have reaped as much wealth as he has."

"It has to do with the tithe the Imperium is extracting on the claims," I said.

"Claims are the same as excavation rights. They are simply

113

made by the one who finds the deposit; the area is limited to what labor they themselves or a small group of the same species can do. The land has to be actively worked for the claim to stick. On most planets, it's normal for the claimants to pay a small tax to the landholder."

"Quint has been abandoned for over two hundred years," I said. "By your own laws, that reverts a planet to non-status. Therefore no previous claims can be repossessed and no tax should be imposed."

I knew this because everyone in the Tin Star Café had said it a million times. The boomers knew their history when it came to non-status planets. It was why there was a rush. A true planetary land grab was a rare thing in these hyper-regulated times, and they hated that they were being forced to pay a license fee to speculate on a declared non-status planet.

"You're talking about the League of World laws and about non-status," Hendala said slowly as though she were carefully choosing her words. "That doesn't exist anymore. Obviously the Imperium has different views about the claims on abandoned planets than the League of Worlds did. So in this case a harvest tax would go to whatever species owned the original claim."

I wished that I had a better command of intergalactic politics. I wish I had listened to all of Heckleck's conspiracy theories. To Tournour's disagreement with the new protocols that he'd been handed down. To Thado's grumbling. But all I knew was what I had gleaned from slinging water at the Tin Star Café when the claims board was being set up.

"The Loor have nothing to complain about with these terms. We have a large swath of Quint so my people are sure to be getting a large harvest tax."

"But not in the right place," I said. "Not where the alin grows."

"The Quinters should be glad that the Imperium is willing to lease the claims back to those that are working them. Everyone wins. If we were still governed by the League of Worlds, I'd agree with your reasoning wholeheartedly and I'd deal directly with you to eliminate any middleman to make a profit on imported alin."

I sank back into my chair defeated. I had no real cards in my hand.

"By Imperium law, the speculators have to accept to pay a tax for harvest rights," I said.

"Nothing is free," Hendala said. "It's the Imperium that rules. Now, if they—we—want those old mining maps to still hold, then those old maps still hold, regardless of Quint's former status in a now-defunct government."

She then waved the conversation away with her arm and offered me a glass of water.

"I don't really care about the claims. And I don't think you do either."

She was right. The claims mattered and didn't matter. I had to think of something new. There were layers to our conversation that were going over my planet-sick head. I knew that there was something not right in the way that Brother Blue was dealing with the claims. I took a sip of the water in front of me to clear my head. It tasted high in minerals.

Minerals and water.

"There is an Imperium officer, Brother Blue, who is asking for a tithe to him for the mineral and water rights to those lands on top of the harvest rights," I said slowly trying to articulate the pieces I was putting together in my head.

Hendala didn't say anything, but her antennae went rigid. I could tell that something I'd said was disturbing her.

"That's not right," she said. "The speculators on Quint are paying a double tax."

She leaned back and looked at me for a good long while in silence. Luckily, I didn't get the sense that she brought me here to kill me.

16

. . . .

Something else was going on here that I couldn't
understand. Something larger.

"You have a private landing pad. That means that you're important," I said.

"Or rich," she said.

"You have an interest in keeping me alive," I said.

"I do," she said.

"You don't want the alin," I said. "You don't care about it."

She smiled. The smile was a genuine Loor smile. There was nothing fake about it.

"I care about the good it can do and the money it can bring. But the alin gives me an excuse to make inquires about the things that I am really interested in," she said.

She loosened her headscarf, revealing more of her face and antennae. She was starting to feel at ease with me.

We were finally getting to it for real. I leaned forward and took one of the snacks, some kind of curdled spread.

"And what's that?" I asked.

"I have reason to believe that the Human representative from Earth Gov is not what he claims to be," she said.

My eyes snapped up to meet hers. Then I remembered that she was the Loor with whom I had said I wanted to file a complaint about Brother Blue. Maybe that was what had piqued her interest.

She could be an ally.

"Your kind is making its place on Bessen and beyond," she continued. "Brother Blue excels at being in the right place at the right time. He has a way of charming everyone around him. He has a way of getting things done."

This was the thread I could pull on. I leaned forward, intrigued.

"The Imperium has changed the way things are done. First, it was the razing of planets, which was unheard of in the past. Now there are rumors of culling the less desirable species. They go in and take everything. But Earth is very protected," she said.

"Do you want Earth?" I said.

"No. I just can't understand how a species like yours, barely starfaring by our standards, rises so quickly."

"Why does it matter?" I asked.

"Because something is not right. Earth colonies get grants and funds and equipment and medicine and aid. It takes away from all of the other species who have been Major for centuries. He's running some kind of scheme, and I can't seem to find a way to catch the beast. And now this extra tax . . ."

I looked up at her. She knew something was wrong, too. She was on my side.

All the hairs on my arm were raised. I had goose bumps. Someone was going to listen to me. It was interesting that an alien would be suspicious because another alien was doing well. Just because the Loor had been spacefaring first didn't mean that Humans didn't have the capacity to thrive. It was small-minded of her.

"Do you know how he does it?" she asked.

I pulled out my data plug.

"May I?" I pointed to Trevor.

"By all means," she said.

I motioned Trevor forward and then put the data plug in it. I managed to project my data onto the flat of the wall across from Hendala. It showed the data that Els had gathered from her ship before it exploded. It showed all of my attempts to communicate with the colonies.

"What is this?"

"The only proof I have," I said. "Ship logs from former Earth Imperium Alliance Officers who were supposed to help with integration but whose attempts to land were repelled. They never visited the colonies. Communication logs. It clearly shows that no one but Brother Blue has any real-time communication with the Earth colonies. Everything was relayed and coordinated through him. But my data is over a year old now."

She didn't say anything as she looked at the scans that flipped on the wall. She sat in silence, but her eyes and antennae betrayed that she was fascinated.

"So what are you saying?"

"There are no Humans on those colonies. Brother Blue lied. He lied to everyone," I continued.

Saying it out loud to someone who had some authority was such a huge relief that I immediately felt my heart lighten. Secrets can be such heavy loads.

She stood up. She looked pleased.

"I've always wondered about you Humans. Always plentiful but invisible. In my youth, when I was on Earth, I saw a population ravaged. Cities left to go back to nature. A people plagued by famine and drought and super storms. Yet, miraculously

119

out here you thrive. And now I know it is based on deception."

"Humans still need to settle the stars and trade with aliens. Becoming a multi-planet species is the way to ensure species survival. That's why I left with my mother and sister. We were hoping that we could show Earth that she should open up from her isolationist stand. To save Humanity we would settle the stars."

I didn't want her to use this information against me, and I worried for a moment that I had sold out Earth.

"Now we have something to talk about," she said. "You must be tired. Get some rest. We have a lot to discuss."

I was exhausted.

She pressed a button, and the Loor from the launchpad came in from a hidden sliding door and led me to a bedroom. I sunk into the softest bed I'd ever been on in my life and, relieved of the burden of my biggest secret, I fell into a deep sleep.

17

When I awoke, my body was adjusted to being on a planet. The light outside could have been dusk or dawn. I checked Trevor and realized I'd been out for two days. It was early morning, and I had space lag. The house was quiet as I wandered through it, marveling at how it was so different than a bin in the underguts or quarters on the Yertina Feray or the quarters of any of the spaceships I had voyaged on recently.

Most quarters on the Yertina Feray were economical in their use of space. Things slid out and tucked in to give a body all that they needed, but in a confined area. Here there was room after room to weave through and windows galore with a view of planetary vistas that took my breath away. I felt as though I could stretch in a way that I hadn't in years. I had been so cramped for so long.

I made my way outside and sat on the porch of the house and looked up at the sky and sun and the trees and the birds. I filled my lungs with the cool, unrecycled air.

Tallara was beautiful. The birds in the sky looked slightly prehistoric to me. The mountains in the distance were like black cut glass. The sky was still that unreal shade of blue. The dirt in the garden was a deep blood red. The trees were bursting with strangely shaped orange leaves. I wondered if it was fall or if that was the natural color of the fauna. It didn't matter. It was beautiful.

I thought of the arboretum and how it had sustained me for years on the Yertina Feray, but that was nothing like a planet. I stepped off the porch onto the strange scrub-like grass and walked to the tiny garden below a trellis. There I dug my toes into the red dirt; real planet dirt.

Excitement coursed through my body. For this moment, despite everything that was happening, life felt good.

I took my time taking in every part of the landscape as far as my eyes could see. I was standing on another planet. After dreaming about it for so long and being so close and so far away, I had made it. I wished that it were something that I could have shared with my mother and Bitty. I took a moment to think about them. To miss them.

Blan was high in the sky, and I shaded my eyes to look at it. I knew it was the same class of star as Earth's sun, but it looked a bit larger in the sky. Was Tallara closer to Blan than Earth was to its sun? I wished I had asked Tournour questions like that.

"You're better."

Hendala stepped out onto the porch. Her antennae folded toward me in a sympathetic way, and she smiled.

"I have missed being on a planet," I said, shaking the dirt off of my feet and joining her on the porch. "Solid ground. Flowers. The cries of animals. It's nourishing. It's so different here from Earth."

"I've been to Earth," she said.

"When? How?" I asked, then remembered that she must have told me when we had talked. Things were slowly coming back to me. Space sickness must have made me foggy.

"Loor youth must go on trips to other systems to expand their understanding of the universe. It's a rite of passage. My daughter is on hers now. I used to do supply runs on cargo ships going from planet to planet. Earth seemed like an exotic stop."

I thought about Earth. I remembered tearing out of the atmosphere and heading to the *Prairie Rose*, docked in space waiting to take my mother, sister, and me away and to a new world, Beta Granade, a planet that Brother Blue had secured from the League of Worlds to promise followers like us a new life.

Hendala took a moment to stand there with me on the porch, pointing out things; the names of flowers, trees, animals, landmarks.

"Thank you," I said. It was nice to have someone care enough to be a planetary tour guide. I couldn't help but smile up at her. It felt so good to have someone mothering me, making sure that I had food and warmth; someone who wanted to show me things. It made me miss my mother something fierce.

"Do you know why the Loor help the Humans?" she asked.

"I've heard rumors," I said.

"It's your smell. Your entire species smells like family."

I wondered if this was why I felt so inexplicably close to Tournour and so comfortable with Hendala. But not all Humans were the same. Brother Blue was nothing like me, even if he was my same species. And I remembered the Loor, Ven Dar, who had died along with Els. I had never felt anything about him. Surely the Loor were as varied as Humans were.

"We're not all the same. We don't all smell the same."

"No, but most Loor can't tell the difference," she said. "We're a trusting species. That's why the Brahar, who share our system, had such an advantage over us during our first contact. They're reptilian, not mammals. They don't have a scent that registers with us. They evolved in such a different way then we did, as life does on all other planets. When we met them, we couldn't understand how alien an alien could be. The stars are very different from the way the poetry of our ancestors described them. Those poets knew nothing about aliens, they only knew the Loor way. It limited them."

"Or preserved them," I said. I tried to think about the things that I'd shed once I'd landed on the Yertina Feray in order to survive and about the Human things that I had kept and lost.

"Many Loor have been seduced by the Humans. They'll believe anything that your species says. They'll remain loyal for no reason. I was one of the first to welcome Brother Blue when he came to Bessen to negotiate the first Children of Earth colony on Killick."

"That was many years ago," I said.

"Yes," she said. "But I was charmed by your funny little species. He was so different than the sad Humans that wander and hitch from ship to ship."

I could not tell her age, but I knew that Tournour was young by Loor standards and that Tallara had a quicker orbit around its sun. But Brother Blue had claimed to settle Killick forty Earth years ago, according to his history about himself.

"But things didn't add up," she spat, her antennae coming to full attention. "Perhaps that's why I take it so personally. I feel invested. Taken advantage of. Or betrayed. I'm afraid of bringing shame to my family for trusting him."

I was nervous that exposing him had made a mound of trouble for Earth.

"The current state of politics is fragile," she said slowly. "It does no good for any species to ruin the status of another. But it also does no good to help."

"Is this what you wanted to talk about?" I asked. I knew that shame was a big deal to the Loor. I knew that as the youngest of his family, Tournour had been sent out to the Yertina Feray to pay for his family's disgrace. But I didn't know much about what that shame was.

"Somewhat. We will talk," she said. "But first, there is a message for you."

"No one knows I'm here except the Brahar I traveled with to the system," I said. "I can't imagine that they'd have anything to say to me. Unless they found the *Noble Star*?"

"The *Noble Star*?"

"It's a ship I'm looking for. A Human friend is on it, I think."

"Another solo Human like you?" she asked, confused. "Not a Wanderer?"

"Yes. A true friend," I said. "He was exiled by Brother Blue's lies. He's an ally. I've been looking for him since I left the Yertina Feray. It's somewhere to go."

She leaned in close to my face, looking deep into my eyes in the Loor way and took my hand and patted it sympathetically. "You're welcome to signal him from here at any time, but this message is not from your Human friend," she said and then led me inside to her office.

She pushed a button, and a screen slid out of the back wall.

It was not the Brahar. Nor was it any information about the *Noble Star*. Instead, it was Tournour who flickered onto the screen in front of me. It was a prerecorded image of him sitting in his office. He was giving a report to the Loor government in a monotone.

"Here," she said. "This bit can't interest you. I'll get to the end."

She moved to fast forward through the message.

"No," I said. "Let it run."

Seeing Tournour talking about diplomatic things and just hearing his voice and seeing his countenance reached right inside of me. Even though he was an alien, his face was more familiar to me than anyone I had ever known. After fifteen minutes or so, the official part of his report was finished.

"Personal postscript to the beings visiting the home of my cousin. Apologies for lack of communication. Arboretum quite empty. Please send itinerary and coordinates for planets or ships where I should send sweets, waters, and salts for trade."

I turned to look at her.

"When you said you were from the Yertina Feray, I contacted my cousin immediately. He confirmed that you were not a registered citizen. He also mentioned that there was a trial order on you."

"That's true," I said. "I'm on the run."

"I gathered. It was his strange subtext that convinced me I should aid you," she said, her antennae folding toward me knowingly.

I blushed. "Tournour and I have a close friendship."

"He and I have a strained one. I don't like to associate with his side of the family. It doesn't do for one of my position to be seen dealing with a cousin who is serving time for family shame. But when I helped you down the lane, I knew why he was so agitated when your name was mentioned. I can smell him on you."

I wondered if all of the times that he'd used his scent to calm me down had altered me somehow.

"While all of you Humans smell like family, I know what *my* family smells like."

My eyes stung. His *cousin*.

"By taking an alien as a partner, he's asking for more shame on his family. He'd do best to stay in exile in the long run. These kinds of affairs are more common for the lower classes of Loor."

"I'm not his partner," I said.

"Don't you care for him?" she asked.

I touched the frozen image of Tournour.

"He is so much to me," I said. "But I hardly know what to make of it. He's a Loor. I'm a Human."

"We Loor take our attachments very seriously," she said. "I try not to judge when it comes to interspecies affairs, they are not unheard of. And you are welcome here, Tula Bane. You can consider yourself among friends."

I took a deep breath of the sweet Tallara air.

"Now to business," she said. "We have a mystery to solve."

18

• •

"Your information says that there are no colonies on
those planets," Hendala said. "My data says differently."

Hendala punched in a number on the screen behind her. It
lit up. There were images of Earth and five other planets with
numbers scrolling by. *Killick, Kuhn, Marxuach, Andra, Beta
Granade.*

"Earth's status in the Imperium is dependent on all of the
good work that Brother Blue does for his people," Hendala
said. "Then again, I've never heard of a species rising so fast.
Five colonies in forty years."

"It doesn't seem fast. Earth's relationship with the stars
has been going on for centuries," I said. "Besides, it's easier to
explain if you raise five colonies quickly by destroying your followers and creating false data."

"Last census confirms. Earth. Current Human home world
population, four billion. Five colonies. Killick, Kuhn, Marxuach, Andra, Beta Granade. Current colony population on all
planets at 1,354,456."

"That's impossible," I said. "Those numbers are too high.
Even if my colony ship the *Prarie Rose* had made it to Beta
Granade we were only sixty-seven. Even if there were
births in the last four years, even if Earth had sent more

colonists out there, that colony would not be much larger now."

She punched another button and the screen zoomed in on Beta Granade. It was strange to see the planet in front of me. I had memorized the map of it on my trip to space. The projected image of the planet orbited until it stopped at the Mur Crater where we were to have started our colony. The stats for the colony came up.

"Beta Granade, population 55,000."

I shook my head.

"No," I said. "Unless Brother Blue has pulled a magic trick, I can't see how the colonies had been populated so quickly."

"You don't believe those numbers to be true," she said.

"I don't believe that there are any Humans on those colonies." I said. "Or at least, if there are, they are not colonies. More like outposts."

"The law is clear. An outpost doesn't count as a colony. He must be fudging the data," Hendala said. "But to what purpose? It's not a sustainable plan."

I shuddered. If he could kill a whole ship of colonists, what else could he do?

"I've personally made the call for a recount for a Human colony census. Yet some Major Species representatives stopped me and persuaded me to let the matter go. So I let it go. No need to bring more shame to my family."

Now her antennae were twitching in a way that I knew meant anger.

"If he corners one part of the map, then he is a power in the affairs of the galaxy," she said. "Do you know how the Imperium does these Minor Species colony spot checks now?"

"I don't know. I never made it to a colony. I've never seen a colony," I said. "I wish I had."

"In the old days, in the League of Worlds we'd send a ship to the planet, meet with leaders, and take tours. Now we fly over the planet and scan for species life markers and biowaste. Your Human colonies, while not thriving and population poor, have been checked and verified. Every time, you miraculously *just* make the requirements for inclusion, and so your influence has begun to grow."

"But where does he get the biomatter?" I asked.

And then it struck me. There *were* over a million Humans in space. They were the Wanderers, hitching rides from ship to ship.

"Would dead bodies display those levels of biomarkers?" I asked.

"I suppose so," she said. "But how would he get the bodies?"

"He's using our Wanderers. He must be."

"Oh my," Hendala said. "He's a monster."

I shuddered at the horror of it, but I knew from my schooling from Earth that Brother Blue wasn't the first leader who had committed genocide.

"He could be dumping them on the planets with no resources, no infrastructure. They'd die there, but the biomatter would still count. He's taking advantage of the fact that the Imperium doesn't go to the colonies."

"Yes. Because the Imperium is too busy fighting to stay in power," she said. "This is not what I was expecting. It's worse."

"My species has the ability to be tricky," I said.

It was a terrible thing to admit. It was true though. I had been tricky. That was how I'd survived.

"Not all Humans," Hendala said. "Some. *Him.*"

"Brother Blue must have help," I said.

"He does. The Brahar help him. The Loor help him. I've even helped him. He is most effective, and he is quick to see opportunity."

"I've helped him too," I said quietly. I had been so eager to help him when I left Earth. I'd helped him get here.

Hendala nodded sympathetically.

"He's got a strategic mind. He was the first to see the merit of the situation on Quint when others were brushing it off as a rumor."

"He has a gift," I said. I couldn't deny that he had a gift, although calling his sick schemes a gift made me feel ill. "I have to stop him. I have to take him down."

"No," Hendala said. "Don't you see? You can't touch him."

"Why not?" I asked. "He's killing people."

"Sad and true. But if you expose him now, you risk Human lives. You put Earth at risk."

"I don't care!" I screamed. "He's a monster!"

I was in a rage. She waited until I calmed down before she spoke again.

"You have to make a decsion, Tula Bane. Are you going to save your species or are you going to exact revenge and doom them?"

I wanted to kill him, but I knew I wouldn't. Not yet. I couldn't doom my species.

"I'm going to warn them," I said.

"So be it," she said.

"I need to find my friend on the *Noble Star*," I said. "He can help me."

She flipped over to the communications array and let me punch in a message. I sent out another message in a bottle, hoping that Caleb would find it.

There was nothing more for me to do on Tallara. I would have to do what my species did best.

I would have to wander.

19

Too soon it was time to go.

I would miss being on a planet.

I spent much of my last few days, when I wasn't preparing to leave Tallara, walking on the paths near Hendala's house.

"Are you ready?" Hendala asked as we entered the shuttle that would take us to the lower part of Togni Station on Bessen. It would be too strange for someone like Hendala to take her shuttle all the way to the top when she had a berth on the moon. I would have to make my own way up the elevator.

"As ready as I ever will be," I said.

"I will get word to Tournour that you've left me in good health."

"Thank you," I said.

With her long arms she pulled me close and crossed her arms behind me. My arms were too short to do the same, but I did the best that I could. Then she leaned her head toward me until her cheek brushed mine.

"Once we part, I can no longer be your ally," she said when she broke away from me. "If you contact me I will deny knowing you. I have helped you more than I should."

"I understand."

"You'll be on your own," she said.

"I told you. I'm solo."

"That's a hard way to live," she said. "Make sure to let some-one in."

The shuttle lifted up into the air and bumped out of the atmosphere. The voyage would take almost a day, so I took the time to verify a hit I'd gotten on coordinates for the *Noble Star*. And then I went through my things.

Hendala had printed out an Imperium uniform for me, the kind that the Humans wore on Togni Station. And she had used her contacts to procure fake papers to help me get out of the system. My fake name was Safti McGovern.

"This will get you to the space elevator so that you can get to a ship leaving our system," she said when she handed them to me. "I can't guarantee them further than that."

I could see Bessen getting bigger as we approached the moon, and then we were there. The shuttle door opened.

"I owe you many favors," I said.

"We are even," she said. "You gave me information. And information is power."

Hendala turned back to me before she exited the shuttle bay.

"I hope that you find peace with your choice," she said. And then she was gone. I wondered if I would ever see her again. I did as instructed and waited one hour before I left to go to the elevator.

Since we'd timed our arrival for the quiet time, the shuttle-pad was empty. I threaded myself through the empty ships, not quite trusting my Imperium Alliance uniform. Trevor fol-lowed close behind me. Each shuttle I passed had its planet's symbol on the side. It startled me when I went past one that had a bright blue Earth on it.

We landed on the outermost launchpad, so it took a few

minutes before we made it out to the lower station proper. I had memorized the map to get from the pad to the space elevator.

I would have to get to the space elevator as quickly as I could to book passage on one of the orbiting ships. I wanted to spend as little time as possible on Togni Station so that I would not get caught by any Humans I might run into. I had not anticipated how confusing and crowded Togni Station would be. Trevor kept pace beside me, but it took longer than I thought to get to the elevator. There were twists and turns and hallways with contradictory signs pointing in opposite directions.

When I finally made it to the main drag, the enormity of the architecture and variety of alien species struck me. On the Yertina Feray, I had always thought that there were lots of different types of aliens, and that was strange, but here the diversity of the types of aliens went way beyond what I had previously known. There were so many of them, but I saw almost no Humans despite knowing that some lived here.

There was no way to blend in. All eyes were on me. All sorts of limbs and antennae pointed in my direction. I had always felt out of place on the Yertina Feray, but here I was self-conscious. I tried to walk as if I belonged to the Earth Embassy by mimicking the way that I'd seen Reza, Caleb, and Els walk, the kind of swagger they had gotten from their Imperium Youth training.

Togni Station was a marvel. It was bustling with aliens. There were windows that went up to a domed roof. Every inch was a building with walkways stretching from one side to another, stories high in the air. Every square was packed with recharging stations, communication hubs, water cafés, nutrient pak vendors, and every other type of store that you could have need for. There were brightly colored flags emblazoned with planets waving in the air, as well as brightly lit signs announcing the offices and embassies that the buildings held. You had to know where you were going because it was easy to get lost.

I was very glad that Hendala had insisted that I program the map into Trevor so he could guide me through the madness.

It was overwhelming. On occasion an alien would say hello to me, as though they knew me. I nodded back at them knowing that they thought I was someone else. It was obvious that the average aliens didn't even know that we had different skin tones or eye colors or kinds of hair. They probably didn't even know what gender I was. They all thought that we Humans looked the same, and I was glad to use that to my advantage.

I had purposely made the path to my destination one that wouldn't take me past the Human Embassy, but I now could see it would have been nothing to be scared of. Just a flag in a window. I had to admit to myself after observing the grand scope of the aliens here who were mostly far from being Minor Species, it was impressive Brother Blue had been able to raise the Human profile the way he did. It made me begrudgingly proud of our species in that we were smart enough to be even minor players in such a galactic tapestry.

Finally Trevor and I arrived at the entrance to the space elevator. From here it was two large doors set in a massive metal structure that went all the way up through the dome to the sky. Looking up at it made my head spin.

I went to the ticket counter.

"May I assist you?" the Dolmav behind the counter asked. He was different looking than Thado; more blue, with larger eyes and blowhole.

"I need to connect with a ship headed for these coordinates," I said.

"I've got one ship headed two systems over. To the Nomi system. That's the closest I've got going out right now," the Dolmav said, shaking his large, slick head, his double chins making wet slapping noises. "Or else you can wait a few days or weeks to catch something going closer."

"No. I'll take that ship," I said. "I want to be on my way."

"You have papers?" he asked.

I pushed forth the currency chit that Hendala had filled and the travel pass and Imperium ID she had prepared for me. We had figured that it was good for three days, at most, which was just barely enough time to get me out of this solar system. Once out, I would ditch the ID.

"Going home for a visit?" The Dolmav asked, not knowing at all where Earth was. I had to remind myself that he was just making small talk. I wasn't prepared for small talk.

"I'm from Earth," I said. It was as close to the truth as I could get.

"You'll have to pay for the robot as well," he said, looking over at Trevor.

I had expected that it would be handled like baggage and wouldn't be a problem, but it was clear that Trevor was my companion, and I learned that most robotic companions traveled as passengers. I nodded, knowing that it would nearly wipe me clean of currency chits.

He nodded and pointed me toward a gate.

I got on board the elevator and strapped in, a single Human among a bevy of aliens. I gripped the arms of my chair as the elevator lifted. It went so fast. A clock counted down the hours that it would take us to get to the top.

I was leaping into the darkness.

20

- -

The shuttle port at the top of Togni Station was small
but felt less cramped and chaotic than lower Togni Station.
Aliens were exiting and entering the elevator, rushing off to
catch their transports down to Bessen. Bright signs displayed
the shuttle and elevator departure and arrival times. I searched
for the name of the ship I was to join up with, the *Jinjon*.

Here, in this place, I was just one of hundreds of aliens on
my way to somewhere else. Some were traveling. Aliens with
too much baggage and families were arguing about little annoying things. Some were commuting. Workers with cases
were reading datapads, worrying about something at some office. It could have been any kind of transport hub on Earth. It
was such a far cry from the reality of my past few years that it
took me a moment to adjust to the fact that this space travel
was a normal day-to-day reality. It was hard to believe that
passes were hard to come by and that the Imperium was actively pushing outward. But even in times of war, people
moved about. And Togni Station was the center of it all because it served Bessen.

"That way," a Per said to me even though I hadn't asked
it anything. My eyes followed to where one of its arms was
pointing.

Wanderers.

There were about sixty Humans huddled together, all different ages. Some were old. Some were children. Most were in between. Even from this distance, I could see that the older they were, the more they were covered in tattoos.

"I'm not with them," I said. "I have a ticket."

I showed him my pass to the *Jinjon* and indicated my uniform to show that I was separate from those other Humans.

"What do I care?" The Per made a movement that looked like it was shrugging all four of its shoulders. And then it wandered off to catch its own transport.

I had never thought that much about the Wanderers other than the fact that they were an embarrassment to Earth. Who were they? Where they'd come from? How hard had it been for them? I knew that they were the descendants from the first intergenerational ships. Those were doomed travelers who'd made it out all the way to first contact and then, desperate and ill-prepared for colonization, had tried to come home. They led the aliens back to Earth, and then Earth had shunned them, not letting them repatriate. But some of these people must have been colonists. They must have been abandoned by Brother Blue, too.

My gate was not too far from where the Humans were. I grabbed a seat and I watched. I was hesitant to approach them. I wasn't ready to jump in and join just yet. I had barely been able to process Reza, Caleb, and Els, who had come to the Yertina Feray a year ago. Seeing an entire group of Humans together made me even more uneasy. They looked like a large family yet were totally diverse in their appearance. They had taken over their area with small tents as though they were camping there. If I was going to accomplish my mission, I needed to think about what I would say and how I would say it. I was dressed as an Imperium officer, so I wasn't sure that I would be trusted. Seeing so many Humans together made me feel strange.

Were they waiting for a ride? Had they come to Togni Station for a reason? Were they trying to get to Bessen? To the Earth Embassy, even? Or were they just between hitches?

I stared at them openly as I thought about how best to warn them about how Brother Blue was using bodies to fake the colonies. Were they safer here in such a public hub or more at risk? What would I say? *"Don't get on a ship."* Or, *"Don't trust another Human."*

I might as well say, *"Don't trust me."*

One of the old Human men pointed at me, which made the others look. I had forgotten to be discreet. I noticed that the parents called their children to come closer. That answered my question. They didn't like me, probably due to the uniform. I wanted to shrink into myself. I wanted to let them know that I wasn't that much different from them.

I was about to go somewhere and alter my outfit so that I could approach them when I noticed a group of three Human Imperium officers talking to the same alien who had pointed me toward the Wanderers.

I saw the Imperium officers give the alien something and then walk over to the group of Humans. An older, large Wanderer woman with long gray hair went straight up to them and began gesticulating madly. It was clear that people here looked to her as a leader, although I knew from Heckleck that Human Wanderers did not have leaders the way that a planet or government did. Just journey leaders. At the end of a journey, a new leader was picked for the next leg. Heckleck had explained to me that in this way, no one person gathered too much power.

She must be their journey leader and that would be marked on her.

I moved forward to try to hear, but was afraid that if I got too close I would be caught by the other Human officers who would know I was an imposter. One of them, an older man who looked like he was in charge, was trying to calm the journey leader while the other two were making the Wanderers line up by age.

The Human officer in charge made an announcement, and there was a bustle of activity within the Humans' group. They separated about a third of the Wanderers. I couldn't help but notice that the officers chose all the healthy young to middle-aged Humans; in other words, the best ones to start a colony with.

My heart skipped a beat, perhaps Brother Blue really was building something on those planets?

As the smaller group gathered their things, there was much hugging and crying and wailing. The aliens who passed the scene either ignored it or looked embarrassed by these lesser beings living such a ragtag lifestyle.

"Humans," I heard them mutter in disgust as they passed me by.

I watched as the officers led the small group away, wondering if the Wanderers felt the way I did when I watched my mother and sister take off on the *Prairie Rose* without me.

The announcement for the shuttle to the *Jinjon* was called, and I tore myself away from the scene and to the gate.

"Will there be any Humans on this voyage?" I asked the Nurlok as I boarded.

"No," the Nurlok said, its whiskers moving when it spoke. "We just dropped off a bunch. They're over there."

"Do you know where they were heading?"

"Do you Humans head anywhere?"

"Some of us do," I said. I pointed to my uniform, grateful for its help in my lie.

The Nurlok muttered a curse under its breath and time stamped my entry to the shuttle.

I took one last look at the Humans who had stayed behind to wait for another transport, and I wondered what would happen to them, with a third of their group gone, only the old and the very young left behind. They still had each other, but gathered together on the dock, they seemed very alone. I saw the large, gray-haired woman who had been in charge leave the group and go up to a gate. She was probably trying to hitch, before anything else happened to them.

I should have warned them. But I didn't. I wouldn't let another group slip by me again.

It would haunt me.

21

. . . .

As a lone Human, I stood out as strange and
untrustworthy, so I kept to myself. I had to be as small and
invisible as I could be. To be unnoticed was to survive.

The Nurloks on the first ship left me alone for the most
part, occupied with their own woes. There was no bartering
here, and my currency chit was very low. Trevor was the only
asset I had, but I didn't want to sell him. It would be too dangerous to be completely on my own. I didn't think I could
bear it.

I booked time on the communications array so that I could
continue my search for the *Noble Star*. While I was there, I
decided to send Tournour a message. Not wanting to use my
own name, I used the false name that Hendala had gotten for
me on Tallara: Safti McGovern.

It was an inventory of sweets, salts, and waters. It was the
only way I could tell him what ship I was on.

*Message: Tournour. Constable. Yertina
Feray.*

Ship: Jinjon

Species: Nurlock

Water: Bitter

Sweets: Low

Salts: Heavy

Inquiry as to return status?

Two days later he'd sent me a message back.

Message: Safti McGovern. Jinjon.

Inventory: Empty without your goods.

Status: Quarantine still in effect. Do not approach the station.

Notes: In thanks for your attention and patience in this matter, please find currency wired from speculator's account. This will be a regular drop. Looking forward to next status report. Hopeful for change in my reply.

Receiving the cryptic message lifted my low spirits. I knew that the currency couldn't be from him. Tournour was already risking his position by having contact with me. Transferring funds from his account would be too noticeable. It was normal to check in with ships about supplies that the Yertina Feray might need. These invoices could easily be buried in a mountain of similar paperwork. But the currency must have been from Reza. With his alin claim, he had enough to spare me an unlimited credit line. I kept my feeling for them both so separate in my mind that it was strange to know that they were still working together to keep me alive. I didn't know how or when I would ever be able to thank either of them.

I vowed that I would send Tournour a message from each ship I boarded to let him know where I was. I wanted someone to know where I was, or else I would go mad from the isolation.

Meanwhile, there were hours to fill and nothing to do. To pass the time I played simple games with Trevor when I wasn't near a window staring out at the streak of stars. My mind had weeks to meander, but I had to keep sharp.

After two weeks, I left the Nurlock ship for a Dolmav one that was heading to the Nomi system where the last coordinates I had for the *Noble Star* were. But I knew that it had likely moved on. I hoped that it had left a trail for me to follow.

"I'm sure they've been looking for you," the Dolmav crewmember said as she helped me through the airlock.

"How do you mean?" I asked, hopeful that there was news of the *Noble Star*.

"We've got some Humans traveling with us."

The Dolmav must have assumed that I was with them and happily brought me down to the quarters where the Humans were. I felt eager. This would be my first chance to let the Wanderers know that they should steer clear of anyone claiming to resettle them.

She banged on the door, and the quarters opened. These were not Wanderers. There were five Humans wearing Imperium uniforms in the room. I had worried about being alone while I was traveling, and now among these Humans I was in more danger than ever.

• •

"Hello," I said when they all looked up at me as I entered the quarters.

"Going out or coming back from a run?"

"Going out."

"I'm Ashland. This is Blattberg, Cullen, and Digger," the one who was a leader said. She was tall and blond and looked like she spent too much time in the Sunspa.

"Safti McGovern," I lied, using the fake name that Hendala had gotten me.

"We're coming back," Digger said. He was a redhead covered with freckles.

I nodded.

"Got about 300 between us," Blattberg said. He squinted when he talked and had a nasally voice.

"A pretty good haul," Cullen said. She looked like she was the smartest one in the bunch. I would have to avoid her.

"I was hoping for 500," Ashland said sounding disappointed. "For the bonus."

My stomach sickened as I realized that they were talking about Humans.

"No one's got 500," Blattberg chimed in. "It's too hard to track them down on ships, they skip around so much."

"It's not like they're going anywhere," Digger said.

"They could be, if they listened to us and stopped just roaming around aimlessly," Blattberg said.

"And then it's not like there are that many suitable for colonization when you do find them," Cullen said.

I had already seen that they were taking the healthy and the young. The ones you'd build a real colony with.

"What's your best number?" Blattberg asked me.

"Fifty," I said, trying to come up with a non-competitive number. "I've only just started."

"Just in from Earth?"

I nodded. "Where did you send them?" I asked.

"We're a Marxuach crew. You?" Cullen asked.

"Andra," I said, picking the colony that I thought was currently the farthest away from us. I took a side glance at Cullen to see if she was buying my lie.

"You're a bit far for Andra," Cullen said suspiciously.

"Like I said, I'm on my way out. I was just at Bessen for some intel."

"And then they sent you out alone?" Cullen said looking at me funny.

"I'm not alone," I said using my bartering skills to shift focus, I pointed to Trevor. "I'm meeting up with my group in two jumps."

"What does it do?" Ashland asked, going up to Trevor and examining it. I quietly sighed in relief that my tactic had worked.

"It's a mining robot," I said. "I'm to give it to the colonies to help with the settlement."

I flipped some switches on Trevor to show how it could mine and perform simple functions.

"You can see how useful these would be on a planet that you're trying to break in. Good for mining, plowing, protection, entertainment. They're going to bring them to every colony."

"That's a good idea," Digger said. They poked and prodded Trevor some more and somehow Digger managed to slide open a very hard to see secret side panel that exposed an orange button.

"Don't touch that," I said, pushing his hand away from the button.

"Why?" he asked.

"It's so that an operator can blow the unit to get through an especially hard piece of bedrock or in the event of a cave in," I said.

Digger put his hands down and backed away. I actually had no idea if that was something that Caleb had fixed, but I wagered he would have.

The other Imperium officers nodded as though that made sense.

"You're going all the way to Andra?" Ashland asked.

I nodded.

"Going to start out and work my way in," I said.

"We're going in concentric circles," Ashland said.

"They don't always let me stop off at a colony, though. How often do you go to Marxuach? I hear they have beautiful lakes there."

I had no idea what kinds of lakes were on Marxuach, but I was betting that they had never set foot on a colony. I wanted some confirmation of my suspicions.

"We don't even have time to go to Marxuach. We just gather the Wanderers we can and put them on alien ships that Earth Gov has hired to transport them there."

Hired transports. Alien collaborators.

"Different colonies, different protocols I suppose."

They nodded.

"Where you from back home?" one of them asked.

"Southwestern United States," I said.

They all chimed in with their home region. I noticed that when each person said their home, their eyes lit up. That's what having a home did to you. It lit you up.

I'd earned their trust, but I didn't want to talk about Earth. I was going to be caught if I talked too much. They would know I hadn't been there for years if I spoke about it.

"I'm very tired," I said. "Space lag." They all nodded in understanding, and I said my goodnights and then zipped myself into my sleep pod. The Imperium Humans stayed up for many hours, and unable to sleep from fear, I listened to them as they played cards and babbled about their missions.

They reminded me of Reza, Caleb, and Els when I had first met them. Young excited cadets making their way out into space. It made me sad that they had no idea that they were being betrayed. I envied them their innocence.

They laughed at how dumb they thought the Wanderers were.

"One fought me tooth and nail! Don't they know that we're taking them to a better life?"

"I hear that all that space travel makes you stupid."

"It makes you stupid."

"Ha ha ha."

"Seriously, those Wanderers should be thankful that we're out here rounding them up and giving them a home."

"They've been away from planet life so long that they've got some strange ideas about it."

"Did you hear that there was a group that went to Bessen to complain about the resettlement project?"

"They are idiots. Good thing we're here to show them how to be civilized."

"Which colony do you want to live on when your tour is done?"

"Me? I want to go to Killick, the first colony."

"Man, I want to go back to Earth."

"I've already put currency for a house on Kuhn. They say that it's greener than any place on Earth.

It was hard to go to sleep to their talking. It wasn't their fault that they were so wildly misinformed. They were ignorant, and I couldn't help feel a bit sorry for them knowing that one day they would realize the horror of the lie that they'd helped to perpetrate. I wanted to climb out from my pod and shake sense into them. But now was not the time. Eventually, I was able to drift off.

When I awoke, I waited until I heard them leave the quarters before I unzipped myself.

I had to get off of this ship soon. The longer I stayed on this ship, the easier it would be for me to lose my cover. I went directly to the Dolmav First Officer to request a transfer to new quarters and then to the next ship.

"I thought you Humans liked to be together," the First Officer said.

"Don't you long for time away from your crew members?" I asked.

He nodded.

"I can pay," I said.

I traded everything I had with me in my bag, three Loor protein paks, an all-planet emergency blanket, some dried flowers from Tallara, and a piece that had fallen off of Trevor.

Within an hour I had my own private sleeping pod and a

151

simple child's jumpsuit that fit me poorly. I commanded Trevor to stand guard.

Then I went and sent my message to Tournour on the Yertina Feray.

Message to Tournour.

> *Message: Tournour. Constable. Yertina Feray.*
>
> *Ship:* Snake's Kiss
>
> *Species: Dolmav*
>
> *Water: Stagnant*
>
> *Sweets: Half*
>
> *Salts: One*
>
> *Inquiry about quarantine?*

And another message in bottle to Caleb and the *Noble Star*.

> *Message to* Noble Star *from Tula Bane*
>
> *Seeking: Passenger Caleb Kamil*
>
> *Request: Rendezvous point*

It was five days before I got a message back from Tournour.

Message: Safti McGovern. Snake's Kiss.

Inventory: Zero Zero Zero.

Status: Blue

Notes: Wind season just begun. Associate safe.

22

. . . .

Between the difficulty of travel, the sporadic messages from Tournour, the failure to hail or pinpoint a location for the *Noble Star*, and the crushing loneliness unlike I had ever known before, I was beginning to get discouraged.

I felt doomed to flail through space like a cork on an ocean. Not having an end in sight, just following the tides of where the ships ebbed and flowed.

The search for Humans was time consuming and exhausting. It took me two more jumps before I hit a ship that had Wanderers on it.

I learned that every ship was different. Some had comfortable quarters. Some had sleep pods. Some had full crews. Some had skeleton crews. Some were large and new. Some were old and could barely run.

All of them were like dropping into mini-worlds with politics and hierarchies that I didn't understand or belong to.

The view was always slightly different or dark on the different ships. While on the Yertina Feray I could feel the gradual spin of the station; with each ship I traveled on, I could feel it gaining speed and slowing down. What I liked on them all was the blur of the stars through the windows as we were moving forward.

Forward.

It was something I hadn't done in so long. I had been so stuck.

Trevor played me music. Trevor played simple games with me. Trevor played the shipping news. But it was a poor substitute for a friend. I missed having friends. I wondered about Thado and the arboretum. I tried to imagine Tournour's day-to-day rounds. I pictured Reza braving the windy season on Quint.

So when the Per crew members confirmed that there were Wanderers in the lower decks, a part of me had hoped that I could at least be social for this part of the journey.

From what I'd seen and heard I knew one thing—the Human Wanderers were wary of anyone that they didn't know. As usual, my first order of business was to send a message to Tournour, secure in the thought that someone knew where I was, and my plea to the *Noble Star*. After that was done, I mustered up some courage and went down to the lower decks.

Before I even got there, I could tell these Humans were a far cry from those I had seen on the space elevator port. They were noisy. They were laughing and screaming and maybe even singing.

I could barely make out the words due to their strange accent.

Oh, make me a golden thread. Make me a golden thread. So I can follow it home. I'm going home.

They were cooking food on makeshift grills. I didn't see livestock, and then I realized that perhaps they caught and cooked the ship's vermin.

One of the Humans noticed me as I stepped into the hall.

155

He made a whoop sound. Others looked up and followed suit, making whoops, which I took to be some kind of greeting.

There was the distinct hubbub as the message was passed down the tents, which they had spread all down the hall of this deck. A bearded man popped his head out from behind a flap and came up to me. As he walked up, he removed his outer shirt to reveal his inked up arms, chest, and back. He hesitated though, when he saw that I was covered up with long sleeves and long pants, and that I had no tattoos visible on my face.

"Where is your story?" the bearded man asked while he sized me up. He spoke in a strange accent—a mishmash of various Earth languages with words that I couldn't understand. Even the nanites had trouble translating since it was so close to my own language, but also not.

Up close, I could see the intricate detail of his tattoos. His bare arms were covered, and so were his chest and his legs. The tattoos even crept up onto his neck. The tattoos depicted ships and star systems. I could recognize some of the ships, a Dolmav freighter on his forearm, a Loor passenger liner on his neck, a Per hauler on his leg. They were all different shapes and sizes, some overlapping one another. They were beautiful. By looking at them, I could almost read this man's journey through space.

"I have no story," I said.

"Everyone has a story," he said, reaching to me to pull off my shirt. I held him off.

"I have no tattoos."

He looked confused.

"You must be from Earth," he asked while his eyes searched me. "Your blank skin tells me so."

"Yes and no."

My skin *was* clear and clean. I had no voyages under my belt. No ships to claim. I had no connection.

"Are you one of them?" he asked, sniffing at me like a dog.

I knew immediately that he meant one of the Imperium Humans.

"No," I said. "I travel alone."

"What's your story?" he asked again, this time more aggressively.

Everyone had stopped what they were doing and stared at me with suspicion. It was unsettling to have so many Human eyes upon me. Not one looked at me with kindness. I was not welcome.

I hardly remembered meeting people like this on Earth. I understood why they were referred to as feral. But that wasn't true. They just had a different kind of Humanity, a fierce and frightening one. I had been that way once, when I was first on the Yertina Feray. It's what you do when you have to survive.

"I've heard that there are more of you from Earth out here," he said.

"There are," I said. "But I'm not with them. I'm solo."

"You're the first I've met," he said.

"You're the first Wanderer I've met," I said.

He softened, as though there was something to that and by being each other's first we were bonded in his eyes.

"Hello," he said.

"Hello," I said.

"This is the only way to know someone's true history," the bearded man said, pointing to his skin.

He explained to me that they all wore tattoos that showed which ships they'd flown on. What systems they'd traveled through. Who'd been their leader. I had heard about that, but it was something else to see it on people's skin. Arms and necks and some faces covered with rocket ships and names and images of stars.

It was the only way to know someone's true history. It was how a Human Wanderer knew what connections to others or to them you might have. I wondered what I would have tattooed on me. The Yertina Feray on my hand. Heckleck on my arm. Caleb on my side. Els on my back. Thado on my bicep. Reza on my belly. The Tin Star Café on my neck. Tournour on my heart.

"I hear from others that your Earth kind want us to hear you. What do you have to say?"

"You have to be careful," I said. "You have to leave the central systems. You have to stay away from other Humans."

"You're Human. You want me to stay away from you?"

"Yes," I said.

"What side are you on?"

"I'm on no one's side."

"Then go away," the bearded man said. "You're bad news. We don't want to travel with you."

I'd done my job. The only thing I could do was find another ship, another Wanderer, another life to save.

23

. . . .

I had to wonder at the madness of my task. Finding Humans who were hitching was difficult, there were so many ships going in so many directions. I had to listen for rumors and hope that my hops would lead me to some tribe to warn and closer to finding Caleb. I convinced myself that every life warned was a life saved. But I had no way of knowing if the Wanderers I found would actually heed me.

After two more months of travel, I saw four more sets of Wanderers on my voyage. Each time, once I'd said my piece, I was immediately shunned for the rest of the voyage.

Not that warning them had been the reason they shunned me. They made it clear that in their eyes, with my blank skin and my non-story, that I was part of the people who had rejected them. I represented Earth. I couldn't make them understand that I was in exile, too. That I was trying to help them. They scoffed at me. Spit at me. Yelled in my face. No wonder the Imperium officers thought the Wanderers were savages.

I was having no luck finding the *Noble Star*, and I was beginning to fear that I would end up wandering forever as well.

It brought back memories of my first months on the Yertina Feray, when I was despised by the other aliens in the underguts. I was cast out and by myself, in an emotional place that I never wanted to visit again. It was hard to bear the fact that I was cared for by Tournour, Thado, and Reza, but it didn't matter. Because out here I was alone again. And because I was always moving, my chances to alleviate my loneliness were thwarted.

To stave off those dark thoughts, I imagined myself back on the Yertina Feray; serving Tournour premium water and holding his hand as he told me about his boring day, listening to Thado as he pruned the trest tree, laughing over some entertainment with Reza that only another Human would find funny.

That would help for a day or two. But then like a wound that never healed, the anger at Brother Blue would return. I would simmer for days, furious at what he had done to my life. But as I moved through the galaxy, looking for Caleb and for Wanderers—seeing such different suns, marveling at gas planets and rocky moons, at ringed worlds teeming with life—I reminded myself that Brother Blue was so small compared to all that I was seeing.

And yet, on most days my spirits were still low. The stress of the journey was wearing me down, and I didn't feel like I had much reason to live.

I imagined stealing a ship and heading toward one of the suns that I saw and burning into oblivion.

After all, I was small against all of this vastness, too. I worried I was going space mad.

I was in the communication center, staring at the newest invoice that Tournour had sent me on a screen when the Kao captain found me. "What is it?" I asked.

"There's a Hort ship passing with a group of Humans that is willing to take you," the Kao said. All of his roundness jiggled when he walked. I knew that he was using echolocation to see me and I wondered what I looked like to him.

"Thank you. I'll get myself ready."

I went to my cabin and retrieved Trevor and the things that I had accumulated on my trip so far. Mostly a grab bag with a change of clothes and protein paks to make moving from ship to ship fast.

I prepared myself for a rough reception from the Hort. Though my long dead Hort friend Heckleck had been kind to me, I knew that the Hort were not the most gracious of species, and I got the impression that they cared for wandering Humans less than most. I expected that Humans would be awarded less than the regular passenger status. The Hort did not travel in comfort, and I assumed that any quarters assigned to me would be the bare minimum of living. Or, more likely, they would throw me in with the Wanderers despite my having paid for a berth. It didn't matter. I was prepared to live on whatever deck they would take me to, even if it meant being with the Wanderers after they inevitably ignored me. That's why I had my own food supply.

The ship's captain, a large Hort, met me at the entrance to the ship. He was much larger than my old friend Heckleck. His exoskeleton was a light brown and his appendages looked as though they had been sharpened. I felt a sudden sense of dread and had the distinct feeling that I'd made a terrible mistake getting on this ship. He did not treat me like a guest. He did not treat me like a hitchhiking passenger. The Hort treated me like a prisoner.

"Take the robot to the electronics bank," he said to the two crew members with him. "We can strip it for parts."

"That's my property," I said. "I paid for a berth."

But there was no one to help me out here with a deal gone bad. I could already hear the other ship unclamping and moving away.

The Hort opened his mouth and stuck out his barbed tongue menacingly.

"Trevor . . ." But before I could issue the command, one Hort pushed the switch on Trevor's neck, and I watched as the light that always made it seem alive dimmed to dark.

"I've mined with that kind of robot before," the Hort said. "And you won't need it where you are going. It's ours now."

"Where am I going?" I asked.

Then two Hort scuttled toward me, holding my arms behind my back with their pincers. I was shoved and jostled by the Horts' sharp appendages as we went lower and lower in the belly of the ship. Their feet clicked on the metal, reminding me of the insects that they looked like.

"A fortune for every Human," the captain laughed as we arrived at a cargo bay door that was heavily guarded. "I'm going to be a very rich Hort."

He made a signal and a small door opened and I was shoved in, the door slamming quickly behind me.

One look around told me everything that I needed to know. This was not going to be like the other voyages. These Wanderers weren't roaming. These Wanderers had been captured and were on their way to a colony to their inevitable deaths.

I was in a cargo bay packed with Humans. It must have been a few groups that had been rounded up. The bay was much too small to hold this many people, and it was too many Humans for just one tribe. I took in the room. There were no windows. The Wanderers had set themselves up as best they

could with their makeshift tents, but with no facilities anywhere for waste or refrigeration, the stink was unbearable, and
people looked sick. I had to cover my nose with my hands because every time I took a breath I wanted to vomit.

Humans were everywhere. Packed and pressed together.
Some alive. I feared that some were dead.

This was a den of hell.

Curious about the newcomer, some Wanderers came close
to me and started to shout in my face as soon as they saw my
blank skin.

"Hey."

"You there."

"What's your story?"

Wanderers near me pushed and poked me, trying to get at
my things, knowing that there were probably things inside that
they could use. They ripped at my clothes. Pinched my clear
skin. There were so many of them.

They were all shapes, sizes, ages, color. They were a blur of
hands pulling and mouths shouting.

In my months of travel, I had never thought that I would
get caught, but here I was. I cursed my naïveté. I had stupidly
thought that if I kept moving, and was mostly on my own, that
I'd be safe. I was wrong.

I had to find a space to think about what I should do next.
Perhaps I could throw some of Reza's credits to the Hort to
get me out of here.

"Stop it," I said. "Please, stop it."

Every time I found a corner where I thought I could be
alone, they pressed in on me, forcing me to move again.

Somewhere I lost my bag. Somewhere else I lost my shoe.
Somewhere else I tore my jacket. They were like bugs biting

me. I just wanted to get away from them, but there was no-where to go.

The crowd's faces morphed together becoming mostly indistinguishable, except one girl who seemed to always be flanking me. She was the only one not yelling, but perhaps that was because half her face was a mottled mess. Half of her hair was missing due to a terrible burn scar that I could see went way down below her collar. I wondered how far down. It was hard to look at her. One of her arms was badly burned, and yet both were covered in tattoos. She must have been in some awful accident. As I went past her, I noticed two terri-fied Humans, not much older than I was, wearing Imperium uniforms, looking shell-shocked. That's when I knew that nothing would get me out of here.

I tried to get ahead of the mob and picked my way until I found a corner with a little bit of space. Exhausted, I gave up being alone and sat down and tried to make myself as small as possible.

A big, burly man pushed me and then squatted down, get-ting in my face. He was so grizzled that I could not tell how old he was. He could have been either thirty or seventy.

"You an Earth girl, Blankie? You come here to sell us like those Imperium lovers? Like them?" he said.

He pointed over to the two Imperium officers who I could see were cowering in the corner. Their uniforms were tattered, and it was easy to figure out that these Hort had swept them up along with the Humans they were supposed to deliver. I felt sorry for them, but I had to take care of myself first.

"You're far from home now," the grizzled man yelled in my face. His breath was rotten. "You're in here with us."

As I tried to move away from him, he grabbed my wrist. I

screamed at the strength and pain of his grip. At first I thought I was done for, but then he stopped, gently turning my wrist around. The gold bracelet I had taken off of Els's dead body with the little charm of Earth peeked out from under my sleeve.

"Take it," I said. I had reached my end. It would be of no use here. I was dead along with the rest of them. "Take it and leave me alone."

I thrust my wrist to him so he could unlatch the bracelet rather than rip it off of me. I braced myself for a violent tug, but instead of taking it, he let my wrist go.

"I'm sorry," he said, taking a step back from me. "I know your story."

Then he shooed everyone away from where I was sitting, and he started talking in low tones to the people around him. The other Wanderers kept staring at me, but I no longer felt threatened. Strangely, I felt safe. The grizzled man took my hand and patted it reassuringly. He smiled; his two front teeth were missing.

I didn't understand what had happened to make him suddenly treat me with respect. But I was relieved as slowly, all of my things were returned to me.

The two Imperium officers inched closer to me, curious at the change, too. Clearly they had been treated just as badly by this group and wanted to know what the difference was now. They were trying to catch my eye, but I didn't want to associate myself with them. I didn't know what was going on yet, and even if these people all came from different tribes, they were not my allies.

I dug into my bag and got out one of my protein paks and some water. I took my time eating the scrap while trying to figure out what to say. To figure out what was going on and how to stay alive. I'd done it before with aliens; I could do it again here with Humans. After I'd had my fill, a ruddy-faced middle-aged woman with a long, dark braid that fell all the way down her back was ushered over to me. I could see that she had everyone's respect. It was clear that she was this journey's leader. The girl with the burned face stood tall next to her. She was probably her daughter or a second.

The woman took my hand and examined the gold Earth bracelet. After a moment she seemed satisfied.

"What's the word?" she asked.

That was surprising. Usually they started a conversation with *what's your story?* I wondered what could be different this time.

All eyes were on me. As though I had some kind of answer for them.

I sensed that they wanted something more from me. I started to offer her my bracelet. "Trade?"

The woman shook her hand, waving my offer away. She didn't say anything, but she was still looking at me expectantly.

"What's the word?" she asked again.

"I don't know," I responded. I had no idea what she wanted from me.

The woman sighed.

"How did you get this?" she asked, pointing at my bracelet. I was getting better at understanding the Wander accent, but still we spoke slowly in a mash of languages to come to an understanding. They did not have the nanites to help them speak Universal Galactic. It was no wonder that they were such outsiders when they traveled. The Wanderers had been traveling since the first intergenerational ships had left Earth over one hundred years ago. Most of these people had been born wandering. Their accent was strange. It amazed me how language evolved and was the same that I spoke, and yet it was so different.

"This?" I said, shaking my bracelet. Everyone pushed forward to hear my answer.

I remembered taking it off of Els's dead body when she had sold me, Reza, and Caleb out to Brother Blue. "I traded a favor for it. Why?"

That was almost the truth.

"What is she saying?" murmured through the crowd. They were all asking questions at the same time.

"She doesn't know anything," the burned girl said to the crowd. "She's not one of them. Move back. Leave her alone."

The crowd was clearly disappointed. They started to dissipate as much as they could in such cramped quarters.

They went back to their business, and I felt relieved without their eyes on me. Large groups of Humans still made me feel uneasy, and this was the biggest that I'd seen since I began my journey. I nodded in thanks to the burned girl for making them go away.

The two Imperium officers stuck close to me. As did the burned girl, who had stayed with the journey leader to make sure that I had space around me. With the crowd now mostly dispersed, I could finally breathe.

"Ednette," the journey leader said, pointing to herself.

"Tula," I said, giving her my name. The burned girl stepped closer to me. "What's going on?"

"They think you're a Gome," Ednette said.

"What's a Gome?"

> *"Oh, I will kiss the pale blue dot. It's just a stone in the sky. When I see the thread, the golden thread comes back through the stars. You know I'm going home, I'm going home."*

I'd heard the burned girl's song before.

"It's a myth we tell over meals. Going home. This is a sign," she said pointing to my gold bracelet.

"This?" I said shaking the gold Earth charm on the bracelet.

"Fifty years ago, every wandering tribe tried to send a member back to Earth to plead our case. To get us home."

I nodded.

"This kind of bracelet is what the Wanderers who manage to get back to Earth or their descendants are supposed to wear when they come back out here to help us find a way to go back home. Back to Earth," Ednette said. "No one has ever seen one return, but we all know what the bracelet looks like. And what the answer is to our question."

"Couldn't anyone make a bracelet like this?"

"Why would they? And even if they did, they wouldn't know the word."

"What is the word?" I asked.

"It's in the song," Ednette said. "It's what every planet is. A *Stone in the Sky.*"

Els. Even though she was long dead, she was still a mystery. Could she have been a descendent of Wanderers? Maybe that's what Caleb meant when he'd said that she'd had to fight tooth and nail to get off the streets and to the stars. Had she really gone to the stars to get the Wanderers home? I touched the gold Earth on my wrist. Perhaps I had misunderstood the reason for all of her horrible actions. Perhaps she had been on a mission that was bigger than her and her heart had gotten lost in the pursuit of her cause.

"I'm not a Gome," I said sadly.

"No," Ednette said. "You're not, but you met one and that is the first time I've ever heard of one coming back out to space. That's something. It means that some of ours actually made it back to Earth. You Earthlings always said that was impossible."

I regretted that Els hadn't accomplished her mission to meet them and bring them hope. Perhaps she had thought she could get them to go to one of the colonies if she were tight with Brother Blue. But in her desperation to help, she might have gotten trapped in enforcing the new lie that he had set. I shuddered at how terrible it might have been for her to believe she was helping the Wanderers to go home and not know that she was actually sending her people to their death.

I had tried to do what she could not. I had tried to help them. But I was trapped here along with them, could not lead myself home, much less them.

"I never believed the Gomes actually existed," Ednette said. "It was more a tale to keep our people moving and hopeful. Not that it matters anymore. We're going to a colony now. We boarded this ship because we are looking for our lost. My husband was recruited six months ago. It's not Earth, but maybe it will finally be a home. Our very own stone in the sky."

"But there are no Human colonies," I said. "We're headed toward death. That's why I'm traveling. I've come to warn the Wanderers to stay away from the colonies."

"Are you trying to keep these new planets for yourself like you hoard Earth?" Ednette asked grabbing my arm.

"No," I said.

"The Imperium Humans only take the young and the healthy. But traders, like these Hort have been searching for Humans. Telling us that they will take the old and the young to the colonies."

It had gotten worse then I thought. Any lowlife with a ship could pick up Humans and get a fee for transporting them to a colony.

"There are no colonies," I said, and this time it was my turn to grab her arm. "There is nothing there. Once the Humans arrive, they die there if they are not dead already."

"My husband is there," she said. "Half my old tribe."

I yelled in frustration. How could I make them understand? Someone had to believe me.

"They're fooling you," I said. "There is a very bad man who is tricking everyone. You'll never settle there, just like you'll never go back to Earth."

That got her listening. Earth was a way to ignite their passion.

"Those planets have no resources. There is nothing there. No infrastructure. In order to settle you need things: grains, supplies, building instruments, medicine. I know because I was supposed to be a settler. If you go there you will only die there," I said.

"But I heard from other tribes, they do a census. They count us up. My husband."

"He's dead," I said.

Ednette was wavering. She knew that her people had been lied to before.

"What's left of the Humans count as population when

scanned from space," I said. "Can't you understand? We're being sent there to cover up the fact that no one is there."

My voice cracked in desperation. I was telling the truth. Every cell in my body was buzzing with the truth. But the truth is meaningless unless it's believed.

"But those Humans with no story came with another group to go to the colonies," Ednette said gesturing to the two Imperium officers still cowering in the corner.

"But, remember Ednette, when they tried to leave, the Hort wouldn't let them. Remember how they howled," the burned girl said looking at Ednette. A look passed between them, as though this girl could read them in a way that Ednette could not.

"Yes, daughter, you are correct. They did act strange. Go to them and get them to tell you what they know."

The burned girl left to talk to the two Imperium Humans. I could see that they shook their heads vehemently. I knew that they knew nothing.

I grabbed at the chance of her growing recognition and repeated myself so that she would understand.

"Wherever we're going, there are no colonies. No resources. No life," I said. "The Imperium conducts a census. They scan the planets for biomatter. Even dead matter counts. And we'll be dead soon enough. We have to get off of this ship."

And then I saw it. Just as I was ready to give up I saw the glimmer of truth dawning on her face. *A high price for Humans. Even cadavers.*

"There's no way off of this ship," Ednette said. "This cargo is closed."

The burned girl came back to us holding one of the Imperium by the collar. She was visibly upset.

"What's wrong, Elizabeth?" Ednette said.

"Brother Blue," she said, her voice high pitched. "He says the orders to round us up come directly from a man named Brother Blue."

"Yes, that's it," I said. "That's the bad man."

"It's true," the Imperium officer said. She was pulling at her curly hair and talking fast as though telling the truth quickly would somehow get her out of here. "We were ordered to round up the young and healthy and bring them to hired transports like this one to go to different Earth colonies."

"We're not killing you. We're helping you to settle. We're getting you out of the sky to find homes," the other officer said. He was tall and thin and had dark eyebrows that made his eyes look sunken.

They were both convinced that they were telling the truth and that Brother Blue wasn't lying.

"There is a reason Brother Blue made sure that you never had to actually deliver the Humans to the colonies yourselves," I said to them both. "Because there is nothing there."

"That's not true. We're trying to help you! I swear! We're trying to help Earth!" the man said.

"He only wants to help himself, to power. To resources. He doesn't care about us. He kills people. He left me for dead on a space station after I found out that he'd sold all of the grain we were to use to start our colony on Beta Granade. And then he killed my mother and my sister by blowing up the ship to make sure it never got there."

The officer began shaking as the burned girl pulled the fabric tighter on her uniform collar so that she started to choke.

"Elizabeth!" Ednette screamed.

"There are colonies," said the female officer. "I swear. I've heard Brother Blue talk about them. I've personally sent hundreds of Humans to Kuhn."

"We pay the transport captains with alin," the man added.

Now Brother Blue's obsession with the alin made sense. He was making currency hand over fist in an unregulated way. It was enough to cover up his deceit.

"You're wrong," I said. "You all bought into his lies, just like I did once."

Elizabeth, the burned girl, let out a moan.

"We're already on our journey," Ednette said, pulling Elizabeth off the officer and close to her. "Our fates are sealed."

"You're on this trip with us," I said to the officers. "And unless we do something, you'll see what's on those colonies with your own eyes right before you die along with us."

24

. . . .

The burned girl, Elizabeth, had stayed back with me as Ednette turned and went away, leaving with the Imperium officers; the man was now shaking.

I was exhausted from my journey and from the adrenaline of being in this strange place and wanted to curl up to try to get some shuteye before I tried to figure out a way out of this mess. I didn't want to stare at Elizabeth, but I couldn't help it since she was staring so hard at me. When I looked back she didn't shy away. She held my gaze. Then she moved and got up toward me. I immediately looked down, trying to show that I meant no offense. The last thing I needed was for her to pick a fight with me. When she stood close to me, I could feel her power. She was sinewy and muscled. She moved gracefully, with complete command. I knew that she could hurt me physically. I had made it through a first wave with these Humans; I just needed to make it through to the end.

I looked back up at her.

"I'm sorry," I whispered. "I don't mean to stare. I'm just having some trouble falling asleep."

"It's okay. It doesn't hurt anymore. If you look at it long enough, people say that they don't see it anymore. They just see me."

She cocked her head to the side and smiled.

"Tula?" she then asked softly.

"Yes?" I said.

"Is it really you?" The burned girl smiled wider, and it was a smile I knew. How did I know that smile? It was then that I looked past the disfiguring scar. It was Bitty, my sister. She was alive.

I jumped up.

"Bitty? Bitty!"

I cupped her burned face with my hands, and I took her all in. Even her hand was burned. The skin was both soft and mottled. There were ridges of red and white and black ink. The landscape of her body was cratered. It hurt me to feel her skin as though I had been burned, too. Then we were hugging and crying, and I couldn't believe that my sister was alive.

"Mom?" I said looking behind her as though my mother would suddenly appear.

Bitty shook her head.

"Ednette called you daughter," I said.

"She's the one who took care of me when I arrived. She taught me how to survive. I would be dead without her."

I felt glad that she had someone to care for her who was unlike me. I envied the fact that she had been with Humans. How much easier it would have been if I'd had a tribe to help me survive. When I looked back up, her tone had shifted and after the moment of excitement of being reunited after so many years, she seemed angry with me.

"Bitty . . ." I said. "What happened?"

"I don't know. Only a few of us made it off the *Prairie Rose*. It was awful. As you can see."

"How did you escape?" I asked.

"I made it to a life pod," she said. "All those annoying drills you made me do saved me."

"Was it an accident or was it sabotage?"

I realized that I didn't know, and Bitty would have a better idea of it than I would. The *Prairie Rose* exploding had haunted me these past three years. It was this great unanswered question. Probably one I would never truly know the answer to. Things happened in space. Accidents happened. It just seemed that since Brother Blue was involved that it was unlikely that he didn't have a hand in it.

She looked at me, searching my face to see if I really believed that it could have been anything other than an accident.

"Do you really think someone deliberately harmed the *Prairie Rose*?" she asked.

"I think Brother Blue never wanted you all to make it to Beta Granade," I said. "He tried to kill me."

Bitty slapped the wall with her hand as this information sank in.

"I wanted to scream every time I heard his name again," she said. "He never answered any of the petitions from the few survivors. I thought you were with him. I couldn't understand why you wouldn't come for me."

All of a sudden her attitude shift toward me made sense. She thought that I had abandoned her. That she could think that I would know she was alive and ignore her was horrifying. I pulled her in again for a hug.

"I wasn't with him," I said. "I found the grain loaded onto the dock, and when I confronted him . . . he beat me. He left me for dead on the Yertina Feray."

The look of betrayal that Bitty had in her face changed to one of sympathy. We both had our scars.

"I had nothing. There were no Humans. I thought I was going mad. I was alone with only aliens for friends. I thought you were dead. I swear to you, Bitty, if I had known you were alive, I would have come for you."

I slipped my hand into hers.

"Tell me what happened," I said.

"The ship made its first skip, and it was fine. Then we made another skip, and the alarms went off. It was during the sleep cycle. I shot out of bed and to the life pods, but there was fire everywhere. I didn't want to go through it but Mom was behind me and shoved me into the fire to get to the pod."

She swallowed at the memory. I could see tears in her eyes.

"Go on," I said. "I'm here now." I had reverted back to being the big sister.

"I was in so much pain that I didn't see anything, just hands pulling me in and a blanket covering me up. We ejected from the ship but Mom wasn't with me."

Now the tears were coming out of her freely. This strong young woman was like a little girl again as she relived the pain. I let her sob on my shoulder until she was ready to speak again.

"We floated for a few days, just tumbling before we were picked up by a ship. Earth Gov wouldn't let us go back home, and we couldn't raise a signal from any colony. Eventually, we found a ship that had taken on some Wanderers, and the tribe adopted us."

"How many of you?"

"Four," Bitty said. "Only four kids in my pod. They've moved on to other tribes over time."

Four out of one hundred and sixty-seven. It seemed a miracle that anyone had escaped at all.

"Ever since it happened, I've been with these Wanderers.

At first I tried to convince them to get to Beta Granade. I was hoping that maybe some others had survived and that you were there. Maybe another ship had come to settle it."

"No one settled," I said. "Those worlds are empty. Brother Blue charmed us out of all of our money and our dreams and then once he'd bled us dry, he disposed of us. We weren't the first. If someone doesn't stop him, we won't be the last."

I hugged her again.

"We're not safe on this ship," I said. "We have to get off of here."

It was good to have a sister again. If I never went back to the Yertina Feray or if I never found Caleb again, then at least I'd be with Bitty. I could bear it now. I could survive this. There was an elation to knowing that I had gotten something back that he had taken away from me.

"I know one thing, Bitty. We are not going to die on a Hort ship at the hands of Brother Blue."

After all of those months of loneliness, I had something to live for. I had just found my sister, and it wasn't so I could die with her. She wiped away the tears with the back of her hand, and just like that, the strong young woman I'd met earlier was back.

"We're getting out of here," I said.

"The Hort won't open the cargo bay door except to dump more Humans in here," she said having pulled herself together. "We've tried. It's impossible."

"There's always a way until there is none," I said.

"You think you can get us out of here?" Bitty asked.

"If I have to die trying," I said.

"How?" she asked.

"Hijack this ship and make it our own."

25

Bitty led me through the cargo bay over to Ednette. When we were young, it was Bitty who followed me everywhere. And when we were on the *Prairie Rose*, I was the one who everyone knew. Here, I could see that like Ednette, Bitty commanded a certain kind of respect. If someone was in her way, they moved. I felt proud that she had survived in her own way; just as I had. She was a young leader and no longer a little girl.

I wondered what our mother would think of us and how we had survived. She would have been proud, I think. Whatever grit she'd had to want to go out into space she'd passed on to us.

"Mother, we'll die here if we don't do something," Bitty said to Ednette.

It was strange to me that she called Ednette Mother. But it reminded me that Bitty was only eleven when we'd left Earth. I was glad that she'd had Ednette to care for her. Just like I had Heckleck to care for me in his own way.

Ednette did not react; she just kept stitching up the fabric that she was holding. Her face was still and stoic, as though she had years of practice at hiding what she really thought or knew.

"It's true," I said. "Let's do something."

"Tula can help us," Bitty said. She was looking at me the way that she did when she was a little girl and thought that her older sister knew everything. I wondered if she might know more than me. She'd been on more space voyages than I had. She looked like she'd been in more fights than I had, too.

"Do you have an idea?" Ednette asked.

"I do. We're going to take over the ship," I said.

"How do we do that?" Ednette asked.

"Our enemies are Hort. I know Horts," I said. "They cannot stand the sound of the Human voice."

"That must be why the Hort mostly never take Humans. It did surprise me when they accepted our passage," Ednette said.

"There was so much money to be made they could not refuse," I said.

Ednette's face sobered.

"The frequency of it reverberates with them in such an awful way that it causes them intense pain. The nanites that most species carry can alter our frequency in conversation, but it can not immediately balance hundreds of Human voices all at the same time. It would give us only minutes, but those minutes could mean life."

"How can I help?" Bitty added.

It wasn't much different then when she asked me when we were children what the game was. We'd march out into the dust, hoping for green fields, but finding only brown, dried foliage. In the distance there'd be the factories, and at night there'd be the stars. During the day, Bitty would rely on me to make up games and find the fun. I led, and she followed. In the past, it annoyed me when she'd asked me that question, but now I could kiss her.

"Bitty, go get those Imperium officers and anyone else you can trust," I said. "We're going to need a team."

"I'll get Traynor, Buzzle, and Thomas," Bitty said, and Ednette nodded in agreement.

"Who are they?" I asked as Bitty darted away.

"They were the journey leaders of the other tribes before I was named for this leg. They know their people."

Bitty came back with them, and I noticed that one of the journey leaders, Traynor, was the grizzled man that had discovered my bracelet.

"Why are they here?" Traynor asked, pointing to the two Imperium officers. "We should kill them and throw them out an airlock. They brought us here. They are responsible for our situation."

"They have a vested interest in getting out of here, and they have military skills that we don't have," I said.

Traynor shook his head in disagreement, but he was alone in his opposition.

"What are your names?" I asked. They were cautious, not knowing what new trick this might be.

"Hanks," the woman said, her blue eyes darting from face to face nervously.

"Siddiqui." He stood at attention as though he was ready to adapt to the situation.

"Do you know how to win a fight?" I asked.

"Who are we going to fight?" Hanks asked incredulously. "We're locked in a cargo bay."

"We're hijacking this ship," I said.

Hanks shook her head.

"You can't get a bunch of savages to fight an honorable spacefaring race," Hanks said.

Siddiqui put his hand up to silence Hanks.

"I'm sure if I could talk to these Hort they'd see that there was a misunderstanding . . ." Siddiqui said.

"There is no misunderstanding," I said. "These Hort have been highly paid to take us to the colonies."

"But that's a good thing," Hanks said. "My great aunt is on Marxuach. She went there with the Children of Earth. We can get there and hitch a ride back to Bessen when the next transport comes."

"I know you've been told one thing," I said. "But you have to stop believing that fiction. I'm going to tell you very clearly that there are no Human colonies, and if we don't stop this ship from going there, we'll be dead."

A wave of understanding finally came over them. Hanks's shoulders slumped, and her eyes got a faraway look as she tried to reconcile reality with what she had believed for so long. Siddiqui straightened, his square jaw set as he made the leap in his mind.

"Weapons," Siddiqui said as he grasped the seriousness of the situation. "Gather whatever weapons or makeshift weapons you can find. We can make a better tactical plan once we know what we have."

"Don't let everyone know," Ednette said. "I don't want to spread any more panic than we have to."

Ednette, Bitty, and the other Wanderers scattered to find what they could. They brought back trinkets and goods that people had hoarded. When we had our makeshift weapons laid out in front of us, it was sobering.

We sifted through and each took knives, clubs, and tools to arm ourselves.

"Could be death," Traynor, the grizzled man, said.

"It's this or death," I said. "You choose."

"I don't like death," he said.

"Me neither," Siddiqui concurred. Hanks gasped putting her hands to her mouth.

"I just came out here to help colonize," she said. "I'm on a peaceful mission."

"Not anymore," I said.

"We die trying," said Ednette. "No matter what the odds." She was this voyage's leader. They would do what she said. It was the rule of survival for the Wanderers. It was a relief to have Ednette's full backing and support.

"The ship is moving again," Bitty said. We could all feel the ship speeding in its acceleration to a light skip.

"I don't know how far away we are from where we are going," I said, trying to calculate from the many ship voyages I'd recently done what the best timing would be for the attack.

"The guards that block us from the hallway. They are our first line out of here. If we can escape the cargo bay, and get to the hallway, then we have a chance at taking over the ship," Siddiqui said.

"What next?" Ednette asked.

"You cannot seduce a Hort. You cannot sway them with sob stories. You cannot play on their sympathies. They are cold and they are cunning. They loved certain kinds of foods that we Humans would never eat and that we certainly don't have. Our situation seems hopeless, but I once knew a Hort named Heckleck who I called a friend. He is dead now but he taught me everything that I know about how to stay alive."

"They don't seem to have any weaknesses," Traynor said.

"Noise," I said and then explained about the Hort and their aversion to the Human voice.

"That's too simple," Traynor said.

"It's true. I learned about it in training. Human voice frequency troubles them. Makes them uncomfortable unless it's modified by nanites," Siddiqui said.

"That's why we're in the bottom of the ship," I said. "It's going to take a long time for us to make our way up to the bridge."

"We'll get there," Ednette said.

"If we make so much noise that it overwhelms them, it could at least give us a first push," I said.

"We can get everyone to do that," Bitty said. "Even the weak."

"Let's get the word out," I said. "When the door opens, everyone needs to make noise—a lot of noise. But everyone else should stay back until we've cleared the hall."

"You want them to fight?" Siddiqui asked, looking back at the Wanderers. Some were so old that they could barely stand. Many were sick.

"Yes," Ednette said. "If we fail, they are dead anyway. Those who want to fight might as well fight."

"They can secure what we've taken as we push forward," I said. "That gives them something to do."

I looked around and noticed that even Hanks was in. Our group was in agreement.

"We'll set the time for attack for an hour after we decelerate from light skip," Ednette said.

We all nodded and headed back to our tents and pods.

"Let's rest up," I said. After a fraught day, I knew I would finally be able to fall asleep with my sister alive.

Tomorrow I was going into battle.

26

. . . .

Our attack would begin in an hour.

The cargo bay was so quiet, as though everyone was saving their voice to be the loudest that it could be.

I passed out the last protein paks I had, and we ate in silence, preparing ourselves for what was to come.

"It's time," I said.

Ednette, Bitty, and I banged on the steel cargo doors until they opened.

"What do you want, Human?" the guard asked.

I made the signal and the cacophony started. Every Human in the cargo bay began to talk, to scream, to sing, yell, yodel, and whoop at the top of their lungs.

In a split second the Hort guarding us went from powerful to powerless. They screeched and scuttled back, and as they did, we rushed forward and pinned them down. We took their knives and immediately our weapons tripled.

We cheered when we took the hallway, but soon, bells rang and lights strobed. One of the Horts must have sounded the alarm.

I did not care. We had to push forward.

"Take care of them," Traynor said. I watched as the Wanderers dragged the Hort guards into the cargo bay. I heard the mournful thrum of music that came from the Hort vestigial wings and then high, piercing screams. I shuddered, but what happened to them was no longer my concern. Ednette, Bitty, Traynor, Siddiqui, and I took one hallway. Buzzle, Thomas, and Hanks went down the other.

I did not know the layout of the ship, so Ednette took point. She'd been on more spaceships than I had. She knew how to figure out the lay of the land.

Stolen knives at the ready, we pressed every button in the hallway until a door opened, giving us a way to move on.

Because the alarms had sounded, I was expecting to see the Hort ready to fight us at every turn. Instead, when we entered the hallway they were running wildly away, looking like they were trying to escape. From us? No. I didn't think so.

"Where are they going?" Ednette yelled.

"I don't know," I said back. "Something is happening."

Something else *was* happening. The alarm was not for us. It was signaling another danger. The Hort scuttled by, ignoring us. We were swimming upstream. The clicking sound of the Hort's panicked appendages on the metal of the floor was unsettling.

Then the ship quickly decelerated and came to a full stop. A strange noise followed, and then an explosion.

"What is that?" Bitty asked. She had a fear in her eyes that I could trace to the burn on her face. It was the fear of a ship tearing apart.

"It doesn't matter," I said. "Keep going."

I was pretending to be unafraid, but inside I was panicking. I had fought for my life in so many ways, but I had never been in battle.

"Let's go," Ednette said. "Let's use this chaos to our advantage."

"Where do we go?" Traynor shouted.

"Wherever they are running away from," Siddiqui said.

"Why head toward danger?" I shouted.

"Because whatever is danger to them is to our advantage," he said.

Ednette made three quick gestures for the team to follow. Whatever was happening to the ship, we were on the move.

We heard a scraping. Something was coming along outside the hull. The ship shuddered. Metal screeching on metal filled the hallway with an ever-deafening sound.

"The ship, it's coming apart," Bitty yelled, eyes wild in full panic.

I tried not to scream.

"No. That's the sound of another ship fast docking," Siddiqui said.

When we turned a corner, there was a flash of light and then smoke.

We weren't coming apart. Someone was invading the ship.

A smoke grenade had burst in front of us. My senses were disoriented, and I fell to the ground. I didn't know which way was up, and there was nothing to see except shadows. I wondered who was here with us and whether they were friend or foe. An arm grabbed me and pulled me up.

"Come on," Bitty yelled.

As I ran I could see shadows as they stepped through the smoke. I tried to make out which species they were, but they all wore elaborate masks to cover the finer details of their faces and forms. In a way, the garish colors and strange masks they wore made them unified. A non-uniform uniform.

"Pirates!" Ednette screamed.

We raced down the smoky hallway hearing only the

thudding feet of the Pirates behind us. They were closing in from all sides and then they burst into view.

I had my knife at the ready. I would fight them if I must. Even though they were attacking the Hort ship, I didn't know if they would attack us, too. We were surrounded by the fleeing Hort on one side and the attacking Pirates on the other.

I froze, and the moment seemed to hang in an eternity until one of them made a hand signal. Everything sped up again as the pirates ignored us and ran off to pursue the Hort.

"Go, go, go!" Ednette cried, jolting me back to the here and now.

Though we all took different hallways, we were at the top of the ship by this point, which led us to the same place. The bridge.

On the bridge, the Pirates were in an intense fight with the Hort who had remained behind. Even though we had arrived, they paid us no heed and continued to concentrate on the Hort.

"They're on our side," I yelled.

"What do we do?" Traynor shouted back.

"Fight," Bitty cried.

I moved forward, my knife flashing.

Bitty jumped in front of me and slashed a Hort's appendage off. The Hort screamed at a pitch that I couldn't hear, but I could feel. Dark liquid spilled to the floor, making it slippery. Bitty shoved the Hort to the ground and with a battle cry sunk her knife into its chest.

"Look out!" I cried as another Hort scuffled over to her. She pushed me back out of the way and then elbowed the Hort in the eye. I turned away as she looped her arm around its vestigial wing, pried it up, and stabbed where I knew the Hort heart was.

"Hide there," Bitty said. "I can tell you're not a fighter."

But she was. Bitty, Ednette, Traynor, and Siddiqui were fighting fiercely. As shell shocked as Hanks had seemed in the cargo bay, she was skirmishing as best she could on the other side of the bridge. She was holding her own but pinned down by two Hort, she could not avoid the sharp appendage that pierced through her back. She fell over, and from where I was crouched I could see her dead blue eyes staring up at nothing.

Buzzle and Thomas were nowhere to be seen. Bodies were everywhere. There was so much screaming; some of it from pain and some of it from fear. I screamed. I had shimmied down even farther by a panel to have some cover but though I was not in the middle of the action, my knife was covered in blood as I slashed at whatever came near me.

Watching Bitty was something else. She was quick. Pinned by two Hort, she ducked and weaved until she and one of the pirates led them to a corner. Then she slashed off the appendages of one of the Hort. While he screamed and scrambled away, dark liquid spraying everywhere, and was finished off by the pirate, she turned quickly and plunged her knife into the other Hort's eye.

Then she jumped on top of its body and kicked open its plating, digging her heel into its soft flesh. When we were young, I had never known her to be athletic, but here she fought with a ferocity that I could barely understand. If I had used my brains and charm to survive on the Yertina Feray, she had clearly had to learn to use her brawn to survive wandering.

Then it was done.

I always had assumed that there would be an eerie quiet in the aftermath of a battle, but it was noisy. People shouting orders to each other. Movement of bodies. The whirring of electronics. The scramble to get the falling ship under control.

The Pirates were finally in charge of the Hort ship. We were now in their hands.

I looked at them, this mix of species, covered in strange masks and colorful clothing, now stained by Hort blood. I think half of the fear they struck was from this mad look they wore. They had helped us, and I was still scared.

One of the Pirates, a biped, came on deck and looked at us Humans and did a sweep of the room. When it turned to me, it slowly removed its mask and showed its face.

Caleb.

"I got your message," he said.

27

· ·

"You found me," I said.

I could hardly believe Caleb was standing there in front of me.

"You were hard to miss," he said. "You left a trail as large as the Milky Way." I moved toward him, but his posse moved in closer as though they would slice me in two if I even hinted at touching Caleb.

"You can't touch me," he said. "They'll kill you if you do. It's the Pirate way."

I took a step back, and they backed down a bit.

Seeing the Pirates in action made me understand why Reza had been hesitant to give me Caleb's ship's name. Having just witnessed the battle with the Hort, I knew that meant he had done unspeakable things. I could hardly recognize him with his facial scruff, long blond hair, and hard blue eyes. He seemed a far cry from the gentle young man I'd known on the Yertina Feray.

He nodded toward the group of Humans on the ship with me.

"Friends?" he asked.

I nodded.

"So you are capable of making and keeping friends," he said.

"I'm still your friend," I said.

"I don't trust you to not try to kill me again," he said. I couldn't tell if he was angry or making a joke. I could not find one thing I recognized in this cold, cruel-looking face.

"I didn't kill you," I said.

"You might as well have," he said. "At least, that's what I know now."

"There were circumstances beyond my control."

"How's Trevor?" he asked.

"He's here," I said. "The Hort took him to the electronics bay."

"That's good to know. I'll be taking him with me," he said. "Then again, we'll take whatever we want."

I swallowed back my sadness as he and the others looked around the bridge with greed in their eyes. I knew I couldn't argue to keep Trevor. Caleb was no longer the boy who sang tender songs in the arboretum and spoke of love for a girl that he hardly knew across a galaxy. He was different now. A Pirate.

"Of course," I said. "He's yours."

He exchanged hand signals and half the group of pirates went off into the ship. Caleb and three others stayed behind.

"What's happening?" I asked.

"I told them that I'd take the parley since you are Human," he said.

Everyone left was staring at us.

"Do you know this man?" Ednette asked.

"Yes," I said. "He's a friend."

"I'm not your friend," Caleb said. "I'm an intrigued acquaintance."

"This is my sister, Bitty," I said pointing to Bitty. I saw a look pass over Caleb's face.

192

"She's alive," he said slowly. He was surprised, and I could tell that he cared about that.

"Yes, and I'd like to keep her that way," I said.

He nodded and then rubbed his face. He looked exhausted.

"I've been trying to figure out what you were doing," he said getting back to it. "Jumping from ship to ship. Your course made no sense."

"I was forced to leave the Yertina Feray," I said. "I didn't have anyone else to turn to. You were the only person I knew. I thought I could ask you for help."

He laughed and shook his head.

"I didn't imagine that you'd joined a tribe. But when I noticed that you'd transferred to this ship, I knew that was bad news for you. Wanderers don't have a habit of ever hitching again if they board certain ships."

"You know about what's been happening to the Wanderers? What Brother Blue is doing?"

"You and Brother Blue," he said. "You are single-minded Tula. I have heard rumors about it, but it's not my concern."

"Of course it's your concern!" I said. "They're Humans. He's killing them for nothing. For power."

"I'm only interested in cargo that I can sell," he said. "Or have use for."

"Who are you?" I asked looking straight at him. After a moment I saw his eyes flick away defensively.

"I came for you, didn't I? I stepped in when there was trouble."

"We were doing fine without your help," I said.

He laughed. It came right up from his belly, and for a moment he looked happy. Like it had been a long time since he'd really laughed.

I hardened my eyes. Nothing about this situation was funny.

"We would have taken the ship eventually," I said. He was making me angry. I had wanted to find my friend. I didn't need this stranger's help.

"And gone where?" he said. "Do you even know how to fly a spaceship?"

"No," I said. "But he does." I pointed to Siddiqui. Caleb took in his tattered Imperium uniform.

"Can you?" he asked him.

"Maybe," Siddiqui said. "Probably. I had simulation training."

"Fair enough," Caleb said. "You can take care of yourself."

"It doesn't matter," I said. "We would have figured it out." But the truth was I had not thought much beyond taking over the Hort ship. I had figured that it would be a hijack, and we could persuade them to fly us somewhere safe. But the Hort were all gone, or dead. They'd been running to their escape pods. What did they care about abandoning some Humans?

I thought that once I found Caleb all of my problems would be solved. I had always known that he would be a leader, and here he was in his element. Commanding. Charming. Seemingly invincible. He was right next to me and yet a million miles away.

In my mind, Caleb was too soft to plunder and steal and he could not roam the stars for any other reason than to try to make things right. I wondered what had happened. It was as though Reza and Caleb had switched places. Hard becoming soft. Soft becoming hard.

"Who is your leader?" Caleb asked our group of Humans. "We should have that parley."

I expected Ednette to move forward. She had been the

Wanderers' journey leader on this journey, but instead they all stepped back and pointed to me.

"You?" Caleb said. "You've finally recognized your leadership qualities. I'm impressed."

"No," I said. "I just got here. I'm not a Wanderer. It's Ednette, she is the journey leader."

I pointed back to her. She shook her head.

"You led us to this bridge," Ednette said. "With or without the Pirates coming, you were leading us to our freedom and giving us this ship. You are in command. That's how this works."

I thought of all the times that I had been ignored by the Wanderers on my voyage. I didn't have the confidence that they would follow me wholeheartedly.

"It's easy to lead when it's fighting for your life," I said. "But I don't have much luck with the tribes listening to me any other time. We should choose someone else."

Ednette knew that what I was saying was true.

"Bitty took the bridge," Traynor said.

"I'll lead, if you will all counsel," Bitty said to us.

We all nodded in agreement.

"You can talk to me," Bitty said to Caleb.

That was how quickly power changed hands with the Wanderers. Bitty would be this journey's leader. The Wanderers on the bridge bowed their heads at the same time to indicate respect for her.

"You're no more than a child," Caleb said.

"There are no children in space," Bitty said. "We grow up too fast."

It was true. I felt so far away from being young even though I still was.

195

"All right then," Caleb said. He knew it was true, too. In the time he'd been out in space he'd grown up by eons.

"Go deck by deck and tell the others to strip whatever valuables they find," he said to the remaining Pirates on the bridge. "But leave enough for these Humans to use on the ship. After that, we'll rest and leave in two full turns."

They nodded and quickly spread out, leaving the bridge.

"Come with me," Caleb said to Bitty.

He turned back to Ednette.

"Organize yourselves with quarters and food on this ship."

Something was not quite right. Instead of safe I felt nervous. Both Bitty and Caleb were so far from the people that I had known and loved.

It made me remember that the largest distance between two people is farther than the farthest star.

28

. . . .

Ednette, Siddiqui, Traynor, and I went through the decks one by one and counted the dead. Sixty-three out of three hundred and fifty.

"That's one full tribe," Ednette said sadly.

After we cracked the cargo door open and let those who'd stayed behind out, everyone went to the mess hall to search through the food and see what was fit for Humans to consume. Soon enough Bitty returned from her parley with Caleb and called her council, all of us who had taken the bridge, together.

"What did he say?" I asked.

"They will leave us with what we need to survive and to make a jump to a system where we can hitch on another ship."

"We'll run into the same trouble," Ednette said.

"Yes," Bitty said. "But now we're armed with knowledge. It may protect us."

"That's a generous deal," Traynor said.

"He's being generous because you are with us, Tula." Bitty said.

"I need to talk to him," I said. I didn't want to believe that he'd come just to leave again.

"I don't get the impression that he wants to talk to you,"

she said. "He said to say thank you for taking good care of his robot."

"Was Trevor whole? Had it been broken down?"

"He just said to say thank you," Bitty said.

"What do we do now?" Siddiqui asked. He knew he was a long way from the Imperium, and he would have to throw his lot in with us.

"We mourn our dead," Bitty said.

"And then we celebrate our new journey leader," Ednette said, looking like a proud mother. She pulled Bitty in for a hug, and for a moment I saw Bitty smile like when we were little girls.

. . . .

We got to the sad task of dealing with the dead.

The bodies were incinerated. The ashes were packed and then scattered, jettisoned out among the stars where they would always be wandering.

Afterward, the Wanderers cleared the mess hall and what instruments could be found were brought out. Songs were sung to mourn, and then songs were sung to celebrate. We all feasted on the Hort protein paks and the grubs that the Hort considered a delicacy, which were not very tasty, but they filled us up.

"Come," Bitty said. "That tattooists are ready. It's time to get your mark."

"My mark?" I said.

"Your ship tattoo," Bitty said. "Now you have a story."

She brought me over to the tattoo artists who had set up in a corner of the hall. Even Siddiqui was in line for a tattoo. But as journey leader, Bitty was given preference and everyone let her go to the front of the line, and she took me with her so we could sit next to each other. The others in line watched and clapped and sang to us as the ink bloomed black on our skin.

"I didn't do anything but try to live," I said to Bitty, as I watched the tattooist work on my arm. The right arm was where your first voyage was marked.

"That's what makes this your ship," Bitty said.

But I thought of my story. Of the *Prairie Rose* and the Yertina Feray. Of all the other ships that I had taken to get here; it seemed strange that there would be no mark for those places.

I almost asked for a different mark, to speak of those ships, but in the end I kept quiet and got the same tattoo that everyone on this voyage did. This mark was just the beginning of my wander. Nothing else would be forgotten. I was marked by them in my heart, where it counted most.

Bitty got something more to her tattoo. She got an extra line, thicker than the other under the ship. It was the mark of this ship's journey leader. Ednette clapped the loudest as she watched Bitty with a mother's pride.

The pain of the needle pricking my skin was a welcome pain, but as it pricked, I felt an intense happiness. This ship would be marked on us all as part of our story. My first tattoo. I hardly knew who I was anymore. An Earthling. A colonist. A gutter rat. A space station citizen. A Wanderer.

The music tempted most to the floor, but I did not want to dance with the other Wanderers who would laugh at my not knowing their intricate steps. Or sing the songs that I did not know. I could only hum along to the pretty tunes.

As much as they had welcomed me, I also did not belong here.

29

● ●

I left the celebration while it was still in full swing,
slipping out quietly to send a sweets, water, and salts invoice
to Tournour who was the one being in the galaxy that I wanted
to share this victory with. I wanted to let him know where I
was, so that someone knew that I was alive. But a one-way
message is unsatisfying. So I settled my restlessness and
roamed the ship as I used to do on the Yertina Feray, trying
to find a good window to look out of.

I paused in the observatory lounge. It was nothing like the
arboretum from the Yertina Feray, but it was the place that
had the best windows. I could see a gas giant in the distance,
some stars, and the *Noble Star* attached to our ship. We were
flying together.

I thought I was alone, and so I jumped at the sound of Caleb's voice.

"I went to the celebration, but you were gone," he said.

"I couldn't join in," I said composing myself. "I am not a
Wanderer."

"What are you then?" he asked, stepping closer to me.

"An alien," I said.

"You don't look that strange to me," he said gripping my
shoulders and bending down to my height so he could look
me in the eyes.

"Did you come to say goodbye?" I asked, a wave of sadness washing over me.

"Not yet. But soon," he said, shaking his long blond hair off of his face. "We should talk. And I knew I'd find you here, gazing out a window."

"I'm predictable," I said.

"No. You're not." He indicated the windows. "But in this you are."

We were quiet for a moment as we looked out at the vast darkness that we were sailing through. He began to hum. That song. It reminded me of becoming his friend.

"I'm sorry about what happened with the cryocrates," I said.

He put his hand up to silence me. Then his shoulders hunched, and he went from looking like this strong man, this ruthless Pirate, to the thin, sensitive boy I'd met on the Yertina Feray. As though being with me reminded him of all that he hadn't done. Of all that he'd had to do to get here. This moment was his weakness.

"You're different," I said.

"That's what happens with time," he said smiling. For the first time since I had seen him again, I saw my friend standing in front of me, my old friend in this now hardened face.

I had only been out here for a few months, and I was also already so changed.

"I don't have friends. I have associates. And we would all double-cross each other if we didn't have a code to live by," he said. "It gets to you."

"We all have a code we live by," I said.

I thought about how I had made rules for myself in order to survive. Things I'd suppressed in order to live with myself.

"It wasn't like what I thought it would be out there. I signed

201

up for something totally different," he said. "Mostly, it feels like I've had to fight my way out of hell."

"I know," I said.

"You don't know."

"Reza came back to the Yertina Feray."

"So he made it," Caleb said with a bit of admiration in his voice. "I wasn't sure that little ship he'd stolen would make the trip."

"He almost made it. He crashed on Quint. He found the alin."

"He's always been lucky," Caleb said shaking his head.

Of course, Reza had not said much about what happened on the Outer Rim, but it was a way to keep Caleb talking.

All beings are nostalgic, Heckleck used to say. *They will talk about the past more than the now.*

"He mentioned some things," I said. Caleb winced.

"He left me," Caleb said. "We woke up and we were surrounded by aliens that we couldn't even understand."

"I know what that's like," I said.

"No, you don't," Caleb said.

"Then tell me how it was different," I said. "I sent you there because it was where you wanted to go."

"But I was asleep," he said. "Do you know how vulnerable that made us?"

I had never thought of that. I had just sent them out in the cryocrates in cryosleep because I wanted to save them. To get them off the ship. I hadn't thought about anything else except giving them the best chance to keep alive.

"The first group we fell in with once we'd been woken from stasis were a species that I had never seen before," he said. "They didn't even know about the Imperium, they were so far out on the Rim. They just wanted to hit some ships. They put us in a training camp, more like a torture camp. They trained us, and we shipped out, ill prepared for what we were up against."

"I know it was hard," I said.

"Hard?" Caleb said. "Our bodies were wrong for all of the gear. But we made it work. Killing is easy. You just do it. I did it so many times that I started to feel nothing. But we weren't getting anywhere. It felt like we were running in place."

I thought about how lucky I had been to find friends in the aliens that had surrounded me. Even in leaving the Yertina Feray, I had Caleb to look for. But I would never forget those first months on the Yertina Feray, where every face was strange and I was utterly alone.

"At least you had each other," I said.

Caleb rubbed his face.

"That was cold comfort in a cold place."

"I know you both had different ideas about how to help Earth to resist collaboration with the Imperium, but once you were out there it couldn't have mattered anymore."

"Of course it mattered. It mattered because we couldn't agree on how to survive. Every day was a battle out there between us, worrying about what was going on at home and how we couldn't do anything. We'd failed."

It sunk in as I watched his face twist with emotions. Humans had a way of hanging on to ill feelings long after time should have let them fade. I knew that best. Here I was, time marching on, changing in some ways, softening in others, letting those like Tournour, Reza, and Caleb into my heart. But I would never stop hating Brother Blue. I knew that it stunted me.

"You'd be surprised what you learn about someone when you are in the far reaches of the galaxy, being trained to be in an army that you don't believe in. You can get anything out of anyone if you are hungry enough, or sad enough, or desperate enough for an escape. It's not that I'm angry anymore. It's just . . . God knows what Reza's got on me."

Some things about Caleb may have changed, but I could see that parts of his heart hadn't. It made me relieved. Perhaps there was some kind of salvation in having a past bond with someone.

"You split up," I said, trying to get the story out of him.

"The ship we were on was boarded by Pirates. They seemed more merciful than the aliens we'd been with and even though they were strange, they seemed less alien. Maybe it was because they had traveled more than the aliens we were with. They'd at least seen Humans before. That makes a difference, you know."

I nodded.

"So you joined up with Pirates," I said.

"We switched sides. I think that was the only thing we agreed on. We were a good team for a while then. Eventually, we joined the *Noble Star*. Our Imperium Youth training came in handy out there. I could always find the littlest ships, the ones that tried so hard to fly under the radar and usually had the biggest loot. One day we hit a small ship and Reza went in first to scout it. Once he got on board, he took off and left me."

He closed his eyes. When he did, everything about his face looked soft. His blond curls. His long lashes. I think it was hard for him to talk to me when he saw my eyes. It was natural for Caleb and I to talk of serious things, but this was hard for him. Confessions are sometimes better when no one is watching. Darkness makes it easier to speak from the heart.

"After he left I thought to myself *I am so far away from anything that I care about.* It was easy to lose myself and to rise in Pirate ranks. You just have to not care about anything and always win."

"You care about things," I said, thinking about the way that he cared enough about us to make sure we had a ship. About the way that while he had ignored my messages, he came through when he knew I was in danger. About how he had loved Myfanwy with all of his heart. "You wouldn't have convinced your crew to let us keep this ship otherwise."

He stiffened as though I had revealed something in him that he didn't want out in the open.

"Sometimes I think I don't feel anything anymore," he said.

I sucked my breath in. That was how I had felt for years.

"Me too," I admitted.

"That's why you just now helped hundreds of Humans save themselves?" he asked. "Because you don't feel? I think your problem, Tula Bane, is that you can't hide behind coldness. You care too much."

Something shifted in me. I had held back from truly caring since I'd been abandoned. But I could not deny that I cared about people. I was glad to be standing here on a ship with a friend, knowing that my sister was safe. I warmed at the thought of Tournour, Thado, and Reza who were far away and yet always in my thoughts. I had to admit that I did care much more than I allowed myself to show.

"Why have you been sending me messages?" he asked.

All of the walls between us were finally stripped away.

205

"I have a trial with a possible execution order on me, and I had to leave the Yertina Feray. I had nowhere to go, so I thought I could join up with you."

"I'm a Pirate. You don't have it in you to be a Pirate."

"I could be if we could hit Brother Blue's ship," I said.

"What?" he said. I had surprised him again.

"We could go and attack his ship when he leaves the Yertina Feray to go to Bessen or Earth. We could get the alin. And if he died in the process, well, that's not a coup. That's just bad luck."

"That's not who you are," Caleb said.

"I want Brother Blue dead," I said.

"You can't abandon these people. If you abandon them, then it will be the same as killing them," Caleb said. "And you won't do that."

"I don't want to be responsible for these people."

Every choice was the wrong choice.

"But you are."

"Why did you bother tracking me down?" I asked.

"I kept seeing all of these other Humans that I let go, but I missed seeing a Human face that I knew. You are the closest to home that I will ever get."

"I'm coming with you," I said. "I'm not a Wanderer. I can't be aimless the way that these people are. I have to go somewhere. Do something."

"Pick another path," Caleb said. "I won't let you become a Pirate."

I could tell that he was serious. And then it struck me. If I could not attack Brother Blue from a Pirate ship, and if the Yertina Feray was denied to me, maybe I could get these Humans back to Quint. They were not safe in wandering in space. They needed a sanctuary to ride out Brother Blue's run on power. Maybe they could work the Human claim. Or Reza's. I could take Brother Blue down in a different way. From within his own ranks.

"If you won't take me with you, then help us to get back to Quint."

"Quint? Why?" he said.

"These people are in danger out here, they'll be picked up again. You know they will."

He nodded in agreement.

"On Quint there is an infrastructure. There are resources coming in to build up a temporary colony. The area of a claim is only good if you have people from your own species working it. They need workers there. Here are workers."

"Why would I want to help them?" Caleb asked.

"When I first met you, you wanted to help to bring down the Imperium collaborators. Here's your chance to help do that."

"I'll think about it."

He turned and left. But I could tell that he was buzzing.

30

• •

Bitty had insisted that we share quarters, even though she was the leader and could be alone if she wanted. I did not refuse. We could barely let the other out of sight, too afraid that we'd lose each other again.

"There you are," she said when I entered the room. "I saw you sneak off."

"I needed to be alone," I said. "Is the celebration done?"

"There are some people still there," she said. "Usually I'd stay, but as journey leader, I thought I should get some rest."

She was younger than I was and yet wiser than me in so many ways. She was brawn and brain. I was heart and hate.

It was strange to share a room with Bitty. There was none of the ease that we'd had when we were young. Not that being sisters was ever easy, but she and I were very different from who we were then. Now we were no longer children. Our divergent journeys had marked us, and I was not used to sharing my space with anyone but Trevor, who was now no longer in my possession.

As she prepared for bed, I could see her burns and tattoos. There were scars on her body I could not help staring at. Her body was tight and muscly, and she looked fit in a way that I never had been. She seemed ferocious, like a wild cat. Her body was a map of her life without me. Her first mark, of course, was the burn from the exploding *Prairie Rose*.

"Was it quick?" I asked.

I couldn't bear the idea of my mother dying slowly.

"It felt quick," she said. "I don't remember much."

She came over to me and sat on the bed.

"Don't be afraid to look," she said. "These are scars. You have yours too."

She put her hand on my heart. Was I that easy to read?

I put my hands on her face and arms. I felt each ridge and wondered if I were as mottled as that on the inside.

"I'm not embarrassed by these," she said. "I've had to fight to stay alive. We all do when we're out here."

Then she pointed to each tattoo, each scar, and told me the story of her voyage since we'd parted.

"The *Dinear. Sunburst. Quantam Grain. Bellio Cane* . . ."

She listed the ships. So many ships.

"You never landed?" I asked. "The Wanderers don't ever just settle on some corner of a planet?"

"No," she said "You know that's not allowed."

It should be, I thought.

"We wander till we go home."

She'd not been on a single planet since she left Earth. I wondered how she would take to my idea of bringing them all to Quint.

"What was it like? Always moving?" I asked.

"You know," she said. "You've been wandering yourself."

"It feels different. I was traveling, not wandering."

"But you've seen how beautiful the galaxy is," she said.

I thought of Quint. And Tallara. And the space elevator to

Bessen. I thought of the suns that I'd seen on this journey. All different sizes. Different colors to my eyes. I thought of the gas giant we were near. There was so much to see.

And still, compared to Bitty, I had seen so little.

We settled down, but I had trouble finding sleep. Bitty's every move at night, her every breath, every sigh kept me awake. My arm was still buzzing from the sting of the tattoo, and my brain was troubled at the burden of being responsible for this ship and these people.

I could not stop thinking about Brother Blue.

I wanted to be home on the Yertina Feray. There was an ache in me that was shaped like the station. Like Tournour. I tried to picture his face. He was the one that I wanted most to talk to about what was happening. I thought of ways that I could get back or get a message to him that was more detailed than a shipping manifest, but I knew that was impossible.

I was sure of only one thing. Quint was the solution. It seemed as though all of the action, the whole center of my universe, was there.

31

. . . .

The *Noble Star* was leaving us. Caleb was leaving. He had not come to say goodbye.

I was hurt. Knowing he would be gone felt like losing a battle in this long war that I had declared.

I stood on the bridge with Bitty, Ednette, Traynor, Siddiqui, and we watched the *Noble Star* as it uncoupled from the Hort ship.

"There she goes," Bitty said.

I felt a twist as I watched it gain acceleration and move away.

"We need to find a destination," Bitty said.

I wanted to put forth my idea of going to Quint, but without Caleb it would be too dangerous, so I stayed quiet.

Siddiqui was leaning over the navigation console, taking his time to study it.

"I'm working on trying to figure out what our best jump will be," he said.

"Do we know where we are?" Bitty asked. "Do we have an idea of where we should head?"

The door slid open. Caleb and a group of three other Pirates came in.

"What's going on?" Bitty said. "You gave us this ship."

Her hand went to her hip to grip the handle of her knife. I put my hand on her shoulder to relax her.

"I thought you were abandoning us," I said.

"You have a way of getting under my skin," Caleb said. "Friends?"

He stuck his hand out to shake.

"Friends," I said as I pulled him in for a hug, relief flooding me. I knew he'd come back because he knew that there was something right in going back to Quint. Having a friend by my side made everything I was hoping to do seem possible.

"We're one skip away from the system that Marxuach is in," Caleb said when we broke apart. "I think we should go there first. See for ourselves what's going on there."

"I'd like to go to Marxuach," Siddiqui piped in. "I have to know if you are telling the truth or lying about the colonies."

There was no need to take a vote. We all wanted to see a Human colony with our own eyes.

"Then let's go," Caleb said.

He snapped his fingers, and the Pirates joined Siddiqui and started preparing the ship.

"What about being a Pirate?" I said.

"The code says that if you leave all of your possessions but the clothes on your back you may leave the crew without punishment."

"What about them?" I asked.

"I told them about the riches that could be had on Quint. They were the only ones smart enough to follow me."

32

. . . .

Nothing could prepare us for Marxuach.

When we skipped into the system, we rushed by the outer planets. We watched the sun, a G-type star grow larger as we closed in on the planet.

"We're receiving a transmission," Siddiqui said.

"Put it so we can hear," Bitty said.

> *Approaching ship. Please be advised that Marx-uach is currently experiencing severe weather conditions. Communication and landing at the colony is not authorized at this time. We expect to be up and running in six months' time. We welcome you to visit us again then.*

The messages kept coming, one after the other. Until, as we got closer to the planet, they started to be threatening.

> *Please be advised that the planet is currently not issuing landing codes.*
>
> *Turn your ship around or else we will be forced to launch counter measures.*
>
> *Approaching ship. You are now considered a hostile entity. This is your last warning.*

Space cannons are now armed. You are now under attack.

"Keep going," I said.

"They're going to shoot us down," Siddiqui said. "I've seen what those space cannons can do."

"There is no one there to fire them," I said. But we all looked uneasy as the planet came into view.

Marxuach was the fourth planet from its sun. It was gray and covered in mountains cut by large rivers and dotted with small seas. There were small green zones hidden in the enormous valleys, and that was where the colony was supposed to be.

No cannons were fired.

"Let's go," Caleb said after we all breathed a collective sigh of relief. "Feet on the ground."

In two hours we would know for sure if we'd been chasing lies or chasing the truth.

Only Caleb, Siddiqui, the Pirates, and I had the nanites that would let us breathe the Marxuachian atmosphere, so we went down, taking Trevor with us. We were quiet as our shuttle entered the green valley on its bumpy descent through the stratosphere.

"There," Siddiqui said pointing out the shuttle window. "I see something!"

I leaned forward and was able to just make out a small set of four buildings.

"There is something there," Caleb said.

"But there's no sign of activity," I said. No one was outside. No vehicles were moving. No land had anything that looked like a farm. No one came outside to look up at our ship, which was landing.

The door hissed open, and we stepped on the ground. We were all a bit wobbly.

Marxuach.

"Let's check it out," I said. We headed for the first building. The windows were dirty, so we couldn't see anything inside. I knocked on the door. There was no answer. We tried the door. It was locked. The same was true for the other three buildings.

"Trevor," Caleb commanded. Trevor rolled to the door and blasted it open. Stale air escaped. We went inside.

It was the base camp for a colony. It had all of the basic equipment to set up a first wave of colonists. But except for two skeletons with guns in their hands, it was empty.

"There is no one here," I said. There was a strangeness to having hoped in a tiny way that I was wrong.

"Where are the people we brought here?" Siddiqui asked furrowing his dark brows. "There were hundreds that I personally sent."

"Let's split up and do a search," I said. I knew we would find no one, but Siddiqui still needed proof.

We each headed in a different direction, making sure that we could keep each other in our sights. In front of me there was nothing but mountains and vegetation.

"Here! Here!" called one of the Pirates. He'd taken the southern direction, heading toward a line of trees. The smell that seemed to stick onto everything thickened as we got closer. When we joined him, we saw what he saw. Beyond the trees was a field, and it was full of decomposing Human bodies.

215

"Oh my God," Siddiqui said as he heaved.

"We can't leave them like this," I said.

"No, we can't," Caleb said. He called Trevor.

None of us objected when he commanded Trevor to burn the trees. We stood and watched as they caught fire and spread to the field, burning the bodies along with it.

Silently we boarded the shuttle and returned to the Hort ship. Sobered from our visit to the planet below. As we blasted off and hit the outer atmosphere to join the stars, we could still see the smoke rising below.

Even though I knew that there would be no colony on Marxuach, I was still in shock at what I'd seen.

We all wanted the same thing now.

We all wanted Brother Blue to pay.

33

We were shaking as we told them what we had witnessed on the planet below.

Every Wanderer gathered in the mess hall to hear our report from Marxuach. They hung on our every word, their eyes stealing glances at the column of smoke that still rose off of the planet.

Disbelief. Despair. Disgust permeated the room as we haltingly told them. Faces found shoulders to sob on. Hands covered eyes as if to unsee the horror. I wondered if it was worse to have to imagine it. Shocked faces stared blankly as they realized that sons, daughters, husbands, wives, friends had been lost. There would be no reunion with them.

"It's too dangerous to live as you have lived," I said to them. "We must not let what happened on Marxuach happen to us."

A murmur of assent washed over the crowd.

"I am taking suggestions as to where we might go to be safe," Bitty said. As strong as she was the burden of this was weighing on her heavily.

I stepped forward.

"We're going to make the dead speak," I said.

There was a collective shout of agreement from the crowd. I raised my hands up to quiet them down. When they were settled, I continued.

"Brother Blue is making his money from alin on Quint. If we can get back to Quint and destroy his source of income, then it won't be so easy for him to ship Wanderers to those colonies to die like that."

"The aliens who collaborate with him will get angry if he can't pay," Caleb said backing me up.

"And that will chip away at his reputation," I said.

"It isn't his death, but it's a start. We have to start somewhere."

"And how will we do that?" Traynor asked.

"Brother Blue is a sucker for a deal," I said. "When I was assisting him on the *Prairie Rose*, he was always going on about the deals that he'd made. We could have Caleb sell us to him to work Quint."

The crowd roared in disagreement.

"We won't be slaves!" an old woman yelled.

"Why don't we just kill him?" someone else shouted.

Others agreed or yelled insults.

"It's true that you'll be nothing short of slaves," Caleb said.

"But we'll be safe from that death," I said. "He'd pay for us. I know he would. Caleb is a Pirate. He's outside of all of these politics. We'll go to Quint. We'd only be slaves in name, not in spirit. From there we'll have time to hatch an attack on him."

"It might be a long game," Caleb said.

"But at least it's a game we can play," I said.

"He'll see you, Tula, and he'll kill you," Bitty said. "I can't allow that. I just found you again."

After hearing of the dead on Marxuach, no one wanted to head into danger and lose anyone again. But we were in more danger in space. I had to make them see that.

"That's where you're wrong, Bitty. He'd see me if I was one Human alone, but if I dress like a Wanderer? He won't see me at all. He doesn't see you as individual people. I'll be invisible."

I put my hands on her shoulders to reassure her that I was right there and not going anywhere without her.

"Humans working a Human claim," Caleb said gently, trying to explain the logic behind the plan. "Keep it in the family."

Bitty looked away from me and out over to the sea of faces that now depended on her judgement for their lives.

"Caleb can show him that he can undercut the Imperium. Show him he can grow his profit, and then we'll snatch it away," I said.

I directed it to the Wanderers who were hanging on to our every word.

"He'll go for that," Siddiqui said quietly. "I've met him. He thinks that we Humans are superior."

Ever since he'd been back from the surface he had barely spoken. It was clear that the truth had shocked him to his core.

I could tell that some of the crowd were moved by him.

"We're just like any other species," Caleb said. "We're the center of our own story."

Caleb appealed to the Wanderers, pulling on the thread of hope that they were beginning to hold on to. He was doing what he was born to do, lead. I jumped in to bring the point home.

"Exactly. And right now, Quint is the new center. Let's use that," I said.

"Tip the center and topple the Imperium," Caleb said pumping his fist in the air in a rallying gesture.

"Why would he think the Pirates were on his side?" someone shouted.

"It's not a part I want to play," Caleb said, walking into the crowd so that he could address the dissenter personally. "But Pirates can be very persuasive."

"Can we even live on Quint?" Traynor asked.

This was the moment where they would tip to join us or where we would lose them all. I had to tell the truth or we'd be lost.

"It would be hard," I said, remembering all that I'd heard about Quint. "And cold. The air is thinner than you are used to, but with the nanites, it would be easier."

"We don't have nanites," Ednette said.

"We can try to trade for doses," I said.

"No, that's where I come in. If he goes for it, I'll convince Brother Blue to pay for them," Caleb said, calming the crowd. "It will be worth it for him if you can work on the planet without air masks. I'll make him see that."

I could see his mind working through scenario after scenario. Everything that he'd been trained to do as an Imperium Youth Cadet was coming up.

"I know how Brother Blue thinks," I said. "He will take the bait."

I looked toward Bitty. She was the one who had to decide our fate. Her dark eyes flicked to each one of us, trying to gauge all the information coming at her.

"We have always said that we wanted to go home," Bitty said.

"I can get my group to agree," Traynor said nodding.

"I think some will settle. But some will always want to

wander," Ednette said, but I could tell by the way she said it that she thought that settling would be good for the old and the very young.

"It is tiring to be rootless," I said, going off of my own experience of traveling these last few months.

"It's true," Traynor said, scratching his beard. "Even when a ship or a station becomes a home, we are never welcome anywhere for long. We are always asked to leave especially when our numbers grow. Then we hitch and are hurried along."

"A planet is a kind of ship," Bitty said, raising her voice and opening her arms as though to embrace the crowd. "We'll go. If we follow her, I know we'll live."

The crowd shouted out their agreement.

As they dispersed, the feeling of the group, which had been so low, began to feel hopeful.

Siddiqui joined me and Caleb.

"What is it?" I asked. I felt sorry for all that he had gone through.

"I can't be invisible in this crowd," he said. "I've met Brother Blue too many times. Worked with him closely."

Caleb put his hand on Siddiqui's shoulder.

"You'll be a Pirate with me. You'll be covered up, and you'll stay on our ship. We won't let him get anywhere near you."

"Thank you," Siddiqui said.

I turned to Caleb.

"Do you think Brother Blue will recognize you?" I asked.

"I never met the guy," he said.

"But he looked at your body in the cryocrate," I said.

"He looked at a dead body in a cryocrate," he said. "I'm not that dead boy."

He grabbed a protein pak from the bowl on a counter and ripped it open.

It was true. There was very little chance that Brother Blue would make the connection between them. But there was someone who would recognize Caleb. *Myfanwy.*

"There is something you should know," I said.

He raised an eyebrow.

"Myfanwy is on the Yertina Feray," I said. "She's Brother Blue's assistant."

Caleb put the protein pak down and wiped his mouth with a napkin.

"She won't recognize me," he said with a bitter edge to his voice.

It was true that she barely seemed interested when I told her that we were friends.

"Are you sure?" I asked. "Everything is on the line."

"She remembers a soft pushover who was moony-eyed for her," he said. "I know now that I imagined a lot of things that weren't there. I always loved her from afar even when she was standing right next to me. I was invisible."

I could tell by the way that he crumpled the foil packet and kicked the table that he was telling the truth.

"I don't want your heart to distract you when you have such a big part to play. She's with him now. She can't be saved."

"You forget, Tula, that Pirates don't have hearts," he said.

Then he excused himself and left.

I could tell though, from the way he walked, that his heart was breaking.

34

· ·

A plan, even when well worked out, is not always simple. To work, it must be elegant.

When the clamps from the Yertina Feray clicked onto the Hort ship and we were finally docked, my heart lifted. I was home.

The doors slid open. Caleb, along with his crew and Siddiqui, now disguised as a Pirate, led the Humans out onto the docking bay in single file until we were arranged in rows, standing in the hangar. We were told to look down, as though we were defeated. But I stole a glance at the space station party that met us, hoping to catch a glimpse of Tournour. At first I didn't see him, but then, a crowd of station officers moved and there he was, mingling with a small team of his officers.

My pulse quickened. I began to tingle as though every cell in my body was coming alive. I couldn't help but smile because his face was the one thing I had been longing to see for months, and now there he was. It was terrible to not be able to run to him.

I stole another glance. His long limbs were bent toward some other officers who were laughing at something he said. They did not seem disturbed that there were slaves about to be sold, and I wondered if this had become commonplace since I left, that workers were needed in the rush.

I had sent him a coded invoice message saying that he would see me soon. He'd messaged back that I shouldn't come, but of course he did not know what the plan was. Now that we were hundreds of Humans led by Pirates, I could only hope that he had an inkling of an idea of what I was doing.

I wanted him to turn so that I could see all of his face, but of course he didn't. I couldn't wave at him or smile. I was to be a Wanderer like the others with no known connection to anyone here.

My eyes shot to the floor again as I sobered up to the situation. This was not a homecoming. I had a role to play. We all did.

There was no room for personal feelings when there was so much at stake, but I couldn't help but worry that all of this time apart had changed him. I worried that he wouldn't care for me in the same way. That he'd found someone else. That he wouldn't be the Tournour I'd learned to care for so deeply. I felt that he was a part of me and thinking that he could be different made me surprisingly anxious.

I pushed those thoughts aside. I couldn't know what he was feeling. But I knew what I was. I had missed him. I had missed the station. That's all that I could know.

It was in this moment that I realized faith was such a hard thing to hold on to. Faith that my plan would work. Faith that Tournour was on my side. Faith that Caleb could act the Pirate enough to fool Brother Blue. Faith that Reza would help me if we made it down to Quint. Faith that we wouldn't be herded onto a ship and sent straight to a colony to die.

"Welcome to the Yertina Feray," Tournour announced. I looked up again at the sound of his voice. Warm to my ears. Commanding to everyone else's.

Tournour motioned for half his team to pat down all the Pirates. If he recognized Caleb, he didn't give it away.

"Clear," Tournour said.

The door opened, and Brother Blue entered with Myfanwy at his side. When he saw her, Caleb pulled his coverings to shadow his face. But despite the fact that I had told him she was here, I knew he was flummoxed. I watched as he composed himself, throwing back his shoulders to give him an air of confidence.

"Brother Blue," Caleb came forward, arm extended. The two men shook hands, and I shuddered.

I could see Caleb stealing glances at Myfanwy. Her face betrayed nothing, not even a hint that she knew him. If Caleb could still be hurt, I'm sure that hurt him. At least it confirmed what he had confessed to me. His love affair with her had been unrequited.

The acoustics in the cargo bay made it so that we could hear most of their conversation.

"I don't know why you would be so bold as to think I need these Humans," Brother Blue said to Caleb. "They should be sent to the Earth colonies to populate them. That's what I pay for. Transport there. Not to me."

"I understand you have managed to secure a small tract on Quint," Caleb said.

"I did claim a parcel from a deceased species for Earth," he said.

"Humans working a Human claim," Caleb said. "We both know that's good business. Your claim is only as good as the area you can work."

He had been so concerned about keeping the colony ruse alive that he'd ignored the potential orbiting right below him.

"You can add settlement to your roster," Caleb said, hooking him and reeling him in.

Brother Blue was silent for a moment as he considered the proposal. I knew that he was no dummy. The Humans would give him a legitimacy that he didn't currently have, and his claim area could grow.

"It's possible that could work," he said trying to sound casual. "What are the terms?"

"You take my Humans then you split the alin profits that they reap fifty-fifty with me."

"That's a bad deal for me," Brother Blue said. "I can get non-Humans to work for cheaper and keep it all. Why should I do that when I could make you go away?"

"You know that claims change easily, and only claims that are worked by the same species stick. You don't have Humans here."

He took a long hard look at Caleb.

"I have some Imperium officers who are working my land," he said. "I don't need these."

"I think you do," Caleb said. "Let's just say, I caught them in the cargo hold of a Hort ship en route to Marxuach."

"A jewel of a colony," Brother Blue said.

"If you like dead ends," Caleb said.

"Seventy-thirty," Brother Blue offered.

Caleb nodded. He should have held out for more, but Brother Blue was pleased.

His whole demeanor changed. He went from hard negotiator to best friend. He laughed and slapped Caleb on the back.

"I've never seen a Human Pirate before," he said. "How did you escape wandering or Earth?"

226

"Well now, that *is* a story," Caleb said. "But one I like to tell over a good drink. Business first."

"Of course."

They continued to talk details. Prices. Workload. Nanites. Coded conversation about how much Caleb knew about Brother Blue's deception.

"I'd like to inspect them for weapons," Tournour said.

"They seem harmless," Brother Blue said.

"It's my job to keep the Yertina Feray safe," he said. "The Imperium charges me with that task."

"You don't trust Humans," Brother Blue said.

"I don't trust anyone," Tournour said.

"Go ahead," Brother Blue said waving him away with his hands. "I don't want to get in the way of Imperium policy."

Tournour stepped forward to help his team, taking the middle row where I was. I was frozen, hoping that he would reach me before one of his officers would. Our eyes locked. If I didn't know him so well, I'd have thought that he was being cold, but his antennae folded toward me in a way that was tender.

After what seemed an eternity, he was there in front of me. His hands moved over my body, checking me for weapons, but every part of him was saying hello. It was torture not to speak. To stare straight ahead. To be submissive.

I did not know what had been going on here while I had been away. I had to trust that Tournour would let me know in his own way in his own time. I had to trust that his messages to me were proof that our bond was still strong.

"Clear," he said it directly to me. That was the only way he could say hello. I nodded slightly to acknowledge him somehow.

Tournour moved on to Bitty and then over again down the row until he was far away from me.

When the inspection was done, Tournour and his team fell back and gave Brother Blue a nod that all was right.

Brother Blue snapped his fingers, and Myfanwy stepped forward.

"This is my assistant, Myfanwy Yu," he addressed us Humans. "She'll be here inspecting you for health and fortitude and administrating the nanites you'll need to survive on Quint and placing bands on your arms."

Myfanwy went down the lines, taking inventory on us one by one. I was covered in Wanderer garb, and we had hand painted more tattoos on my body and face so I could blend in more. My nerves were making me sweat. I wondered if the paint would smudge, revealing me. I had met Myfanwy before. I was standing next to Bitty, and she could sense that I was nervous. She slipped her hand into mine, and I immediately felt better.

Myfanwy stepped up to us. But it wasn't me who caught her attention. It was Bitty.

"You're damaged," she said to Bitty, pointing to her scars.

"I'm strong and I'm healthy," she said. "I'm just not pretty."

Myfanwy laughed.

I saw Bitty smile back at Myfanwy as she moved on to me. I kept my eyes down.

"You're not as hard as the others," she said. "You're soft."

I nodded, staring at her shoes.

I wondered if she was struggling to place me. We'd only met once, but sometimes one meeting is enough to burn a face in the mind's eye. I wondered if I should say something or keep quiet.

"She's just had a child," Bitty interjected. It echoed

228

throughout the hangar. I knew that Tournour had heard the lie, but he wouldn't know if it was true or not. He might not even know how long a Human child took to gestate.

"Where's the child?" Myfanwy asked.

"Dead," I said, this time looking straight at her. Of course there was no child. Bitty's bravery enabled me to look up without fear. If there had been any flicker of recognition in Myfanwy's face, I would have seen it. There wasn't. Whatever flicker there could have been had been extinguished, and Myfanwy was now embarrassed for having pressed the issue. That was one thing that Humans were steady in. It was best to get out of uncomfortable situations as quickly as possible.

"Ah," Myfanwy said injecting and banding our arms and moving on.

Once again I reached for Bitty's hand. I squeezed it in thanks.

"They're fit for work on Quint," Myfanwy said, returning to Brother Blue.

"Good." Brother Blue said to Caleb, "I'll send you the money once they're down on Quint and have done a harvest. They have to prove their worth. They've been traveling for so long that they might not take to planet living."

"You'll give me an advance now," Caleb said.

"I don't have that kind of currency," he said.

"Then find it," Caleb said. "Or when I get to the entertainment deck, I just might tell a whole lot of stories. I've been on the ground at Marxuach. I've seen what you've plowed the fields with."

Brother Blue's smile froze. He took the datapad from Myfanwy and pressed his thumb to it.

"I can give you half now. Half on harvest."

He was going down.

35

· ·

The makeshift spaceport near the landing pad on
Quint was bustling. There was only one town on the planet,
nestled at the center of the Dren Line. It was made up of a
few buildings: a general store, a place to eat, a place to im-
bibe, and a place for pleasure. There was also a law office that
housed a few of Tournour's team. There were no embassies or
representatives here. Most speculating on the planet were
free and wild, as long as you paid your tithe to Brother Blue
and the Imperium.

As I stepped onto Quint, I allowed for a tiny moment of
joy after months of running and uncertainty. I had spent so
many hours staring at Quint, and now I was finally here.

Technically, Brother Blue owned us. To ensure that everyone knew that, we were each fitted with a metal armband to
make sure it was known that we could not leave the planet
freely. They were easily removed but would tear up the skin if
not taken off with a key. The scar would never go away and
would always mark a runaway.

Somehow, despite that yoke, it felt free here. Like anything
could happen.

We were marched out of town and down a dirt road to the
fields that we were going to care for.

I wondered when I would run into Reza. Did he know that

we were coming? Had Tournour warned him? Was he curious about our group? Was he on his field working hard? Only time would bring answers.

For most of the Humans, it was hard going. The walk was painful and slow. It was the first planet that they'd ever set foot on and despite living in different gravities all their lives, planet gravity felt different. Bitty had not been on one since Earth. Almost everyone had planet sickness, but not me. Somehow Quint felt just right. Perhaps it was the cold air or the rocks or the pinkish clouds. I felt sturdy walking on this ground.

"The whole place looks scarred, like it's been through a war," Bitty said.

The landscape beyond the buildings was pocked with deep crevices as though it had been bombed. There were craters and crevices in long gashes along the rocks. Everything was gray, brown or black. It was only far away on the horizon that there was any burst of yellow.

"When the ore started to run out, they did everything they could to get every last bit of it out of the planet. They bound nitrogen to lift it up out of the dirt," I said.

"It seems strange that we're allowed to ruin planets like that," Bitty said. "I mean, we caused so much damage on our planet that we nearly killed ourselves."

"We were bound to do that to Beta Granade when we landed. We were going to change it to suit us," I said. "And look, Quint has rebounded in a way."

I pointed to the lush fields that surrounded us.

"But going to change Beta Granade wasn't my choice or yours. It was our mother's choice. I was a child, and now I am not," she said. "I don't know that I would have agreed with that choice now."

"No," I said. "I wouldn't have left Earth either, but there is a difference between razing a planet for resources, which is what the Imperium wants to do, and cultivating it into hosting life."

"Is there?" Bitty asked.

I wasn't sure in my mind, but I was sure in my heart. When I looked at Quint, left alone for centuries, sprung back and thriving, it made my heart swell. It was something that I wanted to protect. Like this planet was a part of me, and I was its caretaker.

It was strange to think that we were sitting on another planet having a conversation about where we wanted to be. Places that seemed impossible. It was hard to be both sad and angry with our mother for dragging us into this predicament. She was just doing the best that she could by hoping for something better for us.

Along with a few Imperium guards, Myfanwy was with us to settle us into the tract of land that we were going to work. When we arrived at the place, the guards started to set up tents. The Humans could not help. They were laying down, planet sick, and gasping for air, not quite used to the nanites they'd been injected with.

Even though it was cold, I chose to sleep outside and stare up at the stars.

36

I was the first one up.

Sunrise on Quint was beautiful. Orange and pink crept up, peeking over the gray mountains and then lighting up the yellow fields that stretched behind where we had slept.

I sat watching the sun get higher in the sky. The day never got as bright as I remember Earth being, or Tallara, but it was a sun I had grown to love in the last years, and to see it from Quint was breathtaking.

"I need some volunteers to get supplies," Myfanwy said. "You two. You. And you."

Bitty and I, as well as a few others, including Traynor, who was not so planet sick, headed down the road toward town with her. When we got there, Myfanwy gave us each a list and a currency chit to buy some supplies.

"Don't tarry. Meet back here in an hour. You're with me," she pointed to Bitty.

I was not going to buy tools the old fashioned way. I wanted to keep the currency chit for later use. I looked at my list and quickly calculated the trades that I would have to do to get the tools that I'd been assigned. Four.

I felt pulled toward the eatery and longed for something that was home-cooked and not space food. I was not disappointed. A Nurlok was grilling some local hard-shelled insect on a grill, and it smelled delicious.

"One please," I said.

I gave the Nurlok a currency chit but the Nurlok waved it away and nodded at me. I didn't recognize this Nurlok, but I made a mental note of the favor given to me and knew that this was someone I could trade with.

"I owe you a favor," I said showing the Nurlok my list. "I'm looking to trade. I need tools," I said.

He looked me up and down and pointed to the metal armband I wore. I shook my head. As much as I wanted to get rid of it, it would scar me and likely get me in trouble just when I needed to be invisible the most.

"I'm new. But I'm here to stay," I needed something to start trading with, and he probably had something that he wanted to get rid of. I scanned the area behind the counter and noticed the fly-like insects buzzing around the cage holding the insects that he was cooking up on the grill. The cage was filthy with frass overflowing in the bottom of the cage and in a wastebin.

"I can take anything you don't want off your hands. Maybe your frass."

He considered me a moment. Then he let me come through. I filled two bags full of the horrible-smelling substance.

I had something to start with. Sure, it was insect poop, but Thado had always said that any kind of feces was helpful when he wanted to enrich the soil in the arboretum. I had traded many times with ships for their animal feces for him. If I did it right, someone would want this frass, and I would have the currency chit for later.

"Thank you," I said. "What do you want for it?"

"Spices," he said, flipping the ingredients on his grill. The large hard-shelled insect was placed on four long noodles. It was some kind of pill bug, and it was laid on its back with the moist soft meaty substance cut into quarters and stuffed with a mix of a pepper-like vegetables.

I could get spices for frass.

"Then you'll get me tools?" I aked.

He grunted and served me a plate, and I took my bags of frass and went to a corner table and looked out the window as I crunched on the spicy food. I allowed myself to relax. It was dry here, as if the dirt did not want to stick to the ground. It was dusty, and the air was cold. The sun was small in the sky, as though it were just stretching itself a little too far to give Quint any real warmth. Everyone was wrapped in rags to protect against the dust. Aliens crowded the streets, going either toward entertainment, the launchpad with loaded up bags to trade up at the Yertina Feray, or to get themselves some drink or fun. Others were heading out with supplies on the way to their claims.

This time, Quint was brimming with life forms.

As I understood it, Quint was not the same now as when it was mined for ores. Then, when the planet had been surveyed and found to have highly coveted ores, it was marked by the League of Worlds to be mined rather than settled. Planets made bids for tracts of land, and mining robots like Trevor came to work. They were overseen by the aliens who came down to live on Quint to protect their claims. But most aliens back then lived on the Yertina Feray. This rush had aliens down on the ground, working the land in order to keep their claims. A claim only stood if the area was being actively worked. The alin pollen was too delicate a task to leave to robots.

There was one thing that was different about the way that

aliens interacted from the Yertina Feray. As I watched them move about the town, I noticed that they kept as separate as possible. Everyone seemed to stick to their own kind.

When I was done eating, I hit the entertainments tent because I knew that was the place where the most aliens would mix and mingle regardless of species. Someone there would want the frass and give me something in return and a line on where the best spices were. I also wanted to know where the best land was and who the best cultivators were. Knowledge was power.

I scanned the bar, marveling at how much more life and vigor there was in the residents that were on this planet than on the Yertina Feray. There was a real difference to the way that life thrived on a planet. Even on a cold, almost inhospitable one like Quint, there was something about air and sun and weather that made all souls uncurl from the limitations imposed by a ship or station.

While trying to figure out which game table I should infiltrate to start up a conversation, there was a silky low voice that I recognized in my ear.

"You smell like you have what I need," it said.

"Reza," I turned to face him. Every part of me leapt.

"Hello, Tula."

He moved back and leaned one shoulder casually against the wall.

I soaked in his face. His warm smile. His dark eyes. The tight dreads in his hair. My insides quivered as I watched him take me in.

"I hear you're the new game in town," Reza said. He was chewing on a kind of grass. "I hear you work for the Imperium."

"More like workhorses," I said. I was trying to keep calm, but there was a rising heat between us, the one that had always been there. I was excited, but my body reacting the way it did made me feel both good and guilty at the same time.

He fingered the metal band on my arm.

"I'm sorry," he said. "Still, it's good to see you."

The skin on my arm had goose bumps that I tried to ignore. I couldn't help but wish that it was Tournour making me react this way.

"You're looking for some frass?" I said, playing it slow. Playing it cool. But still, I couldn't help but step closer to him.

"Always," he said. "What do you want for it?"

He flashed me that smile that made my insides melt.

"Spices," I said.

"What's your end game?" he asked. He knew there was something else I needed.

"Tools," I said. "For the tract of land we have to work. But I want to keep the currency chit they gave me for myself. You never know when that could come in handy."

Reza spit out the piece of grass he was chewing into a plate.

He took out a datapad and made a calculation.

"Tell that Nurlok that I can give him what he wants, but he'll have to come to my place."

"I need something now," I said.

He laughed.

"Well, you're not going to get it now, Human," he said.

I looked over his shoulder and noticed that the aliens in the place had taken an interest in us. He was playing it up for them, and I was grateful that he could improvise so well.

"Why don't we step outside before we smell up the joint," Reza said.

I followed him outside where we had a chance to talk more freely. I had so much to tell him.

"Reza, I don't know where to begin," I said.

"How about thank you for the currency you're going to keep?" he said. "And all the currency I've sent you."

"Thank you," I said.

"Bitty's alive," I said.

"Your sister?" he said, genuinely surprised and happy for me. "That's great news!" And then he pulled me in for a happy hug. His arms felt so good around me.

"Yes," I said breaking away. "She survived the explosion and had been wandering with a tribe."

"Your mother?"

"No," I said.

His face clouded over, and he looked at me with sympathy in his dark brown eyes.

"What are you doing back here?" Reza said. "How can you belong to Brother Blue and not be dead?"

I quickly summed up what was going on and as I told him what Brother Blue was doing and the dead I'd seen on Marxuach, I watched his face fall.

"My God," he said. "I knew he was evil, but not that evil."

He had to stop walking as he processed it all.

"You actually went there?"

I nodded.

He shook his head in disbelief, and I could tell that he was trying not to cry.

"I have a half a mind to kill him myself," he spat out.

"One more thing. Caleb's here," I said.

"So you found him," Reza said slowly. "I figured he'd have something to do with this. How did you find him?"

"I sent out messages until he found me," I said as we started to walk again.

"How is he?"

"He's different," I said. We were nearly at the eatery, which was filling with aliens for midday meal.

"I told you," he said. "How could he sell you?"

"No. That was my plan. He's here to help," I said.

"Help?" Reza asked. "Help with what?"

"With . . ." I said as he looked at me in a way that went all the way down to my bones. That I was attracted to Reza was very clear, but I did not feel for him the way that I had come to feel for Tournour. "Destroying Brother Blue's source of income so that he starts to lose power in the Imperium."

"But he still skims from the tithe that everyone gives him," Reza said as we got to the eatery. "There are fees upon fees. Everyone stays separate so as not to get more fees."

"We have to start somewhere."

I held the door open for him as we went into the food shop. The Nurlock and Reza haggled over the frass. Then the Nurlock gave me a plate of food to bring to the tools shop.

Reza joined me, and we continued our conversation.

"Where is Caleb now?" he asked. There was no gentleness to the voice. It was bitter. "What's he doing?"

"He's up on the Yertina Feray. Working with Brother Blue."

"Pirating?"

"In a way. Yes," I said. "He's keeping Brother Blue's eyes off of me. Off of us down here."

"I don't deal with Pirates," he said. "That is why I left."

"Reza, you need to get over it. You, Caleb, and Tournour will have to work together now. I can't do it alone."

He took my hand.

"Do you need me?" he asked.

"I need you," I said. It was true. I did. But I needed all of them.

As always he wore his feelings right on the surface.

"I have to go," I said, pulling my hand away from his. My heartbeat had quickened at his touch.

The hour was up, and I could see Myfanwy, Bitty, Traynor, and the other Humans I'd come to town with gathering in the town square.

"Come to the Human camp tonight, I'll meet you on the road and we'll talk," I said.

I remembered what it was like to be with Reza and I allowed myself a small smile.

· ·

Reza showed up at sunset.

"You came," I said.

"I did," he said.

We walked away from the camp down the road a little bit until we were alone by a group of large rocks. It was the first time since I'd left him on the Yertina Feray that we'd been alone. I wasn't sure how to be around him. My body felt strange. I wondered if I should kiss him hello the way I'd kissed him goodbye, but sometimes there is a difference between the tender moment of potentially never seeing someone again and the moment where you realize that you must sort through all of your feelings.

"It's okay," he said taking my hand and kissing my knuckles. "I'm here now."

I hesitated. I wasn't sure what I wanted from him, and I

wanted to be clear headed as I talked to him about what I was trying to do here on Quint.

"I've been thinking," he said. "It's hard to help Earth fight the hold of the Imperium from here."

We looked out down the road at the alien planet we were on. We could hear the Human camp as they sang.

"We're going to do what you want," I said. "We're going to fight."

"You don't know what I want anymore," he said, leaning his head back against the large rock we were sitting on.

"I know that sending you to the Outer Rim was hard. A mistake even. But that was the best solution in that moment. This is a new moment. We either rise now," I waved at the huge night sky, "or we are snuffed out and we lose."

"Fine," he said. "I'll do it because it's you."

He pushed a lock of hair behind my ear.

"I don't really know what I can do to help," he said. "I'm a farmer now, not a fighter. Maybe things would be different if I had gone back to Earth. But I'm here now and I don't have any intel on what's going on. I'm just a guy who trades some spices for insect poop and has a crush on a great girl."

I slapped his broad chest playfully.

"Tell me about Quint," I said. "That will be helpful."

"The fertile spot on Quint is small," he said. "Some people staked claims on the Dren Line. Others are trying to cultivate alin in less hospitable parts just outside that line, but hacking ore out of the ground is different than growing and cultivating. Some of these speculators don't have the touch, and they've lost a great deal of wealth because they don't know how to tease out the pollen or let the plant thrive. The Imperium doesn't want us working together because it doesn't want us to share what we know. It keeps them in charge of the currency flow."

"That's why you needed the frass. It helps the soil."

"Yes," he said. "I experiment. Thado's been teaching me."

He laced his fingers with mine.

"So you're saving the Humans," Reza said. He smiled his big wide smile. The one I loved. I knew we had him. He was on my side. He leaned in close, and I could feel his breath on my cheek.

In that moment, the starlight playing on our features, I knew that peace between us had been made.

"I'll be the noisy wheel," he said, whispering in my ear. "I'll keep Brother Blue's eyes on me so he doesn't see you." Then he put his arms around me and pulled me to him. I could feel my body tense and then relax until I leaned my head on his strong chest and slowly slid my arms around him.

He held me all night, and I marveled at the pure astonishment of skin and heart.

Parts of me felt the same, as though we were one. But I also felt as though I were missing one piece of my true self. I felt like I was missing Tournour, no matter how alien he was. No matter how high up in the sky. Tournour made me feel Human.

"You're me and I'm you," Reza whispered.

I answered Reza with kisses.

But my heart beat out a message in Loor.

37

Part of me loved being around other Humans. While we worked hard during the days in the fields, at night there were songs and laughter. We discovered the pleasure of bonfires and meals shared under an open sky.

The children, though there were not many of them, took easiest to the planet and adjusted to gravity best. Once they'd adjusted, I could see how much they loved the air and the running. They were lucky. Quint was a little lighter than base gravity on most ships, and since they'd gotten the nanites, they did not have to struggle as hard with the atmosphere.

"There will be more of them soon," Ednette said as we watched them together from the field. "A planet gives room to spread. On the hitches we had to keep our numbers manageable."

It made me happy to think that there would be babies born on Quint. It would be the first generation of Humans out in space not born on ships. They would be the legacy of both the intergenerational ships and the colonists. They were really the beginning.

I was the only person they knew who had ever lived on a planet, so they looked to me to help them figure out how to be on one. I had naively imagined that despite the fact that we were basically owned by Brother Blue, the older Humans would take to the land and learn to become self-sufficient. But they couldn't understand the land. They were overwhelmed by the sky like I had been on Tallara. The children had a flexibility of spirit that the adults did not. Even so, it was no lie that Humans were creative and adaptable, and skills that had been long-forgotten through the generations of wandering came easily to some.

I realized that I had survived my odyssey because I had been young. I doubt that my mother would have survived in my or Bitty's place. She understood settling a colony. But surviving by your wits? I don't know that she had that kind of strength.

While we set up camp they would come to me with questions that they thought I could answer. But I only knew what a child would know, and so my knowledge only went so far. Still it was more then they knew, and I answered as best I could.

"What do we do about insects?"

"Where do we get the water?"

"How do you dig?"

They had to be taught how to do everything: how to build a house, how to deal with dirt, how to shade themselves from a sun. Some things I could show them, other things I had to guess. Luckily, the younger, like Bitty, took to it quickly. She was always helping Myfanwy to organize things for us.

"I have other things that I have to think about," I complained to Reza when he got away from his claim and visited me. "I don't know how to build things."

"They look up to you," he said. "This is all new to them."

Then I would give him a look that made him laugh.

"Fine. I'll help," he said.

Reza became a fixture at our camp.

He was instrumental in helping the Humans. At first he did it in secret, after hours, in the makeshift tents, then in the wooden huts, and then in the more sturdy homes. He answered every question about how to live on a planet. I loved to hear him speak about it as though it were something new. Although I had been on a planet before, it felt like my first time.

And eventually, he even convinced Myfanwy to let him take some Wanderers to his claim to teach them his methods.

"He's a good one," Ednette said. "He reminds me of my man."

"No," I said. "It's not like that."

But her and Bitty gave each other a look and then laughed at me.

I still sent messages to Tournour. But I couldn't deny that I sometimes snuck away to be alone with Reza.

I kept waiting for Ednette or someone else to step up as leader. Instead, they seemed more and more dependent on me. And after our first month when everyone had acclimated, they held their tattooing ceremony. This time, the marking was the image of a planet, instead of a ship. It seemed as though most of the Humans, despite the difference between wandering and being planetbound, were glad to be grounded.

I looked at my feet in the dirt. I looked at the gold earth dangling off of my wrist. I looked at my new tattoo of Quint, with the extra bar on it.

I was the journey leader now.

38

. . . .

It was first harvest.

I was in a row of alin delicately scraping the pollen off of
the flower and dusting it into my small bag. We would have a
good haul.

I heard my name being called and turned to see Bitty running toward me.

"He's coming." Bitty burst through the field, and I jerked
my head so fast that a bunch of pollen floated away on the air.
If I cared about the harvest because it would help us, I would
have yelled at her. But this wasn't for us—it was only a part of
our plan to show Brother Blue a big haul. And then destroy it.

"Who?" I asked, shading my eyes from the weak noon sun.

"Brother Blue," she said.

"How do you know?"

"Myfanwy told me," she said. He could not see me. Brother
Blue had to think that everything was going right before everything could go wrong. I needed to have the Humans en-
trenched on the planet to keep them safe. I feared if the harvest
failed too soon, or if he found out that I was here and was the
journey leader, he would uproot them and send them to one
of the empty colonies.

I drew the string on my pouch to secure the pollen and then
handed it to her to add to the haul.

"She's not your friend," I said. It irritated me to see them always together whenever Myfanwy was down here visiting. But I could not deny that there was that spark of friendship between them. And there were so few people near to Bitty's age here.

"She's not as bad as you think she is," Bitty said.

"She works for *him*," I said. But I had to admit, she had been kind to us down here. Making sure that we got the materials we needed. Allowing Reza to teach the Wanderers. Giving us time to organize our own days as long as the tasks got done. And she had never once let on that she knew Caleb, even when he accompanied her down to check on us and get his payment.

"Cover up. You have to hide," she said, and threw me the long covering she was wearing.

I gathered my things and covered myself up so that I looked like a Wanderer.

I watched from down the road as Brother Blue and Caleb arrived at the camp. It irked me to see him come to the fields. Put the dirt in his hand. Turn a flower over and put his nose to smell its fragrance.

From where I stood I could see him laughing and making jokes with Caleb and the other Humans, and I knew that they were growing to like him. It was hard for them to believe that he was behind the atrocities. They could not understand what my problem with him was. He brought down supplies. He listened to their needs. He was making it happen and gaining people's trust. He filled them up with false hopes, as he had with mother and me.

Parts of me ached when I saw him, because he was doing what I wanted to do for the people down here. The thing that truly bothered me was that he was able in a way that I was not. He had currency, and he had Imperium backing. With one hand, he could make things flourish; and with the other hand, he could kill.

I knew that sometimes the Wanderers questioned if Brother Blue was really behind it all. They couldn't understand how a beast could hide behind such charm, or why I wanted to ruin this man. Even though they knew that he had killed their families and many others, they couldn't see it when he was in front of them. I had to remind them.

He's a killer. He's a liar. He's betrayed us all.

Currency was his mistress. So of course he was only visiting because a good harvest would make him even more of it.

When I saw him looking at the fields, I could see something in him that I used to see; that look of a visionary. I could see how proud he was of the Humans and the alin fields. I could see that as much of a monster as he was, in this he was truly excited. You cannot fake that kind of unguarded enthusiasm.

I could not watch anymore and so I walked to Reza's.

"Let me show you something," he said as I walked into his fields. It was acres of yellow petals. His fields burst with flower. I remembered how just my one plant on the Yertina Feray had given me such strength. Seeing it all around me made my sour spirit at Brother Blue melt away a little and my resolve return.

We walked to a small corner of his field where he was experimenting with cultivation. He brought me to a stretch of land where the earth was dark and bare.

"What's this?" I asked.

"This is where my Earth garden will grow. The soil is not right yet. I've been sifting it and feeding it. That's why I needed that frass. It's getting there. Thado is helping me with that."

"I never thought I would see anything like this again," I said.

"It's the first year," Reza said.

I tried to remember what was among the cargo of the *Prairie Rose*. Grain. Potatoes. Corn. Tomatoes. Leafy greens.

"What will grow?"

"I don't know. It will be fun to experiment. But right now I don't have the right kinds of seeds."

"I could get you some," I said.

"You could?"

I tried to calculate the trades it would take. Just calculating the number made me feel like my old self again.

"Absolutely," I said. "Give me a little time."

• •

When we first arrived on Quint, with so many different species coming here, aliens wore their allegiance in patches on their uniforms, or as rings or earrings, or embedded in the fabric of their clothing. Were you from homeworld, or offworld? Were you a Major Species or a Minor Species or no species worth talking about?

They came to work the alin. But they were all running from the Imperium.

The suspicion of trouble and betrayal was everywhere. In town, every species that came to Quint had a story about a terrible thing that their own people were doing to themselves through the Imperium. In a way, everyone here was escaping something from out there. Each species had its quarter in town. The only place to mingle was in the entertainments bar since there was only one. The town was mixed, but elsewhere was separated.

But I was on a mission to get Reza his seeds. And Myfanwy grew to depend on me to go to town and get supplies because she knew that I could make a little turn into a lot. I, in turn, depended on barter and favors to get the best things that we needed. Barter and favors meant that more species were working together without having to work together. We were all depending on each other. The real power on Quint was not in currency, but in goods. Whoever had it could make things happen.

Every trade I initiated made the species that kept apart come together. It was something familiar to me. That coming together was how the Yertina Feray had survived all those years when it was just a skeleton of what it was now.

"Did you notice that there are more and more coming here?" Reza asked one day as we walked through town.

"They think it's safe here," I said.

"You make it safe," he said. "You've gotten everyone to trust each other after running."

"But they don't know what they are doing," I said. "Their fields are failing."

"I could teach them," Reza said.

He had a way with the plants. He'd been there first after all. He'd been prudent in what he cultivated and in what he did. He took care of his soil. He was scientific about it. Between Reza's casual lessons on how to care for the land and the alin and the favor trading that I was doing, Quint was beginning to find its pace.

He taught all of the claimants, not just the Humans and the new arrivals, how to look at the soil. How to care for the leaves. How to water. How to observe the insects that came. He tried to figure out which ones were good and which ones were bad. In his field, life thrived, and the other aliens took that knowledge back to their fields.

We were all starting to work together in secret.

Reza would have nightly gatherings in the field with representatives of all kinds of aliens that lived on the planet. Some were working for him on the sly, and others had their own tracts of land, but they were also learning. Learning the tricks that he had learned. He didn't keep his knowledge to himself. He showed them his method for collecting pollen beads while managing the integrity and bloom of the plant. He showed them the shed where he pressed oil from the alin.

Every time I walked to his field and saw the many aliens milling about, my heart soared. I imagined that this is what it would have been like on Beta Granade. Whenever a Human woman smiled, I imagined my mother smiling. Whenever an alien helped to raise a barn, I imagined that I was getting closer to the life that I had dreamed of living while traveling on the *Prairie Rose.*

"They might outgrow you," I said of the aliens.

Reza laughed.

"Nah," he said. "And if they did, what would it matter? Really, it's better for us all if we cultivate and succeed."

He had a fire in him. While he had given up on his idea of saving Earth from the Imperium, he got pleasure in uniting Quint. It was as though his dream had been rechanneled. And every day he grew a bit brighter with his cause.

We looked up at the night sky, and I could see the station as it passed us by, like a moving star, and I wondered about Tournour and if I would ever see him again.

Despite all of this happiness, he was the thing that was missing.

And there was still the matter of Brother Blue.

But one thing that I was learning on Quint was that a seed takes a long time to grow.

39

· ·

We were bundled up against the dust and the morning frigid air. Days on Quint were only twenty hours, so morning always came sooner than a person wanted. We were moving into the fall on this world, and the angle of the light made it seem as though midday never came.

The alin started to drop their petals. And along with that, something was wrong with Bitty. She seemed to be drooping like the flowers.

"What is it?" I asked. She had always been moody when we were growing up. Always crying and scared. But this was deeper than a childhood fit.

"I find myself restless," Bitty said.

"Me too," I said. It was hard to cultivate patience. I'd been on the planet four months, and while the alin was stored in a shed and the way to ruin it with a mold had been started, it took a long time.

"No," she said. "I mean to travel. It's all I've ever really done."

"You want to wander again?" I asked. I did not want to wander. I wanted to find home.

"Not in the way that I did before," she said. "We weren't the only ship. We weren't the only ones to get trapped. There are others out there."

It was true. As much as I loved having Bitty here, I knew

she was right. But these past months I felt that buzz of creating a community and a home, and I wanted Bitty close to me and to always be a part of it.

"It's not safe now," I said. "You can't go."

But it would never be safe.

"Myfanwy offered me a job up on the Yertina Feray," Bitty said.

"What? No!" I said smacking her arm. "You can't leave me." I didn't want to be abandoned again.

"I'd be back every week. And it's only from here to there, but I'd be traveling," she said.

"I'll think of something," I said. But I thought of how Bitty looked envious when others thrived. Wandering was in her blood. She was always the one who hiked the claim when Myfanwy came, leaving for hours at a time. She did not like to do the chores that kept her close to the camp.

"You really want to go," I said.

"Yes," Bitty said. "I can leave the next time Myfanwy comes."

"I don't like you leaving," I said, holding her hand. "I wish you would stay."

"I'll be happier on the Yertina Feray," she said.

She was a grown person who was free to make her own choices, not the little girl who used to follow me around. We hugged tight. It was hard to let go.

We walked arm and arm back to the camp. In my room, I pulled an object from under my bedroll. It was a cuff that I had made for Tournour out of a lock of my hair, the remnants of the clothes I'd worn on my travels since I'd left the Yertina Feray, scraps of leather and rope. There was no indication that it was from me, but I knew he would know where it came from. He would have a part of me with him.

"Will you give this to Tournour if you can?"

"Gladly," Bitty said, giving me a sly look. "I am so curious about your Loor."

"He's not my Loor," I said.

"That's not what I heard," she said. "That's not what Reza says when you're not around."

"It's impossible to be with an alien," I said. "I'm with Reza. Reza's Human."

"Of course," Bitty said. "Reza's Human."

"Humans are meant to be with Humans," I said.

"Impossible loves have a place in the universe," she said.

"He's there, and I'm here," I said.

She let it drop by changing the subject.

"Thank you," she said. "I'll be your eyes up there."

It would be good to have a spy on the Yertina Feray; someone that I could trust. Caleb was supposed to be up there cozying up to Brother Blue. Get him scared. Get him soft. Get him trusting. But was he doing it? Sometimes I felt he was simply enjoying himself and all the creature comforts that the Yertina Feray offered while I was down on Quint, working the fields.

I couldn't help it. A part of me was resentful. It wasn't his fault. He was doing what I'd asked him to do, but when I thought of him sharing meals, sharing entertainments, and sitting in the Sunspa with Brother Blue as they both got richer, my heart began to freeze. I began to hate my old friend.

"If you're ever in trouble and you need to go, talk to Thado and find out when the next export of Hern is," I said to Bitty. "They always fly under the radar, and you can likely get off the station easily with them and then you can find some Human Wanderers."

She turned to go prepare her things for leaving.

"Wait," I said, and then unclasped my gold Earth bracelet and put it on her wrist. "To keep me with you."

We hugged one more time, and then I let her go.

When she left, I stayed until the ship blasted off. I watched it get smaller in the sky. I watched until there was nothing but clouds to see.

40

● ●

"There is a person from the Department of Extra-planetary Excavation coming to visit Quint," Reza said as he watered his garden. Reza planted other things on his land. He planted Earth corn. He planted Earth wheat. He planted any seed he could get his hands on to make his land bloom. I could see how delighted he was by the small Earth garden we'd started.

"Is she a Loor?" I asked.

"I think so," Reza said.

If it was Hendala then that meant something was shifting at Bessen.

"I have to go meet them," Reza said. "Do business. Tournour is coming."

My heart leapt. I used to wonder how Caleb could talk about Myfanwy who was so far away and still love her. I wondered about that old Earth saying, that absence made the heart grow fonder. It was both true and untrue. I had not had a moment alone with Tournour for nearly a year, but he occupied my thoughts. It was as though no other conversation mattered.

"Can you get Tournour a message for me?" I said, a bit too eagerly.

I saw a cloud of jealousy pass over Reza's face. We had never talked about Tournour, but I knew that my face could not disguise my feelings for him. Sometimes being with Reza only made me feel worse about the fact that I had this place inside of me that held tender feelings for an alien.

"I can't really," he said. "I have to keep it strictly business."

I nodded, biting my tongue. He took a shovel to work out a rock in the ground.

"I'll see what I can do," he said when it finally loosened.

"When are they coming?" I asked.

"Tomorrow," he said.

I went into town, covered up as a Wanderer and hidden in the Nurlok's kitchen, to watch the team from Bessen arrive.

I leaned my head against the glass to watch Reza welcome the group that included Brother Blue, Caleb, Tournour, Hendala, and a group of aliens from each of the Five Major Species. I watched as they all greeted each other, and I saw that Tournour was wearing the cuff that I had given him. That made me smile. I watched as Reza said something to Tournour, and Tournour's face changed. For the rest of the walk he seemed distracted. He was looking around. Looking for me.

"I'm here," I wanted to say. "I'm right here."

When the meeting was over, Reza rejoined me at the Nurlok eatery. After we got some food, we walked back to his place.

I helped him to water the alin, and then we settled in for the night. He reached into his coat and put a data disc down on the table.

"He's gutted," Reza said.

I snatched the data plug, put it into Reza's console, and let it play.

"Hello. This place is cold and, though full, it feels empty without you. I have to

*keep my tongue in check. I have to say yes
to everyone but the one person in the universe I want to say yes to. Forgive this
awful galaxy. And know that while I say no
with every action, my heart beats Tula,
Tula, Tula. Don't respond. Too dangerous.
I can only hope that you are thinking of
me, too."*

"He's not Human you know," Reza said coming up behind
me and slipping his arms around my waist.

"I know," I said turning and burying my face into his chest.
"I know."

I vowed that when this was over, I would spend a month
only talking to Tournour. I was determined to save up conversations for him.

I would tell him about the sky.

I would tell him about the plants.

I would tell him about the birds.

I would tell him about my heart.

· ·

41

"What's it like up there?" I asked. I longed for news of the Yertina Feray, and Bitty was my only way of getting it.

"It's strange," Bitty said. "There's a lot of species pride. A lot of separation. But there are more Imperium people coming. Brother Blue is getting very agitated."

"That's good," I said.

"Myfanwy has me pulling records and deleting them," she said. "The Imperium come and try to get data that we've purged."

"Something is going on," I said.

Hendala and her group had been back a few more times. She never spoke to me, but when I did see her, she folded her antennae toward me in acknowledgment.

"Myfanwy is worried about Earth," Bitty said. "And Caleb says that Brother Blue is stepping up the search for Humans. Caleb is going to go back out and try to find them first."

It was good to know that Caleb was going out to help. But I doubted that he would have any more luck in warning them then I did.

"They won't trust him," I said.

"I made him and Siddiqui this," she said holding up her wrist and shaking the gold Earth bracelet at me.

It was brilliant. The Wanderers would trust someone whom they thought was a Gome.

"He'll lead them here, to you," she said. "They'll be safe here."

"To Quint, not to me," I said.

"The Imperium is auditing Brother Blue," she said. "He's getting desperate."

Things were about to change. After carefully trying to control things, it was time for the chaos to start.

It made me anxious to think of her on her own, but then it made me glad to have a family to worry about. For so long I had only worried about myself.

42

• •

Perhaps the time had finally come for me to be caught.

In order to escape the Imperium scrutiny he was getting, Brother Blue had decided to move down to Quint.

I hid away at Reza's at first, but it was a chore to evade Brother Blue. I saw him in town and on the road and every smile that he flashed made me miserable. He seemed to enjoy the growing town and the newly arrived Humans. He relished it. Looking in on people. Caring for them. As though he were actually the person that he always said he was—not the person who had lied to Earth, to the Imperium, to the Wanderers, and to the countless dead colonists of Children of Earth.

"Why does he stay down here?" I asked. "Why doesn't he just disappear?"

"Things are strange up there," Bitty said. "I don't think he's safe."

The only thing that comforted me about that was it meant soon I would be able to take him down for good.

As more Humans started to trickle down to Quint, at some point we'd outgrow the small tract that could sustain us. We needed to go elsewhere, and I knew just where. The other planets.

Killick, Kuhn, Marxuach, Andra, Beta Granade. They were

sitting there, empty, false towns full of dead people. I had begun to dream that we could get people to live there.

"We're going to run out of resources," Reza said. "Our population is growing too fast." He meant aliens and Humans.

"The new Humans could be trained on how to settle. They could be given supplies and other necessities to cultivate their own land. Then, finally, they can settle in and stop wandering."

"You've really thought this out," Reza said.

"It's possible. It's really possible."

I had seen this dream before. When I heard myself talking about it, I could feel myself come alive.

Brother Blue and I were almost the same.

There was a knock at the door.

"You have to meet with him," Ednette said. "I cannot answer all the questions that he has."

"I can give you a script," I said. "He can't know that I'm here. It's not the right time."

"He knows that there is someone else in charge," Ednette says. "He knows by my markings. And he won't listen to me. He's asking questions about the mold."

We had allowed moisture into our pollen holding bin so that mold would grow and reduce its worth.

"It's time," Reza said.

I finally agreed to meet with him. We'd edged into summer, and so it was hot in Ednette's hut. Or perhaps it was just that I was nervous. I refused to take off my protective gear, as though it would insulate me against the evil that I was about to greet. Reza and Ednette stood behind me, close enough to catch me if I fell. Close enough to hold me back if I lunged.

The door opened, and at first, all I saw was light and shadow. Then the shadow separated into three beings—all Human.

First came Myfanwy and Caleb. The tallest one was Brother
Blue. He looked larger then I remembered. It was as if every
time I saw him, it was through a different lens.

He took off his coverings and looked just as smooth and
collected as he usually did. I wondered how someone so awful
could have eyes that smiled. But there they were, looking right
at me. Looking merry.

He removed his gloves and stuck out his hand to shake mine.

I nearly stumbled back, but Reza put his hand on my shoulder to steady me.

Everyone in the hut knowing my prejudice against him
was staring at me. I shook his hand, and then slowly removed
the scarf over my mouth, my hood, and my goggles and met
his stare.

At first he started, and his eyes lost their arrogant joy. His
face hardened, but then recovered quickly. Even though I could
see hate in his face, I knew he would not show any weakness
in front of other Humans. He had to play it off as though it
being me was part of his plan.

"It's you," he said and then he began to laugh. "Of course
it is."

"There is nothing funny about this meeting," I said.

"Oh, but there is," he said. "It's a good thing you were so
hard to kill, or else I'd be in a real pickle."

"We're only here because we have mutual interests," I said.
"We're only here because it's best if we work together."

The very words tasted bitter in my mouth. I could hardly
believe I was saying them, and yet I knew them to be true.

"Tula, you have the gift." Brother Blue said. "We're doing
good work here."

"I've done good work here. I am on the ground."

263

"Yes," he said. "You've done a remarkable job at filling in the gaps that I can't. I always knew you had something in you, Tula Bane. I saw it when you were a child. You should thank me for encouraging you."

I balked. There was no way I was going to thank this man.

He was talking to me as though I was still his assistant, and part of me almost wanted to fall into that role because it was still familiar. I remembered how to get things done his way, but I hated the way people's attention shifted from me to him. He was more charismatic. He was brighter. I was sullen, withdrawn, and inhuman. Alien. I seemed cold even though my heart was bursting.

He stood there, staring at me. Waiting for me to speak.

"I won't thank you," I said. "I'll never thank you for what you've done to me."

"We have too much work to do." Myfanwy stepped in, doing her best to refocus the discussion. "All eyes are on us. There's to be an audit."

"The Imperium has demanded to see an Earth colony. I need you to perform for me," he said.

"No," I said. "Send them to one of the other colonies."

Killick. Kuhn. Marxuach. Andra. Beta Granade.

"I can't do that," Brother Blue said. "There are issues there."

"What issues?" I asked.

"Pandemic on Andra. Power problems on Marxuach. Terraforming mishap on Beta Granade. Lack of proper receiving buildings on Killick. Light skip block to Kuhn . . ." Myfanwy rattled off the familiar excuses.

I laughed.

"You can drop the act," I said. "Why should we help you?"

"They can't know that this batch of alin has been ruined."

He put his hand on my shoulder as though he were being sincere with me. I shuddered, remembering the last time he'd touched me. Remembering his fists on my body and the cold hard floor of Docking Bay 12.

"You have us marked as your property."

"I'll free you," he said. Then he made a motion to Myfanwy who produced a key from her pocket and started undoing the armbands that had marked us as slaves.

"We work the land, we get the profits," I said.

"A quarter of the profits," he said.

"Earth Gov needs funding," Reza spoke up. "Some profits should go there."

I was glad that Reza had remembered to take care of that Earth was represented in this negotiation.

"Impossible," Brother Blue said. It was so easy for him to wave off billions of people. "If I'm going to get the Imperium to stop breathing down my neck, then we need funding."

"You mean *you* need funding," I said.

"Helping me keep the Imperium from sticking its nose into our affairs is helping Earth Gov," he said.

I nodded. I hated that he was right, but he was.

"We are the true pioneers here. We're full of hope and possibility. We're doing great things for Humanity. We are coexisting peacefully with our alien neighbors," I said.

I laid out my terms and told him my plans and vision for our colony, and made him agree to housing, medical support, schooling, grains. He agreed to it all.

I realized that I'd heard these words before, the speeches. They were what Brother Blue had said to us on Earth and on the *Prairie Rose*. I was saying the same thing, and I believed what I was saying.

Was it the same with Brother Blue? Had his intentions started as purely as mine?

No. We were nothing alike. Or were we?

I shook my head in assent to indicate my agreement.

"Now that we're partners in this venture, you'll see that I always had Humanity's best interests at heart," he said.

"What happened?" I asked. "Why is there no one living at the colonies?"

Brother Blue closed his eyes for a moment and then spoke.

"Killick, the first colony, went fine for five seasons," he said. "And then the weather, the insects, the floods, the soil turned toxic, everything changed. But by then I'd already started a movement. And I liked being the Human mover and shaker in space. I still like it. I liked adding planets to my collection. The other four planets I just sent skeleton crews to, as place-holders. I had every intention to do what I was saying. Things just got complicated."

The only thing I could think of as he told his story was that he did not look like a monster. He looked like an ordinary man.

"It wasn't until Beta Granade that I thought I would start again in earnest with a real colony. But then the League of Worlds fell, and I didn't have time to put actual people on it. I had to get rid of those colonists for the good of all Humans. But now we have a real chance to make it right."

Everyone in the room was looking at me expectantly. I felt as though I was holding all of our fates in my hands. Suddenly I understood about the hard choices that one had to make for the sake of the bigger picture.

"I think I see," I said, taking his hand and shaking it.

I now knew what it was like to sleep with a devil.

43

. . . .

When the inspectors of the Imperium came, Brother
Blue and I were of one mind. Make them believe that Humans were the kind of species they said they were.

Brother Blue stepped forward to welcome the delegation. I cringed at how he turned on the charm, greeting the aliens each in their traditional ways. I saw that he had interacted with them in the same way that I did with aliens when I bartered. Mimicking them in order to get what I wanted.

I looked at the alien speculators who tried to stand with their own kind to put on the appearance of species separation. But it was clear they were mingling with each other as they watched the arrival. A Per was laughing with a Moldav at some joke. Two Nurlock, a Freng, and a Kao were sharing food with the crowd. Two groups of younger Brahar and Hort were kicking a ball around.

It surprised me how much a part of life on Quint mixing had become.

We had grown together through helping each other. We didn't know how to separate. We were a community.

"Why are you mixed together?" the Brahar inspector asked.

"Stand with your own kind!" the Per yelled.

All the aliens looked at each other, confused, and I realized it was because they thought that they were apart. They couldn't see that we were all starting to bleed into each other, even when we were trying to look separated.

A Kao inspector stepped out and examined the aliens in the crowd. His red round face looked over the crowd with disgust. Perhaps fear. It was not difficult to see that we had all adapted to each other's styles.

We were stronger that way, which is why the Imperium wanted us to all go back to our corners. The galaxy was easier to control when aliens were separated and fighting one another for planets, resources, and the ability to expand.

"Let me show you my jewel of a settlement, Brother Blue said sensing the disapproval of the inspectors. He spread his arm to point out various landmarks to distract their attention as the aliens in the crowd reorganized themselves to be more separated.

He did it so smoothly that even I had made sure to step away from the two aliens next to me, and fell into place next to the other Humans.

"Shall we?" he asked when he noticed that we'd all reordered ourselves and led the inspectors by the crowd and out toward our claim camp.

Hendala took the first step toward following him, but she made eye contact with me as she passed me by, rotating her antennae toward me in a stealth greeting. Forming a long line out of town, the Imperium snaked down the road toward our claim camp.

"What's that?" a Dolmav inspector asked.

"No concern of ours," Brother Blue said. "That's not our claim."

"But there are different kinds of aliens working in the field together," the Brahar inspector said. They could understand that there would be mixing in town, just like on a space station or somewhere like Bessen where there was bound to be mixing, especially in the upper power classes. That was not punishable, just undesirable to the Imperium. But working together was a whole other thing.

I looked out at the countryside and could see that a large group of mixed aliens were carefully sowing seeds into a freshly tilled field. We had all helped each other to sow and plow at some point or another. It was tiring work and went so much more quickly if everyone gathered together. I'd forgotten that today there had been a call from a Kao claim for help.

"Are they working together?" the Imperium general, a Brahar barked.

"No, I don't think so," Brother Blue said, trying to move them all along. But the entire party had stopped and was looking at the field. The guards were waiting for orders. The inspectors were talking among themselves.

"We're here to inspect the Humans," Hendala said, trying to move the delegation along.

"Whose idea was it to start working together?" the Imperium general asked Brother Blue. "Was it yours?"

"Not at all," Brother Blue said trying to smooth things over. "We Humans stay on our own land. We don't mingle at all. If you'll notice there is not one Human working that claim."

I looked again to make sure that he was telling the truth, and he was. We had all stayed at our claim for the inspection. I could see now how Brother Blue did what he did. He could convince you of one thing because one day it was true. It didn't matter if it wasn't true the next.

The Brahar refused to move on right away. He called to the guards.

"Separate them," he said. He gave a signal to the Imperium troops. They went up the hill into the field and forced everyone into their own species group, shoving those who wouldn't cooperate into place with the butts of their two-shot guns.

I felt for the Kao speculator, whose field was getting trampled. He would have to start his work all over again.

Brother Blue stepped closer to the general. He was distancing himself from us, and just like he'd done so many times before, moving over to the side that he thought would win. The Imperium was life, and we were death.

"Pers and Dolmavs should not be helping a Kao," the general said. His scales shifted colors as he yelled. They flicked from gold to green.

The Per inspector scolded the Per speculators. The Dolmav inspector scolded the Dolmav speculators. I noticed that Hendala was standing in front of the Loor that had helped the Kao, but she was not scolding them.

"It is unfair for a Kao to benefit from the work of others," the general explained. "It muddies the claim, the value, and the currency."

He spoke as though we were all children. Or stupid.

The Kao was trying to clean up the mess as he listened to the general.

"Here is one thing we can all do together," the Brahar general said. "We can ensure that this Kao gets no benefit from having been helped. We must completely destroy the claim."

He then took a hoe that had fallen to the ground and began destroying and uprooting anything that he could. After a moment of hesitation, all of his guards followed suit. The inspectors, including Hendala and Brother Blue, urged us all to trample the Kao's field.

I did not stamp the ground. I just swayed back and forth in the crowd so as not to be singled out. But when Brother Blue saw me, he grabbed my arm in a menacing way and hissed at me under his breath.

"You will help to destroy this field, or I will destroy you."

"Enough," the Brahar general shouted when the field was ruined. "Let that be a lesson to you all."

"I don't know how one of my own kind would get such an idea," the Kao inspector said.

"It has the smell of Humans behind it," the Per inspector said.

"Likely how they get such good harvests and such good profits," the Dolmav agreed.

We couldn't help but overhear what they were saying about us.

"No, no," Brother Blue said. "Not Humans. Just one Human."

Then he did it. He raised his hand and pointed at me.

"It was her," he said. "Tula Bane. She's been organizing the aliens to work together. I've tried to stop her, but she's persistent. I do not like to punish my own kind, but she's left me no choice."

The inspectors turned to examine me.

I stood up taller. I wouldn't deny it.

"No," Reza said behind me. "It started in my fields. I was the first one here."

The Brahar general stepped up to Reza.

"This is a hard planet, and the alin is tricky to cultivate," Reza said. "I taught everyone here all that they know, and we've all done better by working together."

"Is that true?" the Brahar asked all of the aliens gathered together. "Have you been helped by this Human?"

271

The aliens looked around at one another and then they all looked at me. No one said anything, but it was clear that they were waiting for me to answer. Their faces looked frightened, worried that the inspectors would come and destroy their fields next. This was what so many of them had run away from.

I put my hands out to comfort the crowd and implore the Brahar general to see our point of view.

"We're very few that live here, and we are all far away from home," I said. "Things are hard to get, and so we have to work together, much like you do."

The Imperium inspectors let out various forms of gasps. The Brahar opened his eyes very wide to show me how enraged he was.

"I told you. Tula Bane is the real instigator," Brother Blue said, stepping in front of me.

"Pack up now and leave immediately," the Brahar general commanded to the aliens still gathered in the field. They didn't need to be told twice. They left the Kao with his ruined field.

"I don't need to see anything else," he said.

Brother Blue followed the general down the road, babbling away in an attempt to charm. To me he looked like a dog begging for scraps.

• •

News of what happened during the Imperium audit traveled fast. And within a few days, murmurs in the eatery and the entertainments spots were brimming with frightened aliens ready to take the first ship out of here. Some of the larger speculators gathered at Reza's to discuss how to help the Kao whose field had been trampled.

"We can't let them scare us," I said. "They've done their inspection, but now they are gone."

"We can go back to our way of life," the Nurlok who ran the eatery said backing me up.

"They'll kill us," a Freng said. "My species is not even Minor."

"Or they'll go after our homeworld to punish us," a Calwei said.

"They won't really do that," I said.

"What are you going to do?" a Loor in the corner asked.

"We're going to stay," I said to the aliens.

But we Humans had nowhere else to go.

44

I could see them in the sky. Battleships. They were low in the atmosphere. What were they doing here?

There was a noise, like metal gears coming to a grinding halt. And then there was a flash of light. The field behind me blew up. I could hear the scream of some injured Humans. Where alin once bloomed, there was now falling dirt and yellow petals.

People were yelling.

I looked up at the ships, trying to see where they were aiming. A bright light of a laser blast cut the field again. I unfroze and began to run for the road.

Dirt sprayed around me as I dove for cover behind a large rock. I heard the rumble of the ships as their cannons revved up for another shot.

They did not seem to be hitting the settlement.

Lights streaked across the sky, like a storm of lasers.

"To town!" shouted Ednette.

Soon anyone who was not injured was running down the road to town.

The town seemed to be only place that was safe. Throngs of aliens pushed and pressed into the square. Alien helped alien get to safety.

I pushed through the crowd looking for Reza, hoping that I would find him. Finally I saw him being held up by a Dolmav, who was breathing heavily through his blowhole. Reza was bleeding.

"Are you all right?" I asked.

"They're going for the alin!" Reza said.

After more blasts, we could see the battleships lifting out of the sky and disappearing into space. It was quiet for a moment, and then we could hear people and aliens of all kinds calling for each other. We could see all around us a ring of fire as the fields burned.

"They only hit the alin," Ednette said.

"They didn't want to strip the planet for resources," I said. "They just wanted to get rid of the source of wealth."

I had not wanted the other aliens to suffer, but by having Brother Blue audited, I could see now that it had served to expose all the aliens and their affairs on Quint. The Imperium wanted to make sure that they controlled the wealth.

"They didn't want us getting along," Reza said.

I had no time to mourn for the lost alin, or for all the beings who would not benefit from it. These burning, razed fields meant death to many.

"Form a line!" I shouted. "We save what we can!"

Buckets, hoses, wet rags were found. I shouted instructions to water down the buildings, and Reza organized aliens to help to fight back the fire from the closest fields.

While I ran forward to help, I noticed Brother Blue and others running toward the launchpad to board the last ships off of Quint.

Coward, I thought.

But I could give him no more of my attention. There was work to be done, and a community to save.

These were my people. Human or alien, they were under my care now.

45

. . . .

At some point, a rush is over.

With the alin mostly destroyed, nearly all of the aliens left.

It was stunning how quickly a place could empty out. Within days, there were shuttered houses and shops. Within weeks there was a desolate feeling as the claimed fields around us were abandoned to the elements.

For those few aliens who were still on Quint, there was talk of new seasons and the replanting of the blooms that had survived. But you could see the defeat in everyone's faces. People were pressing out of the fertile Dren Line and trying hard to make things grow in ruined land. The amount of pollen harvested now compared to a few weeks ago was small and the reward nearly nothing.

At the launchpad, it was obvious that more ships were leaving than coming.

There were still a few aliens who arrived late to the rush and still excited by the prospect of speculating. They took advantage of the abandoned claims, but there were not as many as before; and it didn't stop the sense that what was once a buzzing planet was now dying. I was struck with a sadness that everything that I had helped to build up was crumbling.

Brother Blue had disappeared from Quint back to the

Yertina Feray, but we were in the fields trying to salvage what we could. I had managed to give every farm some of the seeds that Reza had. Not just alin, but other things. We were parceling up the acreage and planting things. We sent the children, alien and Human, to gather all the insects that they could and release them into the scorched land. Anything that burrowed and turned. Anything to begin the healing.

Every seed I held felt as though it was a piece of a broken dream I had. I was enraged at how helpless I felt. Quint was ruined. It would take years to get back to where we had been.

In town, all the aliens gathered to hear the galactic news, and it wasn't good. The Imperium had a few planets in their sights as marked for review. They were mostly Minor Species, and Earth was one of them.

"This is my fault," I said to Reza.

"You couldn't have known that they were going to burn the alin," Reza said.

"He's probably up there, restoring his reputation as best he can," I said. "I can't just sit here."

"Well what are you going to do?" Reza asked.

"Listen to the news. It's causing the aliens on the Yertina Feray to react. There are commotions and Hochts nearly every day."

A Hocht was a kind of duel that two aliens of the same species could call on each other to settle a disagreement. I rememebered when I had fought Caleb in a Hocht when I refused to help Els, Reza, and him upon their station arrival. A commotion was when all aliens came out and screamed in a mob. A commotion could quickly turn into a riot if not kept in check. It was one thing to do that when the Yertina Feray was empty and had a low population, but by all recent accounts she was bursting at the seams. If the aliens went back to their worlds suspicious and fighting one another, then that would trickle down to every aspect of interstellar politics and a government like the Imperium would stay in power longer. They had not burned the alin for no reason. They knew they were vulnerable unless they made sure everyone was fighting each other and not rising up against them.

"I need to get up there," I said. "I can calm everyone down, I know I can."

"Why do you think you can do that?" Reza asked.

"Because I'm the one that all the aliens up there trust," I said. Reza couldn't help but agree.

"I got everyone to work together down here," I said. "Now I need to go do it up there."

"I'll get a message to Caleb," Reza said.

I would tell Tournour that I was coming home.

• •

We could see the Imperium battleships in the sky once we cleared the atmosphere.

"They're everywhere," I said, staring out the window as we approached the station. It looked like a flower surrounded by bees.

The Yertina Feray was completely hemmed in. All those ships meant that no one could get out.

"Can you even get us in?" I asked Caleb.

"Never underestimate the will of a determined man," Caleb said.

He pressed a button and began to talk to the docking bay operators.

"You are not cleared to dock," they said. "Please hold your position."

"I've got a standing game at Kitsch Rutsok's," Caleb said. "A full credit line. How about I turn that over to you and you let me slide in?"

"Negative," the docking bay said.

"You're a Kao, right? How about I find you a pleasant little hole for your nest?"

"I do not have the authority to accept your offer."

"You don't need authority. Just push a button and open a door," Caleb said.

He did what I would do. He started trading favors for a way in. He was still not the best at it, and I knew I could do better. I told him to offer the waters that he had. I pitched in my small load of alin. I started giving him thumbs up and thumbs down, increasing or decreasing the amount of moves it would take to get us on board.

We were still circling the station hours later, hoping for a clearance to dock when Tournour broke in. It was not like him to deal with docking matters.

"This is Chief Constable Tournour. Am I talking to the captain of this ship?" he asked.

Just hearing the sound of Tournour's voice made the anxiety that coursed through me calm down.

"Affirmative," Caleb said. He shot me a look, and I knew that something was wrong.

"Your business partner, Brother Blue, has requested to meet you due to irregularities in your agreement, before you are cleared to dock. I can't allow for any aggression to be brought onto this station. You must resolve your conflict prior to boarding."

"Do you have suggestions for resolution?" Caleb asked.

"I suggest that either you leave the system or you jettison the package that you may have with you."

Caleb looked at me. I shook my head no. I did not want to leave the system. He knew better than to argue with me. He knew my mind was set.

"I must deliver," Caleb said. "The package is aboard and too precious."

"I am well aware of that. You must jettison the package or the package will be destroyed upon boarding. This is not a threat. This is a fact."

Then the com went silent.

"Look," Siddiqui said, pointing out the bridge window. "Trouble."

Looking through the window, we could see a small Imperium ship leaving the docking bay, heading toward us. We were quiet for a minute and then Caleb jumped into action.

"We have to get you off of the ship," Caleb said. "I know what to do. Follow me."

Caleb grabbed my arm, and I followed him as he rushed to the airlock of the ship, Siddiqui following fast on our heels. Caleb led me to the bay and started pulling down a suit and gear for me. He measured me with his eyes.

"What am I going to do? I can't leave the ship. Where am I going to go?"

He pointed outside. To space.

"Let's get you suited up," Siddiqui said calmly as he grabbed the elements to make up a spacesuit from various drawers and lockers.

"I can't go out there," I said.

"Yes you can," Caleb said, pulling at my clothes. "You have no choice."

"I have never been in a spacesuit. I have never space walked. People train for years to do that," I said.

"Did you have emergency training when you were on your colony ship?" Siddiqui asked as he helped me into the cooling garment.

I nodded.

"It'll be similar to that," Siddiqui said. "Just like the drills that you were made to do one hundred times."

"Those were to get to pods," I said. "Not to spacewalk."

"You'll step outside with a tether," Caleb said. "You'll hide underneath us, and then when they leave, we'll pull you back inside."

Caleb and Siddiqui started dressing me, pulling the suit tight around me. Asking me about the airflow. Putting the helmet on my head. Asking if I could hear them.

"I need you to listen to me," Siddiqui said. "When you get out there go slow. Very slow. Actually, slow is too fast."

"Okay," I said. But I didn't know what that meant. "Don't make any sudden moves, and try to concentrate on your center. You are your own gravity. Think of yourself as a dancer," Siddiqui said.

"And never let go of the structure. Use your tether," Caleb added.

"To move, go hand over hand, sideways. Up and down are nearly impossible," Siddiqui said. "Your wrists aren't strong enough."

"Okay," I said.

"There is no resistance in space," he said. "That's why you have to go slow."

We could all hear the ship coming alongside of us.

"You have to go," Caleb said. "They're here."

"We'll come get you when it's safe," Siddiqui said.

Caleb blew me a kiss, and then they both backed out of the docking bay and sealed the door. I was alone. I could hear as the air got sucked out of the room. The hatch opened, and I was pushed outside. The tether kept me from free falling, but the door closed and I couldn't help but try to grab for it. I was weightless, and it was silent. I was alone with the universe. My heart was beating so hard I thought I might explode. I was twisting, and I could see the small ship as it docked.

Quint was below me, and I had a sudden sense of vertigo. As though I were falling even though I was floating. I tried to find my center.

Would I get a signal of when to come in? I just had to wait it out. Wait until they left.

I had to know what was going on in the ship. I slowly went hand over hand to a point where I could see the windows.

There they were: Caleb, Siddiqui, and the two other Pirates. A door slid open and in came Brother Blue. I could see him screaming at my friends. They were shoved. Two Imperium guards, both Per, raised their four arms menacingly brandishing their two-shot pistols, one in each hand.

The crew was subdued. I could tell that orders were being given.

Another Imperium guard, a Brahar, started pushing open bins and pulling out things. I watched as others filed down the hall of the ship, finding secret panels. Pulling things apart. They were looking for me.

They all joined Brother Blue back on the bridge, shaking their heads. I could not be found.

I watched as Caleb said something, and I could see Brother Blue's face twist and turn red. I knew that look. It was the look he'd had when I'd pointed out the grain on the docking bay. It was the look he'd had before he'd beaten me and before he killed Els. I feared for Caleb, but breathed easier when I saw Brother Blue smile and turn away.

Then I saw Caleb shout something after him and watched helplessly as Brother Blue stopped and grabbed one of the two-shot pistols from the Per and shoot Caleb.

"No!" I screamed inside my helmet, the sound echoing like crazy.

Caleb crumpled to the floor. Siddiqui and the two other Pirates stepped forward, making surrendering signals with their arms.

"Come in," I said desperately flipping the channels on the radio I had trying to hail someone. My fingers were clumsy in the thick gloves. *"Come in."*

I could do nothing as I watched them get their hands tied behind their backs. I kept hoping that Caleb would somehow get up and be taken away with the rest of them. But I knew in my heart that my friend was dead.

"Hello? What do I do?" I asked. "Where do I go?"

It had been over an hour since I'd exited the ship. I wanted nothing more than to return to it. To Caleb.

A Per stepped up as though he had noticed something outside and I moved to the right out of sight. Minutes later I saw the shuttle disembark from Caleb's ship and head toward the Yertina Feray.

I was stranded in space.

All I could hear was my own frantic breathing. I waited ten minutes and then I slowly worked my way back to the window and confirmed my worst fear. There was no one on board to let me back in. I turned around and looked at the Yertina Feray, but knew that it would be crazy to try to approach one of the docking bays. There were too many ships, and I'd be caught or shot or worse, shoot right by it into eternity.

I only knew one thing: that I did not want to die in all of this black vastness. I turned again and looked at Quint below me and had a mad moment where I thought I could just dive toward it.

Just when I could bear the silence no longer, I noticed a single occupant ship coming toward me. I watched as it became bigger, as it closed in on the Hort ship. I was free-floating and I did not want to be noticed, so I started to pull myself closer to the hatch. The ship must have spotted me because it changed direction. It was a small ship, with an Imperium flag on it. It was heading right toward me. It had guns on its nose. I tried to keep my breathing even.

The ship came up close to me, and we stared at each other. The solar shade came up and I could see the pilot. It was Tournour. Relief washed over me. He made an indication to his head and then put his fingers to the number three twice. Thirty-three. It took me a minute but then I realized he meant the channel for my com set. I dialed in thirty-three.

"Can you hear me?"

I had been holding my breath, and hearing his voice made me burst into tears. As if all of the fear was flooding through me and out of me.

"Yes," I said. "They shot Caleb."

"Don't cry," he said.

"I can't help it," I said.

"Is this a Human thing?" he asked.

"I think so," I said.

Now that I had learned to cry again, it came so easily.

"What can we do to make it stop?" he asked.

I laughed and shook my head and willed myself to stop crying. It was uncomfortable. The tears had steamed up my visor. My nose was running, and I couldn't wipe it.

"I'm okay," I said. "I'm okay."

Tournour was here. I was going to be okay.

"You're going to have to untether yourself from their ship and attach yourself to mine."

"I can't do that," I said. If I unattached myself, I could float away.

"You have to," Tournour said.

It struck me that there had been a backup plan all along. Caleb had been buying me time.

"What do we do?"

"I'm going to nose up to you. Keep you in place. You'll disengage and attach yourself to the outside of my ship. You'll ride me back to the station."

"Like a horse?"

It took a second for the nanites in him to translate.

"Yes," he said.

He nosed the ship so gently up to me. I was astounded at the skill he had as a pilot. I could feel the nose of the ship on the outside of the suit. I unclicked the tether and clicked it onto his ship.

"All right," I said. "I'm secure."

I pulled myself over to him and sat on top of the hull. He thrust forward, barely using any engine. We glided along the bottom of the ships above us so that they wouldn't be able to see us, and we headed toward the station. I checked my oxygen. I still had some air, but it would be tight. The Yertina Feray loomed larger in front of us. A docking bay opened, and we entered, gravity hitting me like a ton of bricks. I rolled off of the ship with a thud to the floor.

Tournour ejected himself from the cockpit and jumped down to me.

He helped me take off my mask.

I hadn't been this close to him in months.

He didn't say anything to me. Instead, he looked at me with his deep dark eyes, and then I reached up and did something I'd never done before.

I kissed him.

46

. . . .

It had been so long since I'd seen Tournour I hadn't
realized how much of myself I'd missed.

"We must hurry," he said, and though he removed my arms
from around him, I could tell that he did not want to let go of
me either.

"Follow me," he said. He led me to the catwalks and the
secret tunnels that Heckleck had shown me when he was alive,
and it made me ache for how everything was now different. We
went up and up and up until we arrived at a lift that was very
small and clearly rarely used. It was no bigger than an average-
sized biped and it could barely hold us both. The door slid
open and we went in. We had to become one in order to fit.

"What are you doing back here?" he asked. "It's too dangerous. The Imperium is clutching onto what power it has by
using force instead of silence. That's always the sign of the end
of a time. Every species is scared for their homeworld and for
their colonies."

"Can we gather everyone at the Tin Star Café?" I said.

"Everyone is frightened," he said. "I can barely keep control of the station. If they were all to gather in one place, I
can't tell you what would happen."

"All those species on Quint, we all worked together. There
was none of that Major and Minor business."

The lift jolted me closer to him.

"As the Imperium feels the noose, they lash out at Minor Species and even my cousin Hendala who is working to expose them from the inside trying to root out the corruption is failing in her attempt to get those in the Imperium to work together to bring it down. Everyone is scared."

"I know we can't do anything about the Imperium, but we can fix this on a small scale. This is our station."

My mouth was so close to his antenna that my lips brushed them. He shuddered. I couldn't tell if it was with pleasure or disgust, but he held me tighter.

"Do you know why I was sent here?" Tournour asked. "What my family's big shame was?"

"No," I said. I had never dared to ask.

"My mother and father," he said. "They thought like you did. They saw the galaxy as a place where we could all work together to bring the best out of each other. They were high in the League. They were Loors of real power. They went to Minor worlds and encouraged them to think that way. To ask for more and to expand, and to join forces with other species."

"What happened to them?" I asked.

"They were killed, of course," Tournour said. "Our lands were stripped, and as I was the youngest, I was sent away in shame to the farthest place as punishment. No one rises from this low on Tallara."

I looked up at him. It seemed strange to me that he had been so hard hearted.

"I used to hate what my parents believed in, that all aliens should be equal. It was terrible to me to be separated from Tallara, assigned to a space station, and to have to work with so many different kinds of aliens. But then I met you. And I understood everything that my parents believed in."

"We are going to survive this," I said touching his face.

"Tell those we can trust, Thado, Kitsch Rutsok, Bitty, to gather who they can, and have them meet us at the Tin Star Café."

The elevator stopped, and the tiny door slid open. The corridor was small, and we were still close to each other, but after being so close, the inches felt like light years apart. I ached to touch him again.

Tournour reached over me and pushed on a panel that opened, and there, before me, was a place that I knew all too well. The underguts.

"You'll have to wait here until I can gather everyone together," he said. "It will take some time."

We moved through the hallway of bins, and I could feel his hope rising with every step. Finally we stopped in front of my old bin. I opened the metal curtain and there it was. It looked so small and ugly and empty.

"I must go," he said. "I have duties to perform. I have to keep the Yertina Feray safe. Stay here and out of sight. I'll send word."

"Will I see you again soon?" I asked. Now that I was with Tournour, Reza was a distant memory.

"There is always hope," he said. "Carry that with you and so will I. If we both do, then the chances of us meeting again are better."

He bowed down to me, and I cupped his face and kissed his forehead. Then he left.

Once he did, the other dwellers of the underguts began to look at me. They all seemed to be new aliens who had fallen low.

I was back to my beginning, but it didn't feel like home.

47

I had been down in the underguts for a few days before there was a knock on my bin. I lifted the metal curtain.

I expected no visitors and I was under orders from Tournour to mix and mingle with no one until I could talk to everyone, but I was restless. My bin felt like a coffin.

I opened the curtain. There stood a Nurlock. *Kelmao.* I'd heard she had taken over the Tin Star Café.

"Hello," she said. She had sureness to what she was doing, even though she was small. She was well-dressed. It made me happy that she had come into her own. She signaled and two other Nurlock stepped forward with boxes that they started to put into my bin.

"What's this?" I asked.

"Your things," she said. Then she smiled timidly in the way that the Nurlock do, pressing her lips so thinly until they disappeared into the barest line.

"I don't have any things," I said.

I opened the boxes. Inside were waters, salts, and sweets.

"This is the portion of the inventory that was left in my store," she said. "It's only proper that it goes back to you."

I pressed my lips to the thinnest they could go in thanks.

"The Tin Star is good?" I said. I missed the bustle of it and the life I'd made there.

"You'll see it soon enough," she said. "I'm to take you there tomorrow at twenty-first chime."

• •

I was the first one to arrive with Kelmao, and she pointed out to me the improvements that she'd made. The Tin Star Café was the same except for more tables and chairs. My three alin plants still hung behind the glass on the window. The door slid open, and Siddiqui walked in with the surviving Pirates and Trevor rolling behind them.

"Caleb would have wanted you to have it," Siddiqui said.

I hugged him and then commanded Trevor to go to the corner. Seeing it stand there, as it cycled through alien music, made me miss Caleb. I couldn't believe that he was dead.

Siddiqui, the Pirates, and I helped Kelmao to set up bottles of premium waters and sweets on the tables for the people who were going to join us to enjoy.

"We should mix them up," I said to Kelmao.

She nodded, and we went about mixing the sweets from different planets onto the same plates and placing the premium and low quality waters into the same cold buckets to imitate what I was going to try to accomplish. It might have been wishful, but as the aliens started entering and were forced to crowd around the same plates and cold buckets, conversations began. I saw Bitty enter with a few other Humans, and she waved to me. Thado and Kitsch Rusok arrived soon after and purposefully mixed with other species. Merchants and old timers trickled in from all corners of the station, and I was pleased to see a good representation of all species present. It was everyone I'd traded with back when I'd first arrived to those from Quint who had left the planet but were still not able to leave the system.

"Looks like everyone is here," Tournour said calling the meeting to order. I surveyed the scene noting that it was exactly the right amount of aliens who could be trusted.

"Planets are given to a species to colonize," I said. "There can be a small amount of other species, but no more than three percent. That's the way it's always been, even before the Imperium."

I was telling them what they already knew.

"It's how they regulate the balance of power," Tournour said. "But this is our station. And we don't need to live in the past."

There were murmurs as the aliens commented to those standing next to them.

"I saw what this Human did on Quint," the Nurlok who owned the eatery said.

"I didn't do anything except make it safe for us to work together," I said.

"You started a community," Bitty said.

"Yes. We need to do that here," I said.

I had done that on Quint. I had brought us together. And looking out on the crowd, I knew I was doing it again. I found some courage inside of me and said what I thought from my heart. So many familiar faces were in the room. Thado. Kitsch. They were here to listen to me.

"If we work together to fight the taxes; to stave off the terror; to protect the species who are smaller in population here on the Yertina Feray and to help them thrive; to share planets, like so many of us did on Quint; or wherever the next rush is, then the Imperium cannot harm us. Not here. And maybe after a while, not anywhere."

The crowd erupted, some agreeing and others disagreeing, many with questions, but everyone was still standing together, not in separate groups. I knew one thing was certain. The conversation had begun. The aliens were debating amongst each other, not taking sides with their own kind. Not caring about Major or Minor status.

Just as I let my guard down to enjoy the lively debate around me, the door burst open. Every alien went for their weapon, and a heat rushed over the room as though there was going to be a riot. Or a war.

But it was not the Imperium.

It was Myfanwy and she was alone, but visibly upset.

"What is she doing here?" I asked Bitty.

Immediately I could feel the tension in the room rise and I worried that we were about to lose what traction we'd gained. Everyone in the room had been burned in some way by the Imperium and, more specifically, by Brother Blue. They had no great love for Myfanwy because of that.

"I don't know, but I know that she's a friend," Bitty said to me loud enough that the gathered group could hear.

Myfanwy pushed her way through the crowd up to me.

"They've suspended Brother Blue from duty," Myfanwy said.

"What happened?" I asked.

"The Imperium are blaming him for all kinds of abnormalities, from skimming currency from claims to undeclared export of a precious substance. To falsifying colonial paperwork," Myfanwy said.

"All true," I said.

"There's more," she said. That was when I realized that her face was pale and she was shaking. "They know that there's a meeting. They thought Brother Blue was organizing a coup against them."

She looked like she was at the end of her rope.

"They've razed Earth," she said.

They razed Earth as they had Quint.

The aliens all erupted. Fear was everywhere. If they came for Earth, then they could come for any of us.

But instead of turning against each other, all the aliens started to make plans to protect our little world aboard the Yertina Feray by making agreements with each other.

I sank into a chair. I'd done it. I'd gotten the aliens to work together here. And clearly the Imperium was scared. It was a start.

But the price had been Earth.

48

It would be a very long time before anyone could go back to Earth.

The planet was devastated, but not destroyed. And while word had gotten to us that the casualties had been high, people had escaped.

But there is nothing more dangerous than a man who's lost everything. And Brother Blue had lost everything. I knew he wouldn't just simply fade away.

HOCHT

BLUE calls out BANE

★ For betraying humanity ★

★ For being inhuman ★

★ For destroying Earth ★

Announcements were posted everywhere. The day had come at long last. I would face him in the ring. I stepped onto the lift and felt as though I were going into the light of a bright sun after being in a black hole. The stands were up, and there was a crowd as I had never seen before.

There were Humans here. There were Humans, Human Wanderers, and refugees from Earth strolling around in the market. They were eating cakes and looking at objects and trading for what they could. And none of the aliens were flinching. They were here just like any other species. And they were a part of the Hocht. I had never seen that before.

I began to realize that I had really started something. They were bartering for supplies at the makeshift market. They were getting pots and pans and rugs and tools. They were trading for the things that you needed for life on a ship for the things that you needed for the life on a planet. My heart swelled.

Killick, Kuhn, Marxuach, Andra, Beta Granade, . . . Quint.

I felt eerily calm, like I had been waiting for this moment my whole life. This time I was not afraid. This time I was ready to fight my enemy.

But before I could get to the ring, Tournour grabbed me and pushed me up into the stands.

"Let me go," I said.

"I won't let you fight," he said.

"Why not?" I said. "I want to fight the Hocht. You can't stop me."

"Sit," he said. "I'm not stopping the Hocht. I'm stopping you."

The announcer called the Hocht. He called the names.

"Bane and Blue!"

I tried to stand up, but Tournour held me down.

297

"Let go of me!"

"No," he said.

The bell rang, signaling the start of the fight.

To my surprise, there were two people in the ring. Brother Blue, in a terry cloth sweat pants suit, an overgrown beard, and a crazed look in his eyes. And Bitty. Bitty in black, looking like a sleek weapon of hurt. I could see on her wrist the glint of gold from my bracelet. When she stepped into position, she looked like a wild cat, and the crowd cheered.

She had just as much a right to fight the Hocht as I did. Brother Blue had cost her much, too.

"No!" I yelled.

I didn't want her to fight my fight. I escaped from Tournour's hold and ran down to the ring. Tournour was on my heels.

Brother Blue began yelling that this was not the Hocht he signed up for. He yelled at Myfanwy to get things right. He yelled at the announcer. He yelled at the crowd.

"Are you here to fight a Bane?" Bitty asked Brother Blue.

"Yes," he said.

"Am I a Bane?" Bitty asked.

"How would I know?" Brother Blue asked.

"I met you on the *Prairie Rose* when I was ten. You took my sister away, and you killed my mother. You took my life away. I have every right to fight you here."

Brother Blue blanched. I saw as he took in her scars, knowing that she must be who she said she was. She was a Bane, and Bane he would fight.

Bitty and Brother Blue circled each other and began to fight and with every blow that Bitty landed, the crowd erupted. They cheered loudly and they clapped and hollered. They booed when Brother Blue escaped a blow or landed one.

I got to the side of the ring, and he saw me. And then he smiled a wicked smile and spat.

"You're like a tick, sticking to this place," he said.

Then he pushed Bitty away with such force that she fell backward. Then he stuck his hand in and pulled something out from his waistband. Hochts were only to be fought with the body, no weapons were allowed, but I saw the knife flash as he lunged for me.

Suddenly, the impossible happened. Bitty was all at once in front of me and then crumpled to the floor. There was blood everywhere, and the blood was not mine.

"He stabbed her!" I shouted.

Bitty was clutching her side, holding the stab wound to staunch the blood. Brother Blue cursed and then dodged the arms that were trying to hold him and made a beeline for the Northmost wing.

"After him!" Tournour shouted to his officers, but he could not hold me back.

I bared my teeth like an animal and dove after Brother Blue. Tournour was close on my heels.

"You monster!" I shouted. I had my sister's blood on me. For all I knew, he'd killed her when he'd meant to kill me.

"Which way did he go?" Tournour shouted. Other officers had joined us now. He gave out quick instructions to do a search and sweep.

But I knew what hallway we were in. I knew where he was going. The docking bays.

"Let's split up," I said. Tournour nodded and turned off to the left. I stopped at a public data console and sent a message to the Tin Star Café and had Kelmao send Trevor to the docking bay. Then I went forward and up.

49

. . . .

I met Trevor as it exited the lift. And then I commanded it to follow me as I pushed forward down the docking bays to see where Brother Blue could be.

The next ship leaving was on Docking Bay 5, but I knew he wouldn't actually leave; he was just looking to hide out until he finished me.

There was only one docking bay that was empty. Docking Bay 12.

I entered.

It was dark.

"Come and get me," I said to the empty hangar.

A second later he emerged from the anteroom.

. . .

He was sick. Wild.

But I had always been wilder.

Wild with grief.

Wild with revenge.

Wild with a desire for all of it to be over.

"I'm here for you," I said.

"I'm going to get you this time," he said. "There's no escaping."

"You can't have me."

I saw him as he approached. He had a knife in one hand and a two-shot pistol in the other. I stayed as still and calm as I could. I had one chance at this. He raised his two-shot gun.

"Trevor, go!" I shouted.

Trevor's security protocol came on and his knives began to whir.

Brother Blue laughed as he watched Trevor roll up to him.

In my rush to do something, I'd mistimed my plan. Trevor was too far away to do any harm. It was as though I'd wound up a toy. I cursed myself.

"This is your weapon?" he said, lifting up his gun, firing one shot, immediately disabling Trevor.

"You should have stayed with your friends, in your café, where you had protection," he said. "Then again, they'd be no help for you this time."

He shot again, this time aiming for me. I ducked behind Trevor just as the phase went by. He was out of phases, but he still had his knife. I had no other weapon except my fists.

"It's over," I said, willing him to give up because that was now my only option for survival. "Your time is done."

He laughed even harder, the sound echoing in the docking bay.

"I'll get off this station and I will reinvent myself," he said. "That's what I do. But you will not survive another day."

I heard as he knocked things over on his approach to where I crouched. The space between us narrowed. Twelve feet. Eight feet. Six Feet. I looked over at the door to see if I could make a sprint for it. He was experienced and I was not. But if I could make it out of the room, I might be able to lock him in and vent him out to space.

But I could tell it was too far.

Brother Blue was right. This time I would die in Docking Bay 12.

His steps were coming closer. He was taking his time because he knew he had me. He was relishing this. I cursed myself for not letting Tournour know where I was going.

I slid my arms around Trevor, preparing myself for my last breaths, when my hand caught on one of his panels. Then I remembered that even disabled, Trevor had one more trick up its sleeve. I could signal for self-destruct overload. I would have less than a minute to get away before I would be killed in a burst of electricity and metal.

"You almost had it right, Brother Blue," I said, trying to distract him as I reached up and slid the panel open, pressing my thumb on the button for the few seconds to activate the sequence. The button glowed orange. Brother Blue, now close enough to use his knife, jabbed hard at my face. I ducked to the left to avoid the blow. The orange light began to flash as the countdown started.

"I accomplished what no one else would have," Brother Blue shouted as he slashed the knife at me again. I dodged to the right. "I gave us the stars!"

I glanced at the door like someone had just walked in. As he followed my stare, I dove for the far side of the room, scrambling behind a crate. Trevor emitted a high piercing warning alarm, and I watched as Brother Blue tried to step back. But he was not quick enough. Sparks shot out of Trevor arcing toward anything that could conduct electricity, including Brother Blue who crackled and lit as he was surrounded by light.

He convulsed and his skin turned from pink to gray. His eyes bulged. His lips burst. His body swelled. Although where

I hid was safe from the charge, I could feel the hairs rise on my body.

Brother Blue fell in a heap to the floor, a mess of charred, melted skin.

He was dead.

Smoke began pouring out of Trevor and its front panels fell off. Then it ran out of power and went dark. Trevor was gone. And losing Trevor felt like losing Caleb all over again.

It was over. It was over. I was done.

The door burst open, and Tournour was there.

"Tula!" he yelled rushing to me. His arms were around me. He released the scent, and while it calmed me, I could not stop crying. He whispered to me, his voice cooing. His arms were lifting me. I was safe.

50

. . . .

There were things to be done.

A new station order began to rise. Aliens started to fill the halls again on the Yertina Feray. It was a place where there was a fresh start for all species. A place for everyone to be equal.

My other dream had also come true. Human colonies were being formed.

The Wanderers would settle the planets and prepare them for the arrival of any more Earth refugees.

In a way, it was everything that Brother Blue had envisioned. It was the sum of the reason why I'd ventured out into space in the first place.

When anyone asked about Brother Blue, Tournour and I said that we saw him board a ship. We knew he was dead, but to the Imperium, he was still out there, with his secrets.

After being stitched up, Bitty and Myfanwy were closer than ever, and I knew by the way that Myfanwy gently rubbed Bitty's back, or the way that they would whisper to each other, that something was growing between them. One day they would be more than friends. It made me feel better that the reason why Myfanwy had never cared for Caleb was a matter of attraction and not the fact that she had never seen what a good-hearted person he was.

They had a task that I knew was essential but wasn't my calling either. They left soon after Bitty was healed from her stab wound. Along with Siddiqui, they took Caleb's ship and crew and set about gathering any Humans they could find to bring them to the five colonies that I was hoping to convince Reza to help set up. We needed a representative in this new way, and Reza was the best equipped to lead.

"Don't you want to come with us?" Bitty asked me before she left with Myfanwy. It was hard to let her go. She was my family, and after all that had happened, I wanted to be with her. But we had different paths now, different dreams.

"I want to go down to Quint and try to make it bloom again," I said.

The truth was that I wanted to bloom again myself. I had seen and done so much, and now I just wanted to go somewhere and be young. I'd had enough of fighting for what was right.

I hugged her for longer than I meant to, releasing her only when I reminded myself that she was still alive and that she would come back one day to visit me.

"I'm sorry about your friend Caleb," Myfanwy said. "He was always kind to me."

"You did know him," I said. "He really cared about you."

"I learned early on working for Brother Blue meant to forget what you knew," she said.

I understood what she meant all too well. It was something I had never learned.

•   •

I was finally ready to claim my future.

Tournour caught up to me as I headed for the docking bay to catch a shuttle down to Quint to talk to Reza.

"You're leaving," he said, pointing to the bags that held all of my personal items. It must have looked to him as though I were going away forever.

"Yes," I said. Since Brother Blue's death and the aliens on the station coming together, he'd been busy coordinating how we would resist and survive while the Imperium took its time to collapse in on itself.

"Reza . . ." I started, but Tournour put his hand up to stop me.

"He's a lucky man."

How was it that Tournour could be so intelligent and so thick at the same time? Here he was, not one hint of jealousy in him, completely ready to accept the fact that I was going to Quint to be with Reza. It never occurred to him that it was the furthest thing from the truth.

"He's the person that can best represent Earth. I can count on him."

He knew that we were going to help settle the refugees from Earth and the Wanderers on all of the Human colony planets.

"Will you go to Beta Granade after? That was your original destination, wasn't it? I know you will do right by all the Human refugees there."

He looked different as he said this. Disappointed almost. As though he were betraying an almost Human feeling when trying to think about where I would go and how that would affect him and his heart. With Tournour, duty always came first. He would expect that from me and never stand in my way, just as I had always understood that about him.

"No. That isn't my home," I said, teasing him with my eyes. I was trying to tell him that there were so many different ways to stay true to one's path.

"Isn't it?" he asked.

"No."

He took my hand and curled his long fingers around mine, and there could be no denying that both of our hearts jumped.

"My exile is done," he said. "I've been pardoned, and I can go anywhere I'd like."

"That's good news," I said. "I'm happy for you. Do you have any idea where you'll go?"

I paused.

"Tallara is beautiful," I said.

He pointed to my three alin plants. They were something to start with down on Quint. The shuttle down to Quint was called, and I let go of his hand.

"Will you be back?" he asked. "Is this goodbye?"

His antennae were flopped in a way I'd never seen before, and his eyes were even deeper and darker than I'd ever remembered.

"You have a terrible time reading me," I said as the shuttle began boarding and I left him staring at me, confused.

• •

"I'm surprised you put my name forth," Reza said as I sat there and watched him pack his things.

"You're perfect for it," I said. "It's what you were meant to do."

The remnants of Earth Gov had wanted me to help lead the resettlement of refugees, but I had refused. It was Reza who had the real skills they needed.

"I'd like you to come with me," he said.

"My place is here," I said.

I could see that he was nervous, as though having to let go of his plan when he crashed on Quint made him doubt his ability. But I had seen the way he'd worked with the Wanderers and the aliens to make their homes. He didn't need me.

"I'm sure they'd like to meet you," Reza said. "Think of it, because of you we have colonies."

"Me and Brother Blue," I said. That was the bitter truth. History would mix our names together, and the story would be muddled.

Reza sat down next to me on the bed and put his arm around my shoulder.

I could go with him. I could tell the real story. I knew I would be celebrated and revered. I would have wealth, power, and prestige. But what good was that? I had never sought it. What I wanted was a quiet life on Quint.

As much as Reza had played the part of being a farmer, that wasn't who he was. His time on Quint was a cocoon, getting him ready for this next part of his big life.

"It's Humans with a place in the galaxy. I want to share that with you," he said.

This was what he was meant to do. Not me. I changed the subject back to the last orders of business.

"When the alin blooms, we'll have currency," I said. "To supplement yours."

He squeezed my hand.

Reza was looking at me with that sweetness in his eyes. It was dark and deep and beautiful and something to get lost in, but it was not where my heart was pointed.

I shook my head. I knew I didn't feel what he wanted me to feel.

"Don't you love me?" he asked. "I love you."

"I do. I really do," I said. And I did. It was such a strange love. A big love. A proud love. "But I see a different road for me."

I looked at the window. At all of Quint.

"You want to stay here?" Reza said. "But there are others who can bring this planet back. Ednette and the Wanderers who are going to stay. You don't have to. You could come with me."

"I don't want to," I said.

"You want to be near him?" Reza said, his voice filled with jealousy.

"What are you talking about?" I asked.

"Tournour. He is not even Human," Reza said.

"If I had wanted to be with Tournour I would have stayed on the Yertina Feray," I said. "I'm here because *I* want to be here."

"He's probably not even compatible," Reza said. "You have to choose . . ."

"Why do I have to choose?" I asked. "Reza, you make me feel like a woman, and I love that about you."

"What can Tournour make you feel like?" Reza asked.

"He makes me feel Human."

Reza made a noise indicating his disappointment in me. But I didn't care. I had lost too much to care what people thought of me.

"Let me ask you a question. Would you stay here with me?" I asked him.

"No," he said after a moment. "My life is out there."

"Then you understand why I can't go with you."

"This planet is a harsh mistress," Reza said.

"But I can make it bloom again," I said. "It's our first Earth colony. I can't leave it. This is where my space journey ends."

He sighed deeply, and as angry as I knew he was, I felt that deep down inside he understood.

"You'll come back," I said. "You'll have to visit and check in on us. And I'll be here."

He pulled me into his strong arms, and we said our goodbyes the only way we knew how. With a soft kiss and a long hug.

Then he was gone.

• •

It only took a few weeks, but I could see it whenever I walked to the edge of Reza's claim. A town was being born.

As it slowly grew, I spent my time making myself comfortable. Reza's house was mine now. I swept the floor and carefully arranged Reza's things, mixing them with my own. Even Trevor, broken down and useless, was there in the corner. It was as if Caleb was there with me, too.

I kept mysef busy with the slow pace of this new life. There were flowers to cultivate. There was community to build. I mentally made a plan for the months and years ahead. What we would need and how we would trade and thrive. I thought of Heckleck and knew he'd be proud.

Every day ended with a brilliant sunset.

As I prepared my supper, after weeks of being alone, I heard the hooves of an animal outside of my door. There were more and more of those larger kind of animals arriving on Quint and so I thought nothing of it. Soon, there would be herds. They would help tame this planet. It made me glad.

I heard a visitor dismount and the creak of footsteps on the porch and in a moment, there was a knock.

I opened it.

It was Tournour.

His antenna moved slowly from side to side.

He had his bag at his feet.

"Do you know what I think?" he asked.

"What?" I said.

"You are my home. You are my world. You are my galaxy."

I smiled at him.

"What if our biology is too different?" I asked.

"Some things are the same."

"It won't be easy."

"We'll work it out," Tournour said. "I don't mind if you get pleasure from being with Reza."

I was in love with an alien.

"But I mind," I said, pulling him inside.

"Why?"

"Because my heart minds," and I tipped my forehead to his, and his antennae folded toward me.

"I adore your strange Human heart," he whispered.

I was home.

I was finally home.

Acknowledgments

• •

To my gentle first readers, Laurent Castellucci, Cylin Busby, Sarah Watson, Angie Chen, Alice Artemis Westover.

To the cluster, the shamers, and the nine piners, you are the wind beneath my word wings.

To Nicole Cloutier at NASA/JSC and Astronaut Rick Mastracchio for the spacewalk space talk.

To Nancy Mercado, who started me out.

To Connie Hsu, who brought it all home. Eternal gratitude for your amazing editing.

To Mimi Simard, who floated me when I most needed it.

To Gina Gagliano, Simon Boughton, and Roaring Brook Press for being so great.

To Kirby Kim for all the cheerleading and care.

To Skylight Books for the constant support.

To Steve Salardino, always.